D0403454

WATCHES OF THE NIGHT

WATCHES OF THE NIGHT

Sally Wright

This first world edition published 2008
in Great Britain and the USA by
SEVERN HOUSE PUBLISHERS LTD of
9–15 High Street, Sutton, Surrey SM1 1DF.

British Library Cataloguing in Publication Data

Wright, Sally S.
  Watches of the night
  1. Reese, Ben (Fictitious character) - Fiction
  2. Archivists - Fiction 3. Detective and mystery stories
  I. Title
  813.5'4[F]

  ISBN-13: 978-0-7278-6618-9   (cased)

All Severn House titles are printed on acid-free paper.

Typeset by Palimpsest Book Production Ltd.,
Grangemouth, Stirlingshire, Scotland.
Printed and bound in Great Britain by
MPG Books Ltd., Bodmin, Cornwall.

For Jessie And Aaron,
who've made me laugh, and given me things to think
about, since the day they were born.

List of Characters

Everett Adams	Alderton University Board Member
Mark Adams	Everett's son
Owen Anderson	WWII Army friend of Graham Lindsay
Jo Austin	Everett Adam's sister
Giovanni Balducci	Art History Professor, University of Siena, friend of Ben Reese
Willy Baylor	WWII Tech-Team member
Alma Bodley	Jenny Hunt's aunt
Roy Bossert	donated coins to Alderton University
Bob Boyd	American who meets Kate in Rome
Walter Buchanan	farmer who boards Ben Reese's horse
June Buchanan	Walter's wife, and a hospital nurse
Alex Chisholm	Scottish historian friend of Ben Reese
Eloise Coffin	library director, Falmouth, Massachusetts
Nick Costella	WWII Scout
Nellie Ferguson	nurse at Leith House
Georgina Fletcher	woman whose death Ben Reese investigated in 1961; subject of Kate Lindsay's novel in progress
George Gunn	Scottish soldier, friend of Ross MacNab
Chester Hansen	Chief of Police, Hillsdale, Ohio
Frederick Harper	President, Alderton University
Ruth (Bodley) Hunt Wharton	deceased wife of John Wharton
Jenny Hunt	daughter of Ruth HuntWharton and Ruth's first husband, Winthrop Hunt

Tess Johns	leader of study trip to Cortona
Dr Jones	Ben Reese's doctor during WWII
Kate Lindsay	writer friend of Ben Reese, nurse in WWII, widow of Graham Lindsay
Graham Lindsay	Scottish WWII Paratrooper killed at Arnhem
Ross MacNab	Scottish WWII medic under Graham Lindsay
Dr Jack Martin	Ben Reese's horse's vet
Dr Melville	Ross MacNab's doctor at Leith House
Ray Mills	member of WWII Tech-Team
Ted Mitchell	leader of WWII Tech-Team
Marietta Mitchell	Ted Mitchell's mother
Francie Mitchell (Gunderson)	Ted Mitchell's older sister
Francesca Mostardini	rare book dealer in Cortona
Maggie Parsons	rents Ben Reese's upstairs apartment
Ben Reese	archivist at Alderton University, ex-WWII Scout
Jessie Gerrard Reese	Ben Reese's deceased English Professor wife
Raimondo Ricciardi	retired Vatican curator, owner of La Fortezza, friend of Ben Reese
Roger Simms	Library Director, Alderton University
Bobby Talbott	American WWII Army photographer
Sarah Thompson	secretary at Leith House
Senora Carlotta Varini	acquaintance of Giovanni Balducci
John Wagner	American businessman known to Phillip Welsh
Phillip Welsh	newly retired Administrative Director of Leith House
Patricia Welsh	Phillip's wife
Richard West	deceased friend of Ben Reese
John Wharton	second husband of Ruth Bodley Hunt

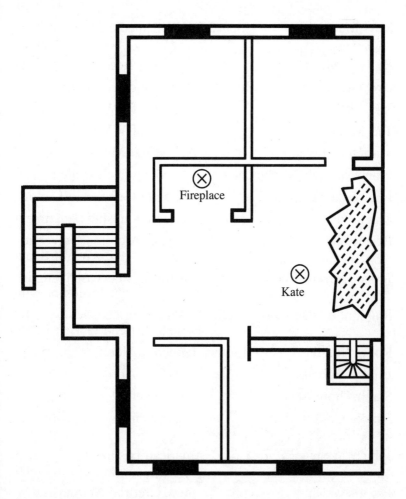

Upstairs of ruined porch building near La Fortezza

One

An American Army combat photographer, a Staff Sergeant named Bobby Talbot, stood in a filthy wet uniform with his back to the Saar River, as chunks of ice floated past on its cold grey skin.

He picked up the beat-up camera hanging around his neck, and said, 'Come on, doc, kneel right down there, right between the two stretchers.' He was watching a short Scottish medic who seemed to be staring past him as though he weren't seeing much of anything. 'Gunn – ' Talbot turned to a taller Scot waiting off to one side – 'you stand behind him. We gotta get somethin' to send your wife before the snow flies. Germany, man, nothin' but cold, snow, and mud.'

The medic still hadn't moved.

And Talbot said, 'I gotta scoot here, doc. I gotta shoot some stuff for *Stars and Stripes*, so if you'd just . . . Doc? . . . Never mind. Gunn, hunker down in front of him and let him stand where he is.

'Least this wasn't much of a skirmish.' Talbot sat on his heels, shoving his helmet back on his head, focusing his .70 mm combat Kodak on George Gunn, who'd squatted in front of the medic. 'Coulda been a lot worse, from what I heard this morning.'

The Yank on the stretcher on Talbot's left mumbled something unintelligible and raised his hand toward his face just as the shutter snapped. Talbot swore without a whole lot of conviction, which still knocked the ash off the cigarette dangling between his lips.

Gunn said, 'Thank you, sir. I'm very grateful. You've my wife's address still, have you?'

'Yep, I'll get it out tomorrow. You got mail delivery in the middle of Scotland?'

'We do. You have it in Michigan as well, do you?'

Talbot laughed.

And Gunn said, 'Thank you again, sir. You're very kind.'

Talbot nodded and walked off, rewinding the film in his camera.

Engineer Sergeant George Gunn fingered the sticking plaster on his left wrist to be sure the dressing was secure, then tugged on his high leather gloves. He put his helmet on so the chin strap wouldn't rub the bandage on his neck, while he watched the blood-spattered medic – Ross MacNab, from Falkirk, Scotland, raised one street away from Gunn.

'You did a fine job, Ross, patching me up. And fancy it being you, lad. Here, the two of us, coming upon each other again, after all this time.'

Gunn waited, watching MacNab with an uneasy squint, scrambling to find something neutral to say. 'The front's thoroughly confused again. The Yanks here as well, all mixed up with our lot.'

MacNab looked as though he hadn't heard.

And Gunn waited even longer this time, while he opened his jacket and scratched under his arms. 'Where were you sent after Arnhem? Bloody botch up that was. Yet we survived, didn't we, lad? You and me. I was attached to the Seaforth Highlanders immediately after the battle.'

Gunn cleared his throat, then glanced at Ross MacNab. 'Is this the lad you dragged from the river?' He pointed to the dark-haired American with the bandaged right thigh, the Yank who'd put his hand up just as the picture was taken. 'Ross?'

Ross MacNab still hadn't moved. He stood between the heads of the two wounded Americans – blood smeared on his clothes and hands, his mouth half-open, his arms hanging at his sides, his eyes dead in an empty face – staring at the grey skin and sunken-looking bones of the Yank with the chest wound on the other stretcher.

Gunn put a hand out toward Ross' elbow, then pulled it away as soon as he saw Ross jump. 'You did very well by us all today, laddie, very well indeed. And it won't be long now till we're home again. Aye, raising a pint together at the Bull. Have they sent you out of the line a-tall?'

Ross didn't answer, and he didn't look at George Gunn. He leaned over and stared at the bloodstain soaking through the bandage on the American's chest till a Tommy whispered 'Medic' twice, ten feet away, on the other side of George Gunn, past the Yank with the wounded leg.

The boy was crying softly when Ross picked up his kit, and screaming half a minute later, when Ross squatted down by his shot-away stomach and pulled out an ampule of morphine.

Gunn watched both of them, scratching the stubble on his chin. Then he picked up his pack, slung his rifle over his shoulder, walked past MacNab without saying goodbye, and went to find his unit.

Ted Mitchell, the American colonel with the leg wound on the stretcher closest to MacNab, had been watching the GI with the chest wound with absolute concentration the whole time Gunn had talked. As soon as he'd stopped, Mitchell quietly, carefully, turned his head to the right to look at Gunn and MacNab.

Gunn had turned his back toward him and was already walking away, and MacNab was holding the Tommy down, trying to stick a second shot of morphine into the base of the boy's neck.

Mitchell examined the bandage that covered most of his own right thigh, making sure it was tied on tightly, before he reached down past the right edge of his stretcher and felt around for his musette bag. It was there. On the ground. The metal box beside it too. And he lay back down, clenching his jaws at the grinding in his head and leg.

He rolled himself as far as he could stand to on to his left side, then opened his jacket with his bandaged right hand and unbuttoned his wet shirt, carefully pulling his dog tags up and over his head.

He pushed himself up on his left elbow, sucking air between his teeth against the pain, as he twisted farther toward the American with the chest wound lying stiff and silent on his left.

Mitchell looked back over his right shoulder to see if MacNab had noticed, but saw him working on the Tommy, stuffing more gauze in the hole in his stomach – and it was then that Mitchell stretched his arm across and felt the American's wrist.

He looked back at MacNab again, before he reached over as far as he could, gritting his teeth, not making a sound, and pulled the GI's dog tags up above the soldier's head.

Mitchell shuddered from pain and exhaustion, but he didn't let himself rest. He shoved his own tags over the other man's face, then pulled the GI's down around his own neck, pushing them inside his shirt.

Mitchell lay flat again, sweating from the effort, and looked over toward MacNab, who was staring down into Mitchell's eyes, while he was closing the Tommy's.

Neither of them spoke. Neither of them made a move.

And Mitchell couldn't tell what MacNab had seen. Or how much he'd understood.

Two minutes later, an American ambulance began backing up behind them, getting ready to load the wounded, just as a unit of GI's marched past, coming back from the line, talking, smoking, equipment clanking, adding noise to the confusion.

MacNab stood, still staring at Mitchell. Then turned and walked away.

Mitchell and the Yank beside him were the last of the wounded loaded into the truck – the second that had come up from an American aid station further up the line. The American with the chest wound was laid on the bottom hanger-bench on the right, before Mitchell was shoved in the center of the floor – both with their heads toward the door.

Mitchell shouted at the two who'd put him in the ambulance that he reported to Army Intelligence and had to have the bag and metal box from next to where his stretcher had been, in order to turn them in.

The driver and the medic raised their eyebrows at each other at the irritation in Mitchell's voice, but said, 'Sir,' finally, half grudgingly, and did what they were told.

MacNab walked up and stood behind the ambulance – big soft flakes of snow falling on his head and shoulders as he stared at the wounded stacked inside the mud-covered khaki truck.

He wiped crusted blood away from the eyes of the Yank with the chest wound, until he said, 'No!' in a high, strained voice, and felt for a pulse in the throat.

The ambulance pulled away, splattering mud and slush on him, while MacNab screamed, 'No! No!' louder and longer, and ran after the truck.

Five or six soldiers watched, British and American both, smoking cigarettes, drinking from cups and canteens, none of them making a move for him yet – watching MacNab stop a hundred yards on to pick something up from the road.

A hand, as it turned out, that he carried with him the rest of the day as he wandered in the direction the ambulance had gone, telling the four or five men he saw that he was taking it up to the field hospital to find the lad it belonged to and sew it back on.

The second American he said that to, a line captain from Third Army's Baker Company, stopped his Jeep and tried to talk to him.

He had to tie MacNab in the passenger seat, finally, when Ross refused to get in, telling him it was for his own good, and that he'd feel better soon. The captain threw the hand in a ditch, then radioed back to headquarters for directions to the closest field hospital.

Monday, December 4th, 1961

Why would somebody do that? Why would you pull a man's eye out after he's died in battle? Then seal it up in preservative and mail it off to his wife?

Ben Reese asked himself why at odd moments all day – that day of bits and pieces. When he'd arranged the packing of paintings being given to Alderton University. And flew home to Hillsdale, Ohio from Tryon, North Carolina. And sorted through mail in his Alderton office, digging out the requests for help a college archivist gets.

He found himself wishing hard that his horse were still alive too, that afternoon, as he walked home in the cold, toying with the idea of driving to the barn to feed carrots to the horses that were left.

Once he was home, he couldn't bring himself to leave, though, after having been away for weeks. So he lifted weights, and did laundry, and stacked wood on the kitchen porch.

Maggie Parsons, who rented his upstairs apartment, had left him a pot of potato soup before she'd gone to visit her grandkids. And Ben put it on to heat, while he thought about the eye in the bottle.

It'd been sent to Kate Lindsay when she was visiting Ben in North Carolina, while he chose the paintings for the university. And Ben could still see her face in front of him, the way she'd been in Tryon, when she'd first heard about the eye.

It was a face Ben liked, when he took time to think about it. Strong. Serious. Interesting. A face he'd watched crumple in upon itself when her mother called and told her about the postman at the door.

The man had just retired from the dead-letter office in St Paul, and he'd appeared, apparently from the sky, holding a package carefully in his hands he'd been trying to deliver since 1944.

It had been mailed from Europe, ripped and damaged, the recipient's name and address undecipherable. 'Physical specimen to be opened by widow' were the only readable words. Which had left the postman unwilling to unwrap it. To say nothing of Kate's mother.

Kate's husband had been killed at Arnhem in September of 1944, and hearing about the package had brought it all back, with Ben standing next to her to see it happen.

He'd known Kate in Wales in 1944. He'd been the best man at their wedding. He'd seen her deal with the wounded and the dying as a practical nurse in an American hospital, while the Allies geared up for the invasion.

But the look on her face, after she'd phoned her mother and asked her to open the package – after she'd heard it was Graham's eye, ripped out and floating in some kind of preservative – was not a look he'd forget.

He'd never seen Kate cry during the war. He'd watched her run out of the hospital and walk across the lawn, fast and furious and driven. But she'd cried in Tryon, when she'd heard about the eye. She'd sobbed against his chest.

That didn't mean that Ben thought he knew her. He hadn't seen Kate since he'd left for Normandy in a sub with a strike force the night before D-Day. Not till this past summer, when he'd been trying to help a student of his investigate the death of a friend. He'd knocked on a door in the wilds of Scotland, and there Kate had been, smiling and waiting for him to really look at her and finally zero in.

Kate had asked him in Tryon to help her find out who'd sent her the eye. And there'd been curiosity in that about the person who'd sent it. But more than that, Ben thought, Kate wanted to ask the sender what Graham had gone through when he'd died.

It won't be easy to figure out. Not after all this time. And I better call her tonight, now that she's seen the eye.

Ben had been taking silverware from a drawer. And he stood and stared at his hands, He'd picked up two of everything. When his wife had been dead for four and a half years.

He said, 'Jessie,' quietly, and shook his head. Then he shrugged his shoulders and dropped the extras in the drawer.

It never goes away, does it? That's not to say it should, of course. Not when Jessie deserves better.

Ben read while he ate, *Pepys' Diary* that night. And it wasn't until he was doing the dishes that he asked himself again why someone would send the eye.

Whoever it was was obviously nuts. But did he like Graham, and Kate too, and think she'd want a memento? Or did he hate one, or both, and do it just to be nasty?

There was no real evidence yet that the eye had been pulled out on purpose. Graham was a paratrooper. It could've popped out from a messy landing. Or been blown out by a blow or a bullet. Or the concussion of an exploding shell from one of the big guns. Ben had seen stranger things than that too many times to count.

But it must've been someone who was in Wales and knew both Kate and Graham. Someone who knew who her parents were. And was with Graham when he died.

It's probably a good thing the package got lost though. It would've been harder on Kate then, right after Graham died.

Ben was standing in his study when he placed the call, scratching the cleft in his chin when he heard Kate Lindsay say, 'Robertson residence,' as though she'd run to catch the phone.

Ben asked how her dad was doing after the second heart attack, and how her mother was holding up. And got good sounding answers to both.

Kate asked if it was convenient for her to describe the package to him then.

And Ben stepped over to his drafting table, grabbed a ball-point pen with his good hand, and arranged several sheets of typing paper in the center of the slanted surface.

He wrote down everything she said in his idiosyncratic shorthand. That it was a clear glass bottle wrapped in cotton batting under four or five layers of plain brown paper. That the outside of the package had been so badly ripped very little was readable – part of Kate's married name (the 'L' and 'd' in Lindsay), two letters in Illinois, the 'v', 't' and one 'n' in Evanston, plus three letters in Sheridan Road. That it hadn't been mailed from Holland, where Graham had died, but was postmarked in England a few days afterwards on the 30th of September, 1944. That there was no part of her maiden name. And no street numbers. And no return address except 'US Army, Europe'.

Ben laid his pen down and rubbed the side of his jaw. 'Then it probably got to England from Europe through American military channels . . . Really? The dead-letter guy went door to door on Sheridan Road? . . . It's amazing he could find you. *And* that he'd try that hard . . . Ah. Then you think it's personal? Because his son was killed in France?

'Wait a minute, what'd you say was on the back of the package? On the outside layer of torn paper? . . . "Personal effects Army personnel killed in action" . . . And on the next layer of brown paper? . . . "Physical Specimen. Only to be opened by widow." And that could only be seen through a tear.'

They talked then about who could've sent it, since they'd known the same people in Wales. When Ben helped Graham train British commandos and Graham helped Ben train American rangers.

'I didn't get to know many of Graham's men individually. But there *was* somebody I kind of vaguely remember who hung around Graham, kind of on the periphery. Someone quiet and shy, who watched you a lot when he thought you weren't looking . . . Kind of a little guy. Short and thin. I remember thinking that Graham worried about him in some way . . . Yeah, but a medic would make a lot of sense too. He'd have access to bottles and body parts, and alcohol to preserve the eye . . .

'So do you want me to give you a grisly piece of investigation to do that might help us figure it out?' Ben shoved his light-brown hair off his forehead, while he laughed at the voice Kate used to say, 'Yeah, I can hardly wait,'

'Try to determine if the stringy parts at the back of the eyeball were cut with a knife, or a scalpel, or got ripped out naturally without an instrument . . . Kate? Are you there? . . . Then you think the little guy sounds like a medic Graham knew?'

Ben was staring at the bay window with the night behind it, not seeing the reflection of the clean white room, or the light from the gooseneck lamp pouring out on the drafting table, or his own face looking pale and still – seeing France and Holland and Belgium and Germany. Seeing bloodstained snow, and bodies speared by splintered trees. Seeing field after field of fatal wounds crawling with flies and maggots. Seeing fresh wounds, and freak wounds, and a quiet wiry medic running from one, to the other, to the next.

'What? No, I'm still here . . . Exactly. What the medics did was staggering. They were *all* unarmed, and a lot of them were conscientious objectors. Some had worked in a pharmacy, or wanted to go to medical school. Some got picked without any reason whatever. But what they all dealt with every day was anything but easy.'

Ben told her then that all they'd had was bandages and morphine. And they'd watched a whole lot of guys die without a chance of saving them. That speed of treatment had been critical, and all the logistics were against them.

'A medic could carry one man. But how far could he carry him? And how did he decide who to pick up, when there were ten men dying around him? I mean, what kind of choices are those? There was no easy way to get the wounded out of the fields, or the forests. There weren't enough trucks, or Jeeps, or ambulances. And the medics bore the brunt of that impossible responsibility every day of the war.'

Ben took a sip from a glass of water, while Kate changed the subject to Graham Lindsay's paratroopers. And then Ben asked her how she'd look for the guy who might've been a medic.

'Is there anyone from Graham's battalion you could still track down? British First Airborne getting wiped out at Arnhem's not going to make this easy.'

Kate told Ben about a friend of her husband's, a Scot named

Owen Anderson, who'd been a battalion level officer but hadn't been at Arnhem. She'd heard he'd become a veterinarian in Aberdeen, and she'd try to call him in the morning to see if he could help.

'If he comes up with a likely candidate, I can call my friend Alex Chisholm and get him working on it too, Kate. Assuming that's something you want me to do. He's got friends in the War Office, or the Ministry of Defense, whatever it is they call it today. From working at Bletchley Park during the war too, and being a historian now, and he might be able to save you some time.'

Kate said she'd like Alex's help. And Ben told her it seemed odd to him that the eye was sent to her parents' address in the States, instead of to her hospital in Wales. Kate explained that Graham had thought she'd be shipped out to a hospital in France, so his men would've thought that too.

'Then someone wanting to mail you something could've decided it was safer to send it to your parents. But that doesn't make it any less strange to send you Graham's eye.'

Ben asked if Kate wanted to examine it then.

But Kate said no. She was tired, after spending all day at the hospital, and she'd rather face it in the morning. That she'd call Ben first thing, once she'd talked to Anderson, before she went to see her dad, and got ready to fly back to Scotland.

Tuesday, December 5th, 1961

Kate Lindsay watched purple finches fight over thistle seed while snow drifted softly off the branches of the redbud in her parents' backyard.

She'd been thinking about the novel she was plotting that was based on the investigation Ben had done of Georgina Fletcher's death in England the summer before, and as she placed the call to Ben, she reminded herself to ask him if he'd have time to answer questions in the next few weeks.

Kate could see him then, the way he'd been in North Carolina, smiling at her sideways with his large grey eyes, as they climbed up a trail to a waterfall near Saluda, making her laugh and forget the severed eye – when she heard his voice on the line.

Kate told Ben that she'd called Anderson in Scotland at the

crack of dawn that morning, and that he'd given her the name of the medic Ben had remembered in Wales.

'He's a short Scot from Falkirk, whose name is Ross MacNab.'

Anderson had been told that MacNab had a breakdown near the end of the war, and was still in a military hospital somewhere. 'He's also heard, but he doesn't know if it's true, that MacNab was seen carrying an arm around, somewhere in Germany. Something not entirely unlike sending me Graham's eye . . . Sure. I've got it right here.' Kate picked up the clear glass bottle and held it a foot from her face. 'It's about four inches high, and probably two and a half in diameter, and I've cut the wax, and loosened the cork, but I haven't opened it up yet.'

She tried to smile, as she set the bottle on the table. 'No, I can do it. Just give me a minute. I'll have to put the phone down.'

Kate swallowed hard, before she pried out the cork, and then pulled a spoon from a drawer. She'd already set a small white bowl on the table, and she fished the eye out of the alcohol with the spoon, then slid it gently into the bowl. She leaned over it, holding her breath, and pushed it around with the old silver spoon, looking at it with the magnifying glass she'd found in her dad's desk.

She tucked one side of her hair behind her ear, and then picked up the receiver.

'Ben? It looks to me like the ends of the stringy things were torn and not cut. They're tattered and kind of ripped looking. Of course, I don't know for sure how they'd look if you'd used a knife, and I'm not about to find out.' She tried to laugh, but her voice was shaky as she turned her back on the bowl and wiped her forehead with the palm of her hand.

'No, I'm OK. Thanks. But what does that tell you? Was it ripped out by natural causes, like a blow to the head or something? That would make it seem less premeditated . . . No, it's not formaldehyde. It smells like regular alcohol . . .

'So what about Alderton's president? Have you had your confrontation? . . . Well, I hope it goes better than you think it will . . . OK. You too. We'll talk when there's news.'

Kate kept her back to the slithery yellow eye, then turned finally, and held her breath again, trying not to inhale the stench of eye and alcohol, and poured the liquid down the drain. She dropped the cork in the garbage under the big white sink, then pulled out a box of aluminum foil and sheared off a ten-inch sheet.

She stared at the eye for half a minute, with her chin crumbling and her dark eyebrows pinned together above her nose, before she scooped it up in the spoon. She set it gently in the center of the foil, then wrapped it up quickly, settling it softly in the coffee grounds mounded on top of the garbage.

She smiled cryptically a second later and stepped closer to the window, where she watched a squirrel on a snow-powdered feeder shovel sunflower seeds in his mouth with both paws.

It's not what I'd call burial with honors. Coffee grounds in the garbage. But life will go on. With or without the eulogy that Graham never got.

Graham Lindsay. Black-haired Celt. Born in Inverness. Tall. Strong. Intelligent. Dead at twenty-six. Squishy, faded, severed eye found floating in a bottle. Only husband Kate Robertson wanted. From the day she met him at age six.

Kate sighed, and shrugged, and told herself to think about the other wives who'd picked up the pieces. Who'd been married for years. Or raised kids alone.

At least I've got work I want to do, and a place to live I like. Ben's coping with worse too. Jessie's only been dead four years, while I got used to missing Graham a long time ago.

Kate tapped a finger on the window and the squirrel froze, staring straight at her, waiting to see what tack she'd take next.

Two

There were no real surprises when Ben talked to Fred Harper, President of Alderton University. It was almost word for word what they'd said in September, before Ben left to pick paintings for Alderton and finish his own sabbatical – aside from one new development, which Ben could have predicted.

Harper wanted one of the donated paintings to hang in his own office. Though he refrained from mentioning it till he'd ushered Ben to the green leather chairs in front of his large polished desk.

Then he posed the critical question: should it be the de La Tour, or the Rembrandt Peale portrait of his brother? Ben told him he'd have to ask Fine Arts what they wanted left in the archives for students doing research before he gave an opinion.

Which was not the answer Harper expected.

It was then Ben mentioned Harrison Hall. Throwing down the gauntlet. Getting back to the conflict he'd come there to take on.

'As I told you this fall, Ben, when I gave you permission to take the remainder of your sabbatical in Georgia – which *I* considered an act of accommodation, by the way – we can't afford to renovate Harrison to meet the new building codes that take effect in January. Harrison has to be sold, and the money used to build an up-to-date dorm for women. I've been speaking to a real estate firm, and they—'

'We can't do it, Fred. The Harrison will expressly forbids it.' Ben went over it all again – the Jedidiah Harrison will, written in 1837, that allowed the university to use the classroom space in Harrison Hall in any manner whatever, but prohibited an outright sale. If Alderton chose not to use the Harrison building, it reverted to the Harrison heirs in perpetuity.

Ben asked why Alderton couldn't convert the building into high-quality apartments for faculty and older adults. 'There must be something money-making *like* that that would justify a loan.'

Harper replied that he did *not* wish to be the next president of Alderton University to take on substantial debt. 'What *I* want is the Harrison will in my hands as soon as possible.' Frederick Harper was leaning back in his high-backed chair, his striped tie off to the side of his sizeable stomach, his pale eyes fixed, his sandy eyebrows tensed, staring at Ben over steepled fingers with cool direct intent.

'I gave you a Xerox before I left for Cumberland, and I—'

'I want the original, Ben. Tomorrow would suit me. Who is this paper restorer you passed it on to? He's had plenty of time to finish the work, and I want it back now.'

'He's a colleague from the Cleveland Museum. He told me then that he had a backlog of documents, and it would probably be close to three months before he—'

'Why didn't you do the work yourself?'

'I was leaving town a week or two later, and I was swamped, and he's developed a new technique that would be particularly suited to documents of that period, on that sort of rag paper, with inks of that type, and it was a great opportunity for me to learn from his techniques. It *is* one of the important documents pertaining to the founding of Alderton, and I thought we ought to—'

'Contact him and get it back.'

'I will. Have you talked to the attorneys on the board about Harrison Hall?'

'I *am* aware of the steps one must take. I don't wish to seem peremptory, Ben, it's not my style, as you know – ' he was smiling at Ben with one of his most affable and conciliatory looks – 'but you must leave me to manage this. It *is* my purview, after all. How are things going with Roger?'

'Roger Simms?'

'Yes, the director of the library. Your superior, you'll remember. How are you two getting along?'

'OK. I've just seen him to say "hi" to since I've been back, but I'm on my way there from here.'

'You must try to keep him better informed, Ben. He seemed to feel, when you went off in October, that his wishes hadn't been considered sufficiently.'

'I talked to him before I talked to you. He said it was fine with him, but to check it with you as well.'

'Did he? He doesn't seem to remember it. Just a word to the wise.'

'Yes. Thanks.' Ben stood up and buttoned his black wool pea jacket.

'You know, Ben—' Fred Harper wasn't looking at Ben. He was pouring himself a cup of coffee from a small silver carafe. 'You *are* Alderton's only archivist. No other person has access to the muniments room. I doubt anyone else knows the Harrison will exists.'

It hung there, in the air between them. Just as it had in September. Till Ben Reese said, 'Maybe. But you and I do.'

Harper looked up at Ben with a thin one-sided smile. 'So you will arrange tomorrow for the return of the original will?'

'I'll call Frank in the morning and tell him you want it right away.'

Everett Adams was the board member to talk to. And Ben told himself to call him that night, as he drove up the long drive on the low hill to the terracotta brick Victorian farm-house that he'd bought after Jessie died.

There were already two cars up by the house, and one he'd never seen before – a big black Chrysler with Kentucky plates, parked behind the mottled Chevy that belonged to Maggie Parsons.

It was wet and raw and blustery, and it felt to Ben like snow was moving in, as he climbed the front-porch steps toward the carved double doors and saw the outline of an upper body behind their etched glass panels.

The right door opened before he got to it, held back by Everett Adams who bowed as he ushered Ben in.

'Hey, what are you doing here? You got a new car?'

'I did.' Everett Adams was a tall thin man in his sixties with friendly eyes and a deeply creased smile that took over his entire face, as he closed the door behind Ben. 'I apologize for intruding, Ben, but—'

'No, don't. You must've read my mind. I was planning to call you tonight. What brings you up to Ohio?'

'I had a last-minute business meeting east of Columbus, and I drove on over to see if I could take you to dinner.'

'I got more than enough for the two of you.' Maggie had stepped into the hall from the living room holding a half-peeled potato.

'Maggie used to manage the Columbus Women's Club, but now—'

'All I get to do is make Ben eat a decent meal once in a blue moon.' She was looking obstreperous, smiling at Ben the way she usually did, like a feisty grandmotherish hen.

Ben laughed and said, 'OK, Maggie. You can take us in hand this once.'

They'd moved to roast chicken from mushroom soup, while they shifted from the general to the specific. From what should've been done six months before to keep Khrushchev from building his wall across Berlin. From reasons for, *and* against, Kennedy sending his 'advisors' over to Vietnam.

They wandered from that to Cumberland Island, where Ben had been working that fall. And the newest crises Adams was facing in his horse van business in Lexington. And the work Adams' church was doing to end segregation peacefully.

Ben locked his hands on the top of his head, the bones in his face strong and sharp looking, his wide mouth serious, his half-shuttered eyes preoccupied. 'Changing assumptions isn't easy. Not in any kind of culture. Business, college, government, race. We point at everybody else's assumptions, and fight every change that hits us. Obviously. Why would I bother to state the obvious?'

'Let me raise *another* question.' Everett leaned back in his wicker chair, his blue eyes watchful, his narrow mouth half smiling. 'Why were you planning to call me tonight? Must've been something particular on your mind. You never do call to shoot the breeze.'

'Don't I? I wonder what that means.' Ben's eyes crinkled at the corners as he grinned at Adams across the table.

'You have a great many interests that absorb your time, and you have a deep distaste for small talk.'

'Ah. Yes. That's exactly right. And there *is* something you need to know as a member of Alderton's board.'

Ben told Everett about Harrison Hall – the Harrison will he'd dug out that fall, the Xerox he'd given Harper, the original he'd taken to a paper specialist at the Cleveland Museum for safe-keeping and restoration. 'Harper seems unwilling to honor it. And now he's pressuring me to get it back, and I can't delay much longer. I hate to say it, but I don't trust him not to destroy the original. Has he said anything about Harrison Hall to the board?'

'No, he certainly has not, and, as you know, there's a board meeting the end of this week. Lord help us, Ben, what kind of folks are we becoming?'

'That's an age-old question. Human nature being what it is.'

'*If* you take the historical view. How can I help with Harper?'

'Tell the board what he's up to before he pushes anything through. The selling of the building *has* to come before the board. He can't avoid that. But I don't trust him to explain about the will.'

'A very sad commentary indeed.'

'Yes. Do you think Harrison could be turned into high-rent apartments? Or maybe converted to medical offices? It's close to the hospital. Away from our main campus. Couldn't we do something *like* that, that'll make a profit to help build the dorm?'

'It's a matter that requires very substantial study. Which should've been begun the moment Harper learned of the will.' Everett drank the last of his coffee and set the cup in its saucer. 'What about you?'

'Me?'

'You could be doing yourself considerable damage getting involved in this, Ben. Wouldn't surprise me if old Fred Harper makes your life a good deal harder.'

'I know. It wouldn't surprise me either. I have tenure, so he can't fire me outright. Which is actually ironic since I'm opposed to tenure on general principles. But what he *could* do, I suppose, is change my classification from professor to library administrator. That would limit my own research more than I want to think about. I wouldn't have sabbaticals. I wouldn't have the summers off. It'd make it a whole lot harder to do work for other people.'

'The Historical Society, for one, as I recall.'

'That. As well as evaluating and restoring all kinds of materials for private and public owners. Fred Harper could make it difficult. And I suspect Roger Simms, the new director of the library, will be only too glad to help.'

'Why would that be?'

'I can't say I understand it completely. But this guy got hired a year ago, and he's a very competitive letter-of-the-law-type librarian, and I get the feeling he'd like me under much more direct control.'

'I reckon you're going to need whatever help you can get. Just don't you give Harper the original will.' Ben smiled at Everett and shrugged. 'I see. Yes, you may well have to. Or disobey a direct order.' He rubbed his jaw with his long thin fingers before asking Ben if he had an extra copy of the will. 'Then I can tell Harper I have one, so he knows he can't get away with destroying the original document. I'll get in touch with the other folks on the board right away too.'

'Thanks, Everett.'

'There's another matter I'd like to raise with you.' Everett Adams pushed his chair back and crossed one leg over the other, as he told Ben that his son, Mark, had served in Italy during the war, and had brought back pieces of antique jewelry he'd taken from a German soldier.

'Mark's intended, from that day on, to trace the Italian family that the ring and brooch belonged to and return the pieces to them. But as the years have come and gone by, and his own engineering work has become more demanding, he now knows he doesn't have the time, *or* the experience.'

Mark had asked Everett to ask Ben if he'd be willing to try to trace the jewelry and return it to the rightful owners, if he paid Ben to go to Italy.

'I'd be *very* interested in doing that. I could go over next summer, if he can wait that long, or maybe even over spring break. I'll have to see how things go here.'

'Well, I reckon I better be going, Ben. With it snowing the way it is, I want to be in Columbus before the roads get bad.'

'If they're nasty now, just turn around and come back. Let me get you the copy of the will.'

They both took their dishes to the kitchen, while Everett said he'd get Xeroxes made for everyone on the board and hand them out before the meeting.

'Course, there is another approach that might be interesting.' Everett Adams smiled sardonically as he buttoned his black wool suit coat. 'We could *not* tell Harper that you've talked to me. Then we can see how dishonest he is by whether he mentions the will on his own. If he doesn't, we'll know a good bit more about him than we did before.'

'That's a good idea, except that—'

'If he's *that* dishonest, we surely don't want him sitting in that office at Alderton. We just barely survived the rascal we had before him.'

'But if he doesn't know you've got a copy, he may get rid of the original.'

'True. I wasn't thinking of that.'

'Come with me to the study.' Ben walked through the kitchen door, past Maggie's inside stairs, turning left into the center hall that ran toward his front door between the dining room and the study. 'It's a tight position to be in.' Ben unlocked a file drawer, then pulled out an unmarked file. 'I ought to tell him I've given you a copy. I owe him that as my employer. Or I *would*, at least, under normal circumstances. But the good of Alderton has to come first, and seeing how he acts is obviously worth doing. I just don't know how to do it yet.'

Ben usually slept like a stone, when he didn't have one of his dreams. But that night, without one, he woke up at two – and still lay staring at the ceiling at four, ready to get up and move.

His house was the last one on the west edge of town, with fields and farms winding off on his right, as he walked south down his long sloping drive, toward the sleeping street. Ben would've liked to head into the country, but there weren't sidewalks in that direction, and the edges of the road were piled with snow and ice. So he turned left toward the sidewalk that started at his nearest neighbor's.

It wasn't cold enough for the snow to squeak, but it glittered in the street lights, sifting down like diamond dust in the smallest breath of a breeze.

He told himself to pay attention – to feel the bite of cold on his skin, to let the stillness seep in, to listen in the thick soft hush to the muffled rhythm of his boots, to the distant moan of a fast southbound freight – and let his mind drift.

He thought about books he'd been reading. And paintings he'd unpack the next week. And then found himself listening to Jessie laugh, as she held on to him while they sledded fast

down a high hill, the way they used to at a friend's farm –
till Ben saw he was standing by the post office, opposite
Alderton's campus.

The Coffee Cup was on his left, across the narrow side
street. The windows were lit, and there was steam above the
ceiling vents. And Ben decided on a cup of hot chocolate, as
he rubbed his hands against the cold.

He opened the door to the Coffee Cup, and stood on the
mat stamping snow off his work boots – when he saw a tall
dark-haired man walking out of the men's room.

Ben whispered, 'Mitchell!' before he could stop himself –
feeling his blood beating at his brain, while he stood there
frozen, staring at the stranger, watching him pick up a mint
by the cash register, listening to him make small talk, watching
him buy a paper and take it to the table at the back where
he'd left his sweet roll and coffee.

Ben yanked the door open and stepped out again into the
cold, then walked around the corner, leaning back hard against
freezing brick, never noticing the post-office truck pulling out
across the street.

It wasn't Mitchell. He knew that. Different mouth. Different
voice. Different way of holding his head. Not the same condescending arrogance he remembered from when Mitchell talked
to his men.

But why is my own reaction this intense?

*Years of asking, 'Why didn't I do something after I got
back?'*

*I should've tried in the hospital. There must've been some-
thing I could've done if I'd really taken it on.*

Ben was walking again. Faster this time, back up the hill
toward home. Not noticing anything but the firestorm in his
soul.

*What could I have done, though? Other than writing a
handful of letters that asked a few lame questions when I
couldn't have proven a thing. I couldn't then. And I can't now.*

*Which still avoids the pivotal question. What would I do
now? If I did see Mitchell walking down the street? Could I
keep from beating it out of him?*

Or crushing his windpipe with the edge of my hand?

Or driving the bridge of his nose into brain?

Three

B en Reese had been trucked over, out the Ardennes, and had slept four hours total in the last three days.

Two of them at the end of that afternoon, when he'd slept in a tent for the first time in weeks. On a canvas cot. Under a clean dry army blanket. Burrowed in like a hibernating animal. Wrapped in the dry safe comfort of it. The peacefulness. The luxury of it. That would've been hard to explain to any civilian anywhere, anytime in the last hundred years.

Now he was having trouble making himself move. Making himself wake up and open his eyes and get ready to do it again.

But he did. Finally.

Groggy and cold, he swung his feet to the ground and sat on the edge of the cot holding his head in his hands. His scalp was sore and itchy, and he rubbed it and scratched it all over, after sitting there motionless longer than he thought he ought to.

He blew his nose on a dirty handkerchief, and worked at loosening his fingers, seized-up and stiff in the cold. Then told himself it was time. To pack up what he'd need, and go eat whatever he could find.

Ben sneezed three times and rubbed his eyes, then pulled his helmet on over his dirty wool liner. He checked the knots fastening the wires around his waist under his outside coat – one wire coated with diamond dust, the other smoother and thicker.

He strapped his Colt .45 over his coat, under his right arm (the heavy 1911 Army issue Colt most GIs preferred) – one strap over his right shoulder, the other around his chest, grip aimed forward so he could grab it fast with his left hand.

He wiped the blade of the hatchet his dad had made him

(with a curved pointed pick *and* a steel blade that he always carried on patrol). Then he slid the handle through the left-side loop of the belt he wore over his hip-length coat.

Ben slung his old Springfield competition rifle over his left shoulder, checked his pockets to make sure he had everything he'd need, buttoned a fresh pack of Camels into one, and stepped out into a cold dusk in an already dark forest.

He filled a canteen with coffee in the mess tent (CW Washington coffee – powdered, bitter and strong), added his last half-shot of schnapps to help fight the cold, grabbed two cans of C-rations, and walked over to the fire where the technical guys he was taking out were talking among themselves.

Ben sat on the first folding stool he'd seen in a month, and stretched his fur-lined boots close to the fire, boots he'd liberated from a dead German officer sometime in December. Not a second too soon, either, with the cold the way it had been – and still was now. He drank his coffee, and ate his dinner, and listened to the technical guys talk.

One of them, Ray Mills, had just been sent in from another team, and he'd been asking about procedures, listening to the colonel in charge, a guy named Mitchell, who'd been telling them where they were going, and what they needed to find. They'd stopped that discussion as soon as Ben sat down. All he'd heard was, 'Tonight's not as important a site as what we'll be getting to farther into Germany, but with the line here now . . .'

Ben knew there was something wrong. Something going on between the three of them. The third guy in the team, Willy Baylor, who'd been with Mitchell awhile – he was staring at Ray Mills while Mitchell talked, giving him a look that said, 'This guy's doin' the talking, and he's in charge, but I'm telling ya, everything you need to know ain't gettin' said.' Ben saw it. He could read it right there in his eyes, as though the words were printed in the air above his head.

He watched Baylor and Mills glance away from each other, silently wary, body language talking, lighting Luckys and warming their hands on their tin cups, listening to Mitchell tell them how important it was that they search the site the way he said.

Ben finished his C-rations, cleaned the fork of his Swiss Army knife and shoved it in the coat pocket with his wire cutters, listening and looking at his watch, wondering when the new kid would decide to show up. The scout he'd only met once, who'd been assigned to him for training more than anything else (like ninety per cent of the others he'd worked with in the last two months). It was almost 21:00 hours and the kid was cutting it close.

Then he saw him, coming around the corner of a tent, crossing the camp, looking around for Ben. Ben lit a cigarette, while asking himself what the kid's name was. *Rick maybe. Something like that. No, Nick sounds closer. I need another blast of coffee.*

Ben finished the rest in the canteen as the boy hunkered down, and said, 'Hey,' to Ben, and held his hands toward the fire.

Ben looked across at him and nodded. 'It's time we got ourselves organized. Ray Mills . . . Willy Baylor . . . Colonel Mitchell . . . they're all technical guys. Nick Costella here's a scout.' Ben pointed around the circle as he said each name, then looked at Nick again. 'Ray, Willy and Colonel Mitchell are T-Forces. They're armed, but they're not army. They haven't had combat training. And we're taking them out to a site they have orders to investigate.

'It's roughly eight kilometers north-east of here, still in woods, from the reports I've seen, in between small scattered fields, west of Schleiden and Gemünd. There're SS patrols all around here, and there's no predicting them, *or* the line. Which is very fluid right now, and shifting really fast, so anything could happen.'

Ben took a drag on his Camel, as he looked around at the rest of them. 'Once we leave camp, there's going to be no talking. No noise of any kind. The first sound you wouldn't hear in a woods and I turn us around. Everybody got that?' Ben studied the group around the fire, making eye contact with every one of them. 'Good. OK. There'll be no smoking either, needless to say. Nothing like a Camel to bring a Kraut running.' Ben smiled, inhaled his own, and then stuck the butt in the snow beside his stool.

'Now, the object of this – ' Ben was looking at Nick – 'is to get in, secure the site, let the T-Force people get whatever information they're after, and get them back here as fast as possible. With weather coming in, and patrols the way they are, we've got to get back here by four hundred hours. Five hundred at the latest. Any questions?'

Ben gazed at the group around the fire. Nick looking small, wiry, and jumpy, eating a chocolate bar and staring hard at Ben. Ted Mitchell standing, looking tall, smart and sure of himself, holding a canvas musette pack in one hand. Willy Baylor, large and calm-looking, was watching Mitchell, flexing his fingers in his leather gloves, trying to get the blood moving. Ray Mills, his wire-rimmed glasses hiding his eyes, his teeth tight on his lower lip, sat fastening the straps on an empty battle pack.

Ben reached in his pocket and pulled out a small tin. 'We've got a half-moon tonight with heavy cloud cover coming and going. A lot of the time we'll be in woods, so before we go, I've got some stuff here I'm going to put on us to help us see each other in the dark. We've got to stay together. We can't afford to get separated.'

Ben unscrewed a lid and stuck his finger in a phosphorescent fluid, then dabbed it on the sight of his old Springfield, using the same finger to dot the front and back of his helmet just above the lip.

He marked the tech team's helmets too, and then turned to Nick. Who asked him what it was, and where he'd gotten it.

'You go to scout school in Louisiana?'

'Nope. Training's lots shorter than it was.'

'I used it in the Bayous there. Foxfire, *they* call it. Phosphorescent algae. This is something like it I picked up in Holland.'

'Could I speak to you a moment?' Ted Mitchell was asking Ben.

And when Ben had finished, he walked over to Mitchell and followed him away from the other men.

'Sergeant, I understand that you're in charge from here on out, until we get to the site. But I want to make it very clear that there I'll be taking over.'

'Right. Investigation of the site is under your command. I'll be the one to say when we pull out of the site, though, and I secure the buildings before your team goes in. If security's involved in any way, you do have to answer to me, Colonel. If you'd like to read my orders, you may.' Ben was unbuttoning a pocket inside his coat, getting ready to pull out his papers, when Mitchell shook his head.

'No, I understand, you have the responsibility for the safety of the mission. I wanted to clarify the ordering of my men once we're on site.'

'They're nothing to do with me.'

'Good. No offense intended, Sergeant.' Ted Mitchell smiled at Ben, his brown eyes careful-looking in the firelight, before he glanced away.

'No offense taken, Colonel. One other thing. When your men are looking through the buildings, even if there're blackout curtains up, I want them to use flashlights, not turn on the electric lights. I've found it a useful precaution.'

'Agreed. We're prepared to do that.'

'Good.' Ben glanced at Mitchell, then turned to the rest of the men. 'I've got to check in with headquarters, and I'm going to get some coffee. I'll be back here, ready to leave in fifteen minutes. That would be – ' Ben was looking at his watch – 'twenty-one-thirty hours.'

The rest of them checked their watches. And then they watched Ben walk away, and pull on the fur-lined gloves he'd taken off the German with the boots.

Ben stopped and looked back again, and said, 'Baylor, could I talk to you for a second?'

'Sure.' Baylor trotted over to where Ben waited, and walked on with him toward headquarters.

'What's the deal with you and Mills? There's something between you two and Mitchell, and I need to know if anything's going on that'll affect how we work tonight.'

'Mills is new, and he doesn't know Mitchell, and I'm not sure that—' Baylor stopped, but kept his eyes on Ben while he lit himself a Lucky Strike.

'Go on. Mitchell's not going to hear anything from me.'

'He's too lucky. Three or four go out, one or two come back. Always him. Always Mitchell.'

'And?' Ben was looking at him hard.

'It's like . . . I don't know, I haven't been with him that long. I've only been over here a month, but some think he's a jinx. And some think maybe he doesn't *want* everybody to come back.'

'Why? What kind of reason could he have for that?'

'I don't know, and I've thought about it plenty. One thing I do know, he always takes the labs himself. Checks out all the scientific stuff, even though we're technical too.'

'And?'

'A couple guys came back with bullets in the back.'

'That can happen in a firefight. That doesn't necessarily mean—'

'I know.'

'There more to it, or not?'

'I don't know what to believe, but there's something about him. He takes care of himself, that's for sure.'

'Yeah, but you got to, on one level.'

'Sure, it's just . . .' Baylor inhaled and looked over his shoulder at Mitchell.

'You ever come up against mines?'

'Twice.'

'You tell him that's what I talked to you about, looking for mines and booby traps tonight around the site. Asking if you'd run into them before. You bring it up with him yourself, OK?'

'OK. You expecting any?'

'If it's a military installation, you can bet on it.'

'It's not.'

'That's what I figured. Don't worry about it. Nick and I'll look out for them. You go on and get ready.'

Ben started off toward headquarters, watching Mitchell out the edges of his eyes. Watching Mitchell walk the other way watching Baylor the whole time.

It was quarter to eleven and dark as it'd been that night when they got to the driveway to the plant, coming at it sideways from out of the woods. It was mud and gravel, half-covered with dirty snow, running straight between tall fir, tire tracks and frozen footprints cut in the whole surface. Which meant there wouldn't be traps or trip wires. Making the approach easier.

Ben motioned the rest of them to stay in the shadows of the trees. And then he slid from one tree to the next toward the tall two-sided gate in the high wire fence topped with barbed wire.

Circling the fenced-in compound, he examined the ground along the fence from twenty feet away, lying on his stomach at irregular intervals, studying the surface, looking for signs of wires or booby traps – till he'd made a careful circuit of the whole block of buildings.

He studied them too as he passed – the two old brick buildings (with black metal windows and black metal doors) built at right angles, the sheds and garages strung along the third side, making a U-shaped courtyard with the open end toward the gate.

There were no lights. No sounds. No dogs roaming the premises. Nothing like a military site, or a high-priority scientific plant. This looked like a typical business, locally owned most likely, in the country outside a village.

It looked as though it'd been there a while too, in the same configuration and condition. There were no signs that the contents had recently been moved for safety (from bombed-out cities all across Germany) the way munitions and major research sites were being transported to the country.

Though this plant *was* well hidden, and at least two miles from the nearest village. There was a house half a mile away that might've belonged to an owner or manager. Similar brick. Similar age. No chinks of light around the black-out curtains. No sounds at that hour of the night. Wisps of wood smoke in the air. Children's footprints in the yard. Car frosted over in the drive. No one up. No one out. No dog in the yard. A path leading from the plant toward the house, which Ben found, close to the front gate of the plant, as soon as he circled back to that gate – where he stopped and examined the chain and padlock.

He didn't want to cut it if he could help it. The longer the impression lasted that no outsiders had been there, the safer it'd be for everyone concerned. And he pulled out the bundle of picks he carried, and picked the lock fast. Then he slid inside the gate, motioning Nick to keep the tech team right where they were in the trees.

The large building on the left looked like offices. The biggest building, opposite the gate, with block and tackle above double doors, looked like a manufacturing plant. There was no name or logo identifying the business anywhere Ben could see.

He made a sweep of the courtyard fast. No time wasted. No extra moves made.

And then he checked the front door frame of what he thought was the office building for wires or detonation devices, before he picked the lock.

It was pitch dark inside, with black-out curtains across the windows. And Ben checked the rooms, one office after another, one lab after another, using a flashlight with a blue glass filter – examining every doorway and floor for wires or traps of any kind, unlocking all the drawers and cabinets before he left each room.

When he'd been through all of it, the basement up through the second floor, he walked out and signaled Nick to bring the team in.

He waved them into the labs and offices, left Nick guarding the courtyard – and unlocked the biggest building.

There was nothing threatening there either. No trip wires. No detonators. No dogs or guards. Just glass-making furnaces. Annealing ovens. Different kinds of glass-blowing equipment – metal rods, metal shapers, chairs with metal braces for working the rods. Boxes of vacuum tube bulbs, crates of vacuum tubes in various stages of completion, spools of copper wire, wire-drawing dies, boxes of electrodes, blocks of tungsten, bins of silica and potash.

There was metal-fabricating equipment too. Drill presses, grinding wheels, polishing and bending tools. Piles of scrap metal. Bins of broken glass.

There was a metal door in the end wall, and Ben unlocked that, to a smaller room more like a lab, with electrical equipment and metal boxes and parts he couldn't name.

The technical team had been sent to Stoltz Electronik to look for useful developments in vacuum tubes, and anything having to do with the new work being done on developing transistors. And to find out too if there was work there related to the monitoring of communication – radio, aircraft, or telephone.

No one could predict what they'd find. All the Allies knew for sure was that Herr Rudolph Stoltz, the owner and founder of Stoltz Electronik, was a well-respected audio engineer who was believed to have been on the verge of important new discoveries before Germany invaded the Sudetenland. Scientific intelligence sources, including American inventors and business developers advising the Office of Strategic Services, felt certain that Herr Stoltz's work would be well worth finding.

Ted Mitchell had used the number and size of the buildings as justification for searching the labs himself, and he'd sent Baylor to examine the assembly building, and Mills to the basement and the first floor offices to look for research and raw material orders.

Mitchell started in the main laboratory on the second floor of the office building, scanning the cabinets and lab benches with a practiced eye, considering the vacuum tubes and capacitors, rolls of wire and other electrical components, reading lab diaries as he went (having taken eight years of German).

He spent the most time on the lab books. And it didn't take him long to see that if there *was* breakthrough work being done at Stoltz Electronik it wasn't being done in that lab.

At least this scout unlocks every lock. This scout who talked to Baylor. Who notices things he shouldn't. Baylor wouldn't look me in the eye after that, so something got said I should know about.

He opened the door at the far end of the room and stepped into a smaller lab beyond, where there were similar benches and glass-fronted cabinets, as well as floor-to-ceiling metal-doored cabinets that took up a short-end wall.

Mitchell opened the door beside it leading into the lab director's office, where he found a drafting table, a large organized desk, and a medium-sized metal safe with a key-lock door that the scout had left open. Mitchell started with the shallow drawers under the drafting table, pulling out prints and electrical schematics, studying them on the slanting surface.

The prints in the first three drawers didn't interest him, but when he got to the fourth, and studied both the prints and schematics, he nodded slowly and said, 'Wow!' in a low half-reverent whisper.

He folded them and put them in his musette bag – then moved to the desk and the safe.

He put two lab books from the safe into his bag, along with four metal reels that were wound with coated paper. He looked through the metal cabinets in the small lab next – where there were toilet-paper-sized rolls of a cellulose-like material he couldn't identify, next to five metal boxes, almost two feet square, with heavy removable lids.

He studied the boxes carefully, contrasting and comparing, before selecting one.

The team reported in by the front door of the main office at 0200 hours, as instructed by Colonel Mitchell.

Mills had found nothing that seemed particularly significant, but he'd put together a stack of purchase orders detailing materials purchased, as well as suppliers used. Baylor had brought a cross-section of vacuum tubes and electrical parts, and two metal boxes.

Mitchell examined Baylor's boxes, selected one, and gave it to Baylor to carry. He told Mills to carry the other, the one he'd brought from the small upstairs lab.

Then Mitchell walked out to the courtyard, and told Ben Reese they were ready to leave.

The cloud cover had lightened, and they moved quietly, shifting from tree to tree, from shadow to shadow, in half-moonlight, pausing when Ben motioned them to, staying where he told them to stay, as he swept the area in front and to the sides, while Nick guarded their rear.

They had to cross one narrow curving one-lane road, cutting south-east to north-west through the woods. And as they got near, Ben halted them, and went ahead to scout.

He could hear a vehicle in the distance on his left, on the south-east side, half a mile away maybe, the noise of it carrying eerily in the quiet cold night.

Car probably. Nothing big. No tank. No personnel carrier.

SS patrol most likely. German voices. Talking. Laughing. Louder than they should.

Ben melted back into the shadows, his rifle in his left hand, butt down on the toe of his boot.

An open car, a Volkswagen panzer wagon, a lot like an American Jeep, rolled in from Ben's left and slid to a stop thirty-five feet in front of him, twenty feet to his left.

Damn. Four SS. Machine gun mounted on the rear.

There was a tire-mounted flat on top of the hood, half-hiding the driver and passenger, and there were two men on the flat back, machine gun between them.

The officer in front laughed at one of the soldiers in back, then talked to him out one side of his mouth, a cigar clamped in the other. The soldier in back handed a liter beer bottle to the officer, climbed down off the car and walked to the side of the road (the other side from where Ben watched) to relieve himself against a tree.

Ben studied each of the SS, listening to the banter, trying to evaluate levels of alcohol and alertness, hoping hard that they'd just drive off – when something cracked behind him.

A tree branch, or a stick on the ground from the sound of it, stepped on by one of the team.

The SS driver opened fire, as the officer catapulted behind him to the far side of the car. Machine-gun bullets cut through the woods half a second later, ripping trunks and branches, spraying splinters as deadly as shrapnel – as Ben sited on the German driver and shot him in the chest. He signaled Nick Costello, fifty feet behind him, to get up beside him fast.

And Costello got there, crawling part way, crouching too when he could, while Ben laid covering fire.

Ben told Nick to take care of the squad – and went off to circle the SS.

It was a nasty ten minutes – Ben dodging left through the trees, sprinting across the road seventy feet south-east, snaking around behind the VW, shooting the two handling the machine gun just before Costello shot the officer in the face.

Ben checked pulses, took papers and weapons, then grabbed the key to the panzer wagon. He sprinted back across the road, and dropped the weapons near Costello, who was staring blindly at Mills, lying crumpled and dead at his feet, his glasses blown ten feet away.

Mitchell wasn't noticing. He was leaning on a tree with a .45 in his hand, his eyes burning on adrenaline. While Willy Baylor lay dying on a slick of snow and mud speared with broken tree branches, cut and splintered by machine-gun fire.

Ben knelt beside him, picking him up, talking to him, cradling his head on his left arm, watching him drain away – till Baylor opened his eyes, and focused on Ben's face.

He tried to say something when he saw Ben, straining to get air into ripped lungs, finally managing to whisper, 'Mitchell ... lab ... alone ...' He choked, and blood gurgled in his throat. But he gathered himself together again and whispered, 'Luger,' so quietly Ben could hardly hear it, even with his ear down next to Baylor's face. Baylor kept struggling to say something else, his lips working to form the words, his eyes talking to Ben.

But then his face fell against Ben's coat and he died before he could get it out.

Ben held him for another second, then closed Willy Baylor's eyes, and laid him down on the ground.

He took one of Baylor's dog tags off the chain around his neck. And sat on his heels for half a second, before he glanced at Mitchell's back. Then Ben tugged Baylor's coat and shirt up so he could look at his wounds with his flashlight hidden under Baylor's coat.

Luger. Two bullets in the back. Close range.

Closer by a lot than you'd expect.

Ben picked up Baylor's pack, and went to examine Mills.

One bullet to the brain. Luger possibly. Not as close range as Baylor.

Probably closer than across the road.

Ben took one of Mills' dog tags, picked up Mills' pack, then handed the pack to Mitchell. He grabbed one of the metal boxes, motioned Costello to pick up the other, and started moving out fast.

They made it back to camp without hitting another patrol, which was more than they'd had a right to expect, after the noise of the firefight.

Ben dropped his musette bag at his own tent, then started over toward Mitchell's with Baylor's pack and metal box. Mitchell was standing outside it, taking off Mills' pack, setting his musette bag on the ground beside it, his Colt .45 strapped around his waist on the outside of his coat.

Mitchell hadn't seen Ben – who'd come up behind him – and when Mitchell leaned over, his coat tightened across his waist and hips, and Ben saw a bulge underneath the cloth. He yanked the coat up without saying a word to Mitchell and pulled a German Luger out of the holster strapped to Mitchell's waist.

Ben stood there, smelling the barrel, even though Mitchell had already spun around and was standing with his fists clenched, staring right at Ben.

Ben was looking at him cold and hard, and Mitchell got right up in his face before he hissed, 'What do you think you're doing, soldier?' in a too-quiet belligerent voice.

'Your friends were shot with a Luger, Colonel. Both of them in the back, which was kind of interesting, from closer range than I would've expected, and yours has just been fired.'

'I shot both handguns tonight. The SS were firing Lugers too, in case you hadn't noticed. What are you tryin' to say, Sergeant?'

'That I'm thinking about it.' Ben didn't say anything else. He stood and looked at Mitchell for a minute. And then walked off to headquarters.

He wrote a report that stated the facts without making accusations. He handed in the dog tags. He described the location of the bodies. Then he asked to talk to the intelligence officer alone.

The officer looked at him, asked his radio operator to leave the tent, and waved Ben into a folding chair.

Ben didn't know the guy, and he sorted what he had to say carefully before he said it. He made no accusations. He confirmed what he'd written in the report, then asked him to find out what he could about Mitchell. Nothing official. Just questions up the line. Like what kind of record he'd had since he'd been in Europe as a TASK officer. Did anything seem fishy? Did an inordinate number of his team members die? Whatever anyone could find out would be greatly appreciated.

The intelligence officer read the report again and asked a couple of questions, before he said, 'If it's any consolation, *you* won't be having to deal with him again. You're getting shipped out in less than an hour. You, and eleven other scouts they're bringing in from all over.'

Ben thanked him for the help, took the orders the officer had pushed across the desk, and stepped outside the tent. He walked a few feet toward the mess tent, sat on his heels in the snow, lit a Camel, and opened his orders.

He walked on to the mess tent and filled his canteens with coffee. Then grabbed two tins of C-rations and went back to the tent to pack up.

Four

When Ben looked back on December the 8th later, he could see that the phone call from Alex had been the single most important event, because of its connection to the danger and death dealt with in the next three months.

At the time, he saw it differently. The way we do when we can't see around the corner, and can't get past the way life stings right now.

It was a day that seemed interminable to Ben, filled as it was with nasty little realities. Not the cataclysmic trials that make you step up, but the pinpricks, the flea bites, the paper cuts of personality that leave you staring at the ceiling late at night.

The inside world opened under him at four that morning, when he woke up wondering why he couldn't hear the sump pump, and found six inches of water flooding the basement floor.

The outside world stepped in at six (when Ben was on his second cup of coffee, having already replumbed the spare sump pump and squeegeed a roomful of water) – when Alex Chisholm (the eighth Earl and thirteenth Thane of Balnagard), a good friend of Ben's since the Second World War, called from Dunkeld, Scotland to tell Ben what he'd learned about a medic named Ross MacNab.

Official British military records were bare bones affairs, yet, in discussions with several acquaintances, in and out of government, Alex had learned that Ross MacNab had been sent to a military mental hospital (Craigalston, to be precise, outside of Buchlyvie) in 1945 and released some-time in 1953. What had happened to MacNab since then Alex couldn't say, except that, according to the records at

Somerset House, MacNab had never married, and wasn't yet deceased.

Everett Adams called Ben seconds after Alex hung up to say he was worried that Leonard Foster, the board member who'd recommended Harper for the presidency, might tell Harper the board knew about the will.

An informal meeting late the night before had stated that the sole intention behind not telling Harper was to evaluate how honest he'd be on his own. Foster had ultimately promised he wouldn't approach Harper. But Everett hadn't been convinced, and wanted Ben to be prepared.

The board meeting started at nine that Friday with the usual puckering of lips and planting of kisses on the ones who matter by Frederick Harper, while Ben looked on in disgust.

He listened with some small part of his brain for the kinds of information he had to take down as the non-member secretary of Alderton's Board of Trustees, watching Frederick Harper try to curry favor and still look important himself.

It wasn't until Harper got to Harrison Hall that Ben took down what he said verbatim. When he started by describing the new building codes, and went on to the expense of redoing the existing structure, the need for a new women's dorm, the desirability of selling the building and directing those funds toward the aforementioned dorm. Harper talked of the types of buyers who might be interested, the findings of a real estate appraiser and the sales agencies already contacted, the leasing of temporary classroom space, and the rearrangement of more.

'Yet, as all of you know well, you who have attained prominent positions in the world by virtue of persistence and hard work, life is rarely so uncomplicated. Dr Reese here – ' Harper nodded blandly in Ben's direction – 'has recently presented me with a copy of a will belonging to the donor of Harrison Hall, which substantially ties our hands in the matter. In fact, the original will was placed in my hands only this morning, moments before we entered this room.'

Harper went on to describe the terms of the will in some detail, and Everett Adams leaned over to Ben and whispered, 'Look at Leonard Foster.'

The plump, pink, hairless-looking face and head, the round

glasses and the soft rosy mouth nodded and smiled encouragingly at Harper, till Foster's eyes turned to Everett Adams with a cool smug look that said you can't touch him now. He's doing just what you wanted.

But there were more constraints Harper had to deal with as well. For a board committee was set up to study Harrison Hall. And Harper was told to return the will to Ben by the end of the day.

Three hours after the board meeting, Ben had to listen to another bureaucrat, Dr Roger Simms, as he straightened a perfectly squared stack of memos and dropped a pencil in his desk drawer. 'I presume you've now learned to schedule an appointment properly. It was quite unprofessional of you, Ben, to stick your head in the door Tuesday afternoon.'

'I did knock, you know. Maybe you couldn't—'

'I was on the phone with an extremely important call.'

'Yes, so you said at the time.'

'An issue of even greater significance needs to be addressed as well. You should have consulted me about your sabbatical this fall before you spoke to President Harper.'

Ben said he had, when they were walking down the hall in early September. He'd explained then that he hadn't finished the sabbatical he'd begun the previous November because he'd come back three weeks later when his good friend Richard West was murdered. 'I stayed and worked all spring. Remember? I was a witness in the murder trial and couldn't go back to England. I was only asking for part of this October and all of November, when I was actually owed seven months.'

'I have no recollection of the conversation.'

'I s'ppose I should've put it in writing, but you said, "Fine, no problem, just check with Fred." So I did. And it didn't occur to me that I had to go any further.'

'Didn't it?'

'I did mention it to you again before I left, after I'd gotten the OK from Fred, and you didn't say anything then. But it was hectic in the—'

'I want to see your artifact lists, with all values stated, as soon as possible.'

'I'm updating the lists, but—'

'The values are indecipherable, as you very well know. The

descriptions are generally accurate, though they do leave out substantial detail.'

Ben explained to Simms that he had to take precautions for security reasons when describing artifacts and giving their values. The approaches he used were recommended in the security courses he'd taken at the Brooklyn Museum of Art.

'Because if somebody who's here as a student, or working temporarily, is casing the joint as it were, looking for lists of what's worth stealing, the values can't be discernible, and the descriptions can't give every detail. I can give you the key to the value code, I suppose, though the previous directors of the library didn't think it was within their purview, since they were librarians and I'm the only archivist.'

'It's within my jurisdiction, regardless of whether it seems appropriate to you.' Dr Simms leaned back in his chair, stretching a rubber band between the fingers of his small neat hands, his feet dangling above the floor as he tipped the chair back toward a wall of books. 'Monday should give you enough time. Things have changed, Dr Reese. It's my opinion, and that of others whose opinions matter here, that you've had too much independence for far too long. Discipline is going to be brought to this library, whether you like it or not.'

'I see. Well, if that's all for now, I have to meet Fred Harper.'

'President Harper?' It was a peevish voice, high and shrill. Which Ben chose to listen to as infrequently as possible.

'I can't see you now.' Fred Harper was standing in the hall outside his office holding the door closed behind him. 'I have a board member in my office.'

'That's fine, I can—'

'Here's the will.'

Ben took the flat cardboard box from Harper's hands, pried the lid up carefully and glanced through the sheaf of heavy linen pages, sealed with wax and ribbon.

'Thanks, Fred.'

'I won't forget this, you know.'

'No, I didn't think you would.'

'I can *almost* understand, *almost*, that you might have thought you ought to tell the board about the will, but not informing me of that is completely indefensible, and it won't go unrewarded. You may have been here longer than I, but I

can promise you that you'll be leaving sooner.' Harper had
turned his back on Ben before he'd finished the last sentence,
and closed the door behind him before Ben could respond.

Ben called Kate in Scotland an hour later and told her what
Alex had told him. Kate said she'd ring Owen Anderson again
and ask if he could track down anyone else who might know
where MacNab was.

Ben described the board's decisions, and the confrontation
with Harper. And then he heard the best news of the day –
that Kate's last book had been nominated for a Wilkie Collins
Award by Suspense Writers International.

Sunday, December 24th, 1961

'Ben! It's good to see you.' Walter Buchanan had just filled
his son's horse's water bucket, and was about to fill the one
that belonged to the only boarder horse left, since Ben had
had to put Journey down earlier in the fall. 'You had any luck
finding a new horse?'

'Nope. I've looked at four or five, but none of them was
what I wanted. How are the boys doing?'

'Fine. Ready to eat like always. You come out to see me,
or the horseflesh?'

'Well . . .' They both laughed, before Ben said, 'It's
Christmas Eve. I didn't have anything I had to do. Not till I
drive an old guy I know over to midnight service. So I thought
I'd come out and give these two some apples, the way I used
to with Journey.'

'Max, here, could use some spoiling too. He's the new
boarder's horse, but he ain't getting much attention, and I
think he's bored. Weather's been good enough till last week
that he coulda been out some on trail rides and what not, if
the riding area was froze hard. That's what I wanted to see
you about. He's a real good horse. Real personable.'

Ben had been patting Max since he'd fed him an apple,
sliding his hand down the side of his neck, while the big
chestnut gelding had snuffled Ben's other palm with his soft
gentle mouth, keeping one eye on Walter, waiting for him to
walk toward his feed bucket – which was when he rushed off
to get his grain without taking time to blink.

'Lady who owns Max? Lady from Illinois who's here teaching for a year? She's got illness in her family up in Michigan, and she's real busy and on the road with that, and she'd like somebody to ride him, and give him some attention while she can't. I told her about you, and she asked me to talk to you about it.'

'Yeah, I'd like to do that. I miss being around horses a lot.'

'To tell you the truth, I don't figure she really wants him anymore. Guess she fell off last year in Illinois and got hurt pretty bad, and maybe she's lost the urge.'

'That happens. And if you don't have time to ride them, they get out of shape, and spookier, and it's not a good situation.'

'Yeah.'

'What is Max, thoroughbred and . . . ?'

'Half-thoroughbred, half-quarter horse. He got the best of both, in my opinion. He's real smart, and he's sensible, and he moves *real* well. Least it looks like it to me. People who do dressage like you, I don't know what you'd think.'

'The level at which I ride dressage hardly deserves the term.'

'So what're you doin' for Christmas?'

'Maggie's cooking me a turkey before she goes to her daughter's, and the guy across the street's coming over. His wife's in Indiana. Her mother's got cancer and can't be moved, and he's got to go to work here the day after. I'm having a couple of single people I work with too. And then I'll drive up to Michigan to see my folks on the twenty-seventh.'

'Don't sound like a whole lotta fun.'

'Maybe I'll come out and see these guys too.'

Max was chewing his grain, grinding his lower jaw from side to side with a faraway look in his eyes.

Ben walked into his kitchen from his back porch, filled a kettle and put it on to boil, then set a pan of Maggie's pot roast on to heat beside it.

He sat at the table by the window and started sorting mail from the day before – circulars and ads on the floor, Christmas cards in one stack, bills and business in another – till he got to an envelope from Scotland. Kate. From Loch Rannoch.

Dec 14th

Dear Ben,

Snow's been falling since last night and the phones went out this afternoon, although not before I made the phone call I'd been trying to make for several days.

I spoke to Owen Anderson last Saturday, and he called people he knew, eventually learning about George Gunn. Gunn was in British 1st Airborne with Graham and Ross MacNab, and he grew up in Falkirk not far from MacNab.

I didn't reach Gunn on the phone until today, but he's turned out to be *very* helpful. He gave me the name of the expensive private mental hospital MacNab is in, and gave me a little background. He hasn't seen MacNab since Germany, but he does write to him two or three times a year. MacNab has answered, but not with any regularity.

MacNab's parents are dead, and neither they nor he would have been able to afford the hospital, and his fees are paid by a benefactor he writes about obliquely in very glowing terms. The identity of the benefactor is apparently a deep, dark secret. Ross is very grateful to be where he is. And he writes coherently when he decides he wants to.

The last time Gunn saw Ross was after Gunn was hit by shrapnel and stumbled upon Ross near the site of a skirmish in Germany where MacNab was patching people up. Gunn says Ross was clearly having a breakdown of some kind at that time. He's heard since that Ross was carrying around a severed arm when taken away to an aid station, apparently later that day.

As soon as the phones are back on I'll phone Leith House and make an appointment to see Ross MacNab. I'll try to make it for the second or third of January. I've got to finish the plot outline now, as well as the rest of the proposal that goes along with it. I wish typewriters weren't the way they are. The inability to edit and correct is enough to make me stutter.

I hope you have a really good Christmas. We have a great time here usually, even when the power goes. It's the English Christmas I always dreamed of as a little kid when reading English novels. Graham's father and I go out into the forest and cut down our own tree.

We cut holly in the woods, and buy mistletoe from a sheep farmer we know. And it's beautiful. Timeless. Breathtaking for me, in a way – eating roast beef and Yorkshire pudding and looking down across the loch to one white slate-roofed cottage in the middle of a pine forest on the other side, while we listen to Handel and Bach with elderly friends of David's, and one or two friends of mine.

I hope it doesn't sound like I'm rubbing it in, but having seen where we live, I thought you might like a glimpse of Christmas here. Anyway, I hope yours is just as good, if not as sensorially spectacular.

I'll let you know what I find out as soon as I see Ross MacNab.

Thank you for all your help.

I hope things are better at Alderton.

Kate

Ben read the letter twice before he realized the pot roast was scorching and sprinted over to the stove.

Five

Sunday, December 31st, 1961

He was a tall man, crouched down, sitting on his heels, with a waxed khaki canvas rain jacket hanging to the ground around him, watching with travel-sized binoculars from between two evergreen shrubs.

He'd been waiting for half an hour, halfway along the long north side of a large oval pond circled by woods and wild undergrowth, focusing hard fifty yards away on the west end of the pond. He sat motionless, silent, hardly breathing, concentrating on a section of bushes that almost hid a wooden bench.

He lowered the binoculars for the fourth time in ten minutes, shoved the black stocking cap back from his forehead, then wiped the sweat from his eyebrows with the back of a leather-gloved hand.

He quietly pushed a canvas backpack further away across half-frozen ground, then tucked his coat under and sat on it cross-legged, readjusting his binoculars. He ignored the ducks on the pond, and the scattering of birds swooping and darting, pecking at seed heads and dried winter berries. He set his elbows on his knees instead, and pushed the binoculars hard against the bones around his eyes.

So where the hell can he be? He's never late. Why would he be late today?

The tall man told himself he was overreacting, and that it couldn't help but get in his way. That something unexpected must have happened. Something perfectly ordinary that had nothing to do with him.

Getting in a sweat over this doesn't make sense. If I can't get it done today, I'll make it happen tomorrow. Although rescheduling the . . .

Damn! Come on, you little . . . Wait . . . There . . .

There he is!

He still sat cross-legged on the ground and watched, straining to see what he could between bushes, breathing shallowly, bending forward, his black-gloved hands gripping the binoculars in his lap.

A short red-haired middle-aged man, neatly dressed in three-piece tweeds under an open waxed-cloth rain jacket, brushed a leaf off a long teak bench with a small nervous hand.

He turned around toward a large high table and stared intently at the surface, telling himself to study it carefully to avoid another mistake.

He'd set the paints out properly. He'd uncovered the water jug. The thermos was out of the way on the bench. The sandwiches still in their wrapper in the satchel. The seedcake tucked alongside. The watercolor pad centered on the table. The binoculars out of their case as well.

All's present and accounted for, laddie. There's no need to feel flustered.

He told himself for the third time that having to go back for his watercolors was nothing to be disturbed about. That they'd slipped his mind the way they might any normal person's. He must calm himself down, and relax his shoulders, and slow his thoughts a wee bit, and put things in proper perspective, the way Dr Melville had told him to, time out of mind.

Forgetting your paints does not presage another black period. Not of the sort you had last autumn. Remember what Mother used to say as well. 'Turn your mind to the good you've been given.' The goodness of your benefactor. Who brought you here, and pays the accounts, year after year. Which you deserve in no way a-tall, and can never hope to repay.

The kindness of the staff couldn't be overlooked. Nellie Ferguson in particular. The freedom to organize one's days, to paint, and study and listen to fine music. The coffee made to one's liking. The teacakes from Dunblane. A lovely church service earlier that morning with an excellent sermon for approaching the New Year.

You've a very great deal to be thankful for, laddie. A very great deal indeed.

Aye, and there's the rub. The provision that's been made. When I deserve nothing a-tall, after all I've done.

The short slight man set his elbows on the table, then took his head in his hands. He held the sides of his woolen cap, his fingers clenched and white, his head hanging limply above the block of watercolor paper, his eyes closed and his teeth clenched.

He rocked slowly in a circle, one way and then the other, making a small sad noise in his throat between a groan and a whimper.

It's not right, you know it's not. Living here in ease and comfort, when all those brave lads you maimed and killed, who'd looked to you for help, who put their trust in you alone, lie dead in cold, dark, solitary graves that only you could . . .

He told himself to look at the trees, to relax his hands, and take a deep breath, and listen to the birds in the thicket. *You must remember what Dr Melville says. All medics had a very hard time of it indeed. The need around us was perpetually greater than we could cope with, and the sense of failure is difficult to overcome.*

And he did have a rare treat to look forward to. Graham Lindsay's wife was coming to visit in two days' time. It would be lovely seeing her again. If he didn't act like a terrible ninny, tongue-tied and hopeless, as soon as he cast his eyes upon her.

I do hope I can screw up my courage to apologize properly, to raise the issue and face it squarely. For I did mean well. I did mean it as a keepsake. I was simply not thinking a-tall clearly at the time.

It must have been a terrible shock. To open the package and see it floating.

But you weren't to know what you were doing then. Watching poor Graham die the way he did. Watching all of them die at Arnhem. You're not to think of that anymore. You know too well what comes of it.

Ross couldn't imagine why Kate would want to visit. He hoped she hadn't been holding it against him, and only now learned his address.

Dr Melville had said there was nothing to worry about. But Ross hadn't told him precisely what he'd done. He'd only hinted in the vaguest terms.

Still, it's time you set to work, my lad. You've wasted too much of the morning.

MacNab's small eyes stared intently at the pond, at the dense shrubs and grasses and thicket all around it. One hand slid into a coat pocket and picked up a stub of soft sketching pencil, while the other reached for the watercolor paper. There was a teal on the pond. There were thrush and flycatcher and more than one member of the titmouse family in and out of the bushes. And the surface of the water, edged in ice, rippled in shadow and sun.

Then he pictured Kate again, and his face turned pink, and he laid the pad down. He said, 'I can't imagine it,' very softly and very slowly and shook his head and swallowed. *Seeing Kate Lindsay after all this time.*

He'd just begun to draw again – the cattails on the far side of the pond, the background shapes behind the male teal, the stronger curves of overhanging boughs – when he turned to his left and listened.

Now, what can that be? It sounds like a hippopotamus trampling through the undergrowth, a great huge clumsy beast . . . Look at that now! They're all flying off, all of them, frightened by the . . .

'Ross?'

Ross MacNab spun around, his narrow chest heaving, his face a confused terrified child's – until he'd stared for half a minute. Then relief and something like pleased disbelief washed across his flat thin face. 'It can't be, can it? Is it you? After all these years?'

'I hope I didn't startle you too much.' He was a tall man, dark-haired, with a broad strong face, wearing a khaki canvas jacket, carrying a brown canvas backpack with a stocking cap sticking out the top.

'You'll have noticed I didn't say your name. I never do, exactly as I promised.'

'I'm not surprised. I knew I could trust you from the start.'

'With all you've done for me, I'd be a poor specimen indeed if I couldn't be counted on for that.'

'It's good to see you out by the pond. I remember the time when you wouldn't go outside. I've kept up with you, you know. I've been kept informed. I've heard about your hobbies. I know what you like to eat. And I know you're doing a lot better now.'

'Dr Melville has seemed pleased this winter. Once I recovered from a bitter spell earlier this past autumn. You've come all the way from America, have you? Here. Please. Let me move my thermos.'

'I'll put it over here.'

The tall American had already sat on the bench next to Ross, and he picked up Ross' thermos, and set it on the ground beside his own knapsack.

'I never ask after you. I've never said one word. I've kept to our agreement in every single particular.'

'I know you have. I've never doubted it for a moment.'

'It's the least I could do, as you well know. I'll never be able to thank you enough.'

'Nonsense. If it weren't for you I'd be dead. So do they treat you well?'

'Aye, they do. They couldn't be more pleasant. I have a lovely room with views of the forest. I'm able to fix my own schedule. I can garden. I've been allowed to make my own wee blind where I can paint the wildlife on the pond.'

'That's why I came here. I heard you come to the pond every morning.'

'Aye, at nine. Unless it's raining very heavily, or it's too cold to sit outdoors.'

'Oh, before I forget, I brought you a treat from Hamilton's in Dunblane. Seedcake to have with your coffee.'

'You're too kind. You are indeed. Their seedcake is very much like the sort Mother used to bake for my birthday tea.' He was careful not to mention that he had those cakes brought every Saturday from Dunblane, and had one in his satchel now.

'That's what I was told. That your mother had made them, and you loved them.' The American laughed as he reached down for his knapsack on the other end of the bench from Ross. He asked Ross about the birds that could typically be found around the pond, while he took out a brown paper parcel of seedcake, as well as a thermos exactly like Ross'.

He set his thermos and the parcel on Ross' painting table, then asked Ross what it was that had just flown above their heads across the glade. He picked up Ross' thermos and slipped it in his own backpack, while Ross told him it was a teal, and peered through the break in the blind. 'So you only started painting once you came here? Here's your coffee. I've already poured it. And here's a cake too.'

'Thank you very much indeed. Aye, I began by taking a water-color class here at Leith House, but I very much enjoyed looking at paintings as a wee lad as well. I used to go to the library and study books on famous artists. It's very peaceful, you know. Painting landscape, and animals in nature. It makes one observe in a way one couldn't before. The cake is lovely, by the way.'

'Good. I'm glad you like it. Could you move the thermos over to your side? There's not much room for the bag of cakes.' The tall man passed the thermos to Ross with a gloved hand and watched Ross wrap his fingers around it. 'I hear it's gotten a little easier for you to talk about the war.'

Ross dropped his eyes toward his cup, and paused for several seconds before he said, 'A wee bit,' as though he'd had to consider it.

'I also hear you're about to have a visitor.'

'I am. The very first visitor I've had since I arrived. She was a lovely young girl, Kate Lindsay. An American nurse, you know. She was stationed in Wales in . . . 1944.'

'Why's she coming all of a sudden?'

'I've no idea a-tall. I was very surprised indeed. She told the woman who manages the offices when she rang-up that she'd recently spoken to someone she knew who'd mentioned I was here. I expect she's being kind.' Ross looked embarrassed then. As though he couldn't imagine someone coming to see him out of anything other than pity.

'She'll probably want to talk about the war.'

'I won't. I shall have to explain that I can't.'

'She probably liked you, when she knew you, and hopes you're doing well.'

'I wouldn't have thought she remembered me a-tall. I used to watch her from afar, and listen to her talk without having the nerve to say a word. I knew her husband better. He was a very fine man indeed.'

'Was? He's dead now?' The cool dark eyes were watching Ross, the handsome mouth settled in a self-possessed line.

Ross MacNab nodded. And then looked out through the break in the blind.

'You better pour yourself some more coffee, you look like you're getting cold.'

'I think I will have another wee cup. I could drink out of the thermos, you know, and you could use the lid.'

'No, I never drink coffee. I've never liked it. How have you gone about studying birds?'

Ross answered while the American leaned back against the bench, his long arms crossed across his expensive-looking jacket, one large ankle resting on his other knee.

He saw Ross' eyes begin to droop, after he'd asked him about the composers he liked. And why he preferred water-color to oil.

He saw Ross' shoulders slump and his hands fall heavily in his lap. And then he asked Ross how he scheduled his days, and where he got the records he listened to, and what kind of books he read.

It took Ross several minutes to answer all those questions, speaking slower and softer as time went on, with more pauses between sentences, with obvious effort at organizing his thoughts and enunciating words without slurring.

The American poured Ross the last of the coffee, holding the thermos from the very bottom with one large black gloved hand, watching him drink it down very slowly, as he told Ross again how much he owed him, and how grateful he was, and how glad he was that Ross was happier than he'd been before. 'Man, I didn't realize how late it was. I've got a business meeting in Stirling and I've got to run. It was good to see you. I couldn't be this close and not stop in.'

Ross nodded hazily and smiled.

'Don't tell anybody I dropped by, though. The bargain's still on.'

Ross nodded, and said, 'Of course. Don't know why, I'm beginning to feel quite sleepy . . . I didn't rest terribly well last night . . .'

'It's that kind of day too. And it's really relaxing, sitting here in the woods. No, don't get up. Stay right where you are. Watch what's happening on the pond.'

Ross straightened himself against the bench, looking as though there was something else he was trying to say.

'Oh, I've got to get my knapsack.' The American leaned over from the end of the bench toward the knapsacks lying on the ground, and slipped the seedcake out of Ross' pack into the one he'd brought. 'I don't know when I'll see you again, but you keep up the good work, and if there's anything you need, you know who to ask.'

Ross was looking at him as though he thought he ought to make himself stand.

'Don't get up, please, just sit there and enjoy the view.'

Ross was smiling when he whispered, 'Thank you.' Very softly, very slowly, in a high, slurred voice.

Six

K ate had been looking at the soft gentle quick-folding hills on the southern edge of Perthshire, thinking about ways to describe how the landscape can change in Scotland from one mile to the next – when she yawned twice, and asked herself why she'd been so exhausted the day before, driving from Loch Rannoch to Dunblane.

Finishing up the proposal. Working too many hours. Thinking about MacNab in the middle of the night. Wondering how to ask about Graham without upsetting Ross.

That's why I'm so edgy now. I should've arranged to talk to his doctor before I talked to him.

There it is. Leith House. Tastefully carved in stone.

The man at the gatehouse unlocked the gate to a winding wooded drive that was more than half a mile long. Which Kate drove slowly, looking at trees and shrubs. She stopped at the end in the car park, and smiled for a minute at the view straight ahead of a large, cream-colored, slate-roofed house with pepper-pot turrets at the corners.

She walked the rest of the tarmac drive into a large gravel courtyard, which she crunched across, with a feathery stomach, toward the only arch in the harled front wall.

She could feel her heart thundering in her chest, as she stepped under the carved stone crest above the broad archway that ended at a locked iron gate. A guard in a small office on the right came out and let her in, then pointed across a stone-paved courtyard toward the wing on the right.

Kate hesitated in its paneled hall, smoothing the collar of her cream silk blouse, before she opened the office door facing her on the left.

'Mrs Thompson?' Kate was looking at a short sturdy woman

in a blue sweater set and tartan skirt who was standing at an open file drawer, staring straight at Kate.

She asked Kate about the drive down, and offered her tea as well. Then Kate asked if she could talk to Ross' doctor. And was told there'd been an unlooked for event, and that Kate might wish to sit down.

'I'm frightfully sorry to be the bearer of bad tidings.' Mrs Thompson looked uncomfortably across the top of Kate's head, cradling her elbows in her hands. 'But our Mr MacNab died New Year's Eve morning. I do apologize for not ringing you. I'm afraid your visit slipped my mind until this morning, when you would've left long since.'

'Ross MacNab died?' Kate watched Sarah Thompson push her navy blue plastic glasses up her nose and fold her hands on her desk blotter. 'How?'

'Ah, well, that's the tragedy of it. We never expected it, none of us here at Leith House. He went off to paint by the back pond, taking his lunch as usual, and it was there he . . . well . . . it seems he took his own life.'

'Why? Had something happened to upset him?'

'We haven't the foggiest notion. He was allowed the freedom of the grounds, you see. There was no thought he'd injure another, or try to leave himself, and there never had been the first hint that he might make away with himself. Certainly not in the last seven years at least.'

Kate still hadn't taken it in. But she heard herself ask how Ross had died.

Sarah Thompson hesitated. She cleaned her glasses on a spotless handkerchief and sipped her tea before she spoke. 'We presume he'd been saving up his sleeping medication. Pretending to take his Nembutal tablets when he was given them at night, and hiding them away somewhere terribly clever, since that's precisely the sort of behavior staff are trained to detect. Dr Melville seemed as surprised as anyone, and he's a wonderful doctor, he truly is. He's been treating Ross these eight years and more to very good effect.'

'So Ross took a lethal dose of sleeping pills when he was out by the pond?'

'He dissolved them in his coffee, and then drank every drop.'

'It makes me feel terrible for him.'

'He had very definite schedules for himself. It was highly unusual when he hadn't come back to his room by teatime, and one of the orderlies went to look for him. Well, there he was, you see, by the wild pond, sitting on his own special bench, slumped across the table. He'd apparently been dead for several hours.'

Kate said, 'I see,' but she didn't. She was staring out the Palladian window beyond Mrs Thompson's head, wondering if her coming to see him had sent Ross over the edge.

'Do you think it would be possible for me to talk to Dr Melville? I wouldn't take much of his time, but it would help me a lot. I know I should've made an appointment earlier, but—'

'I suppose I could *enquire*.' Sarah Thompson looked hesitant, but as though she wanted to help too. And then she reached toward the phone.

'May I ask you one or two questions first?'

'Aye, though I fear I may have said too much already. I rather suspect I'm still in shock.'

'I have personal reasons for wanting to find out whatever I can about Mr MacNab that go back to the Second World War.' Kate didn't say anything else for a second. She looked at her lap and sighed. 'My husband was killed at the Battle of Arnhem. Ross served as a medic under him. The details are kind of complicated.'

'It was a terribly trying time.'

'Yes. Is there a person you would've contacted in case of some emergency? I don't know, a doctor, or a lawyer, someone interested in Ross' case?'

'There *is* a lawyer who was to be notified in any emergency. But that sort of thing you must ask Dr Melville.'

Kate nodded, looking shell-shocked, empty and tired and sad.

And Sarah Thompson watched Kate as though she knew what it felt like. 'I believe I may say that the former administrative director of Leith House, Mr Phillip Welsh, he was in touch with the solicitors.'

'Oh?'

'It was his responsibility to oversee the financial arrangements, and he might have been of some help. Mr Welsh is no longer with us. He resigned a fortnight ago. The twentieth, I believe. Quite suddenly. His last day was the twenty-seventh.'

'Would it be possible to give me his phone number and address?'

Sarah fingered the cameo brooch pinned on the shoulder of her cardigan without looking at Kate. 'I don't see why not. If he doesn't wish to speak to you, it's his decision to make.' She pulled a revolving card file closer, and wrote the address on a slip of paper she then handed on to Kate.

'Thank you. You're very kind. What sort of person was Ross MacNab? When I knew him he was somewhat shy.'

'Oh, aye, very mild-mannered. Very gentle. Very quiet. He was interested in a great many subjects as well, and he used his time here to good advantage.'

'That's good. I was afraid he just sat around staring at a wall, or something.'

'Oh, no. No. Though he did become quite flustered when having to make decisions. Coping with change in his schedule was difficult. And he could slip back to hardly speaking from one day to the next when especially worried or upset. Generally, he seemed very grateful to be here, where the grounds were lovely and he could be alone and do his "work," as he called it. His painting and his wildlife study. One never would have imagined that Ross would take his own life.'

'I remember him as kind of a watcher who seemed to like people, but didn't know how to make the first move.'

'That's a very fair description. Though after his breakdown I expect his difficulties communicating became a great deal worse. That was very unprofessional of me. It's not my place to offer opinions. You need to speak to Dr Melville, and I shall see if it's convenient.'

'Was I surprised Ross MacNab took his own life?' Dr Fergus Melville thrust his lower jaw out beyond his upper lip, while he tugged at his left earlobe. 'It wasn't inconceivable that he would do such a thing. He had very dark periods. Autumn was especially difficult. The fall of 1960 was a wretched time in particular. December could be hard on him as well, and March, generally, though the timing wasn't exact from one year to the next.'

'Why were some times harder than others?' Kate had unbuttoned her green wool suit and was pulling the skirt down across her knees.

'One can't say with certainty, but I suspect it may have been related to specific events in his war experiences. Arnhem in September 1944. Holland in December. Breakdown in Germany in March of 1945. Of course, *I* thought there had been considerable improvement in Ross' condition since 1960, and I didn't anticipate a breakdown such as this. I can certainly conceive of specific circumstances which might have made depression likely, but as matters had been progressing, it came as a very great shock.'

'Do you think it was my fault?' Kate was staring at the black leather purse in her lap, her thick, dark, chin-length hair falling across the left side of her face, half-hiding her eyes.

'Your fault? Why would it be your fault? Because you were visiting? And your fear is that a person from the past, related to the war in his memory, caused an emotional crisis for Ross?'

'Yes.' Kate looked at him then, her blue eyes strained and her mouth tense as she crossed her arms across her middle.

'I suppose an argument could be made for such an interpretation, but *I* wouldn't make it, I can assure you of that, and neither should you in my opinion. He seemed very pleased you were coming to visit. He mentioned your husband, and knowing you in Wales. No, I would be very surprised indeed if your arrival had anything a-tall to do with it.'

'He killed himself two days before I was scheduled to arrive. Couldn't he have been afraid of what I was going to ask him?'

'He might have been, I suppose, but he didn't give me that impression.' Dr Melville lit his pipe and squinted through the smoke at Kate's strained-looking face. 'May I ask why it is you decided to visit?

Kate told him about Graham's eye, meeting Melville's own to begin with, then staring down at her lap.

'Yes, I do see. That must have been a terrible shock.' Dr Melville nodded his broad furrowed face, clasped his hands on top of his sandy-blond hair, and stared absently at the ceiling. 'If Ross hadn't wished to see you, it's quite likely, in my opinion, that he would have asked us to ring you and cancel your visit. He avoided risk or stress of every kind. He refused to engage in situations that caused him alarm or apprehension, which, under the circumstances, was very wise indeed. He wasn't an irrational person, you know. He was highly intelligent and commendably self-educated. Quite able to order his activities according to his own particular wishes, except in his bleakest periods.'

'Would it have been likely that he would've been the one to send me the eye?'

'Possibly. What was your relationship with Ross during the war? Assuming you don't mind my asking.'

Kate explained what little there was to explain.

And Melville stood then, and moved to the table beside the bay window, where he poured two glasses of water. 'I would say it's entirely *possible* that Ross sent you the eye. He was deeply disturbed by his experience at Arnhem. His first experience with battle. An especially horrific one as well. The sense of inadequacy and impotence many medics felt in such circumstances cannot be underestimated. Though that still is not to say that Ross *did* send you the eye. Merely that I believe it possible.'

Kate nodded slowly, and then looked directly at Melville. 'I *have* heard that when he broke down in Germany he was found wandering around carrying a severed arm and saying he was going to take it to the owner and sew it back on.'

'It was a hand, actually. One which he found by the side of the road. Ross was eventually discovered by an American officer and taken away to an aid station.'

'That does seem similar to sending an eye in a bottle.'

'It wouldn't be inconsistent, certainly.' Dr Melville's bright blue eyes, set in a ring of wrinkles, gazed consideringly at Kate. 'Was the eye severed deliberately? Or did it appear to have been forced from the skull by accidental external trauma?'

'It didn't look to me as though it had been cut out.'

'Well, in *my* view, it would have been quite unlikely that Ross would sever an eye himself and pack it off in the post. But if he *had* been sufficiently traumatized, if he *was* in a state of sufficient disturbance, and he *was*, I should say, at Arnhem. He might have, under those circumstances, picked up an eye, if it had been . . . well . . . if it hadn't been normally attached.'

'I see.' Kate sipped her water and set the glass on the desk.

'I wouldn't have thought Ross capable of any premeditated planning, but in an act of the moment, if he considered it an act of kindness, he might have done something very much like that. Sent the body part of a person he admired to the dead man's widow as a keepsake.'

Kate nodded and said thank you. And tried to think what else she ought to ask while she had the chance. 'How did Ross happen to come to Leith House?'

Dr Melville fingered the file in front of him for a second, and then dropped his horn-rimmed reading glasses into the breast pocket of his navy blue suit. 'A solicitor wrote asking if space were available. Leith House had opened its doors as a clinic of this sort in 1949, and though it filled quickly, there were occasional vacancies, as you might imagine.' Melville paused to relight his pipe. 'Ross was brought here in 1953 from the military hospital where he'd resided since 1945.'

'Who brought him?'

'A doctor, now deceased, from Aberfeldy. How he came to be involved in the case I never heard. He brought him in a hired car from Craigalston Hospital.'

'And Ross' fees were paid by a benefactor of some sort?'

'Yes.' Dr Melville smoothed his reddish-blond mustache, setting his thumb and forefinger in the center and sliding them out to the sides.

'Do you know who the person is?'

'I don't, as it happens. And if I did, I would not be at liberty to say without the requisite legal instruction.'

'I'm sorry, I didn't mean to be nosey. I'm just . . . it seems so odd to me. An unknown benefactor, it's like something out of Dickens.'

'It does happen, though. We had another patient here with a benefactress. It's one of our most successful cases. She left us in a much improved state. One isn't always able to observe such improvement, and it's a great consolation when one does.'

'Yes, I'm sure it must be. Would it be possible for me to ask you to describe Ross' condition? I wouldn't want you to violate any sort of confidentiality, and I don't know if it's right of me to ask. I'm interested in war trauma. I have a good friend who was a scout in Europe, and other acquaintances as well, of course, and I'm curious about what it's like.'

'I am free to make certain observations, with Ross now deceased. Were he alive, I could not be nearly so forthcoming. I can say, in general terms, using very large strokes of the pen indeed, that he was haunted by the horror of the war, his terror in the face of it, and his sense of having failed utterly to save and heal as he'd intended. Medics were terribly vulnerable in the midst of the carnage, yet responsible all the while for *saving* lives in thoroughly impossible situations.'

'I can't imagine going through a battle, much less worrying about caring for the wounded.'

'I rather suspect nearly all medics suffered from a sense of inadequacy and impotence. The number of wounded appeared infinite. The resources the medics had at their disposal were limited. Such a sense of overwhelming responsibility, and the impossibility of living up to it was a very difficult state to manage.

'Some medics soldiered on, as it were, and were able to return to normal life without observable signs of disability. But many suffered debilitating manifestations of their battle-field experiences. Stuttering. Shaking. Uncontrolled weeping. Psychosomatic ailments such as the inability to speak or walk. Behaviors such as those sometimes persisted for months and years at a time. Ross MacNab did not begin to speak again until early 1947.'

'Is that a long time for that condition to hang on?'

'Aye, it is. He was a gentle, shy, anxious, introverted person who feared risk and responsibility. He was very sensitive. Very artistic. The only child of quiet, unassuming parents. His mother was forty when he was born. His father was fifty-two. The mother's life was centered on Ross. The father worked as a clerk in a small suburban indemnity firm. Ross had grasped early that they both hoped for a very quiet, very modest life for him. Inherent traits, perhaps, in them, worked upon as well by the deprivations of the First World War as well as the Great Depression. Though I hasten to add that such a perspective is merely my own interpretation.'

Kate nodded and said she understood.

'Certainly Ross realized early that they hoped to see him in a steady, routine office job of some sort, pursuing simple everyday hobbies. Collecting stamps, perhaps. Marrying a sympathetic young woman, and raising their children close to his parents. Yet Ross' aspirations were for an artistic career. Whether he would have followed his own inclinations if he hadn't been injured in the war, I couldn't say.'

'But he had gotten better since you'd been working with him?'

'Oh, aye, I would have said so, yes, definitely. Though,

recent developments lead one to wonder.' He smiled and tapped his short, broad fingers on the wooden arms of his chair. 'In addition to the various forms of psychoanalysis I employed, I tried to encourage him to work out a way of ordering his days that gave him real satisfaction. The immersion in hobbies which would help keep him interested, and as free of stress as he was likely to be. Clearly I misjudged his condition, and missed significant signs of distress.'

'They must not have been easy to see.'

'Perhaps, and yet that *is* my job.'

'Did Ross leave a suicide note?'

'No. No, he did not.'

'But you are satisfied that it *was* suicide?'

Dr Melville stared at Kate in silence for a moment, before he said, 'Why would you ask such a question?'

'Well, it sounded as though you were surprised he'd killed himself, and I just wondered if you . . . if you had any doubt at all that he did.'

'I can't imagine the alternative. It couldn't have been an accident, not with the amount of Nembutol in his system. Concentrated as it was in the dregs of the coffee in his thermos. Foul play would seem highly unlikely. I see few means, and no motives whatsoever. The procurator fiscal had no doubts a-tall.'

'That doesn't mean he's right. They aren't always, are they?'

'No.' Dr Melville pulled his reading glasses out of his pocket and read the last page in the file in front of him before he closed it again. 'I expect the most logical position I could espouse at this moment is to say that it's highly probable that I didn't fully recognize, or accurately analyze, certain aspects of his condition. One would *like* to think that were not the case, but thinking what one wishes to think is frequently damaging, is it not?'

'I know. From my own long and painful experience.' Kate smiled and picked up her purse. 'I don't mean to be insulting, but I don't meet too many doctors who seem as willing to consider their professional behavior nearly as critically as you.'

'I manage on certain days a great deal better than on others.'

'So do I.' Kate slipped the strap of her purse over her shoulder, and thanked Dr Melville for his help. She hesitated though, before she got up, and said, 'Does it seem likely to you that Ross wouldn't have written a suicide note? Wouldn't he have wanted to explain to you, if no one else?'

'I'm sorry to say I don't know. I would have thought Ross would have written a note. I doubt he would have wished anyone here to feel they had failed. He was especially fond of Nurse Ferguson. But that's no more than speculation on my part.'

Kate nodded, and then sighed. 'I don't know why I feel it as strongly as I do, but I wish very much that I'd known Ross better. The quiet, sad man I never took time to talk to back when we were all in Wales. I feel sorry for him. I'm a writer so I get interested in questions about who people are, and why they make the choices they do. But I think it's more personal than that in this case. Anyway, thank you, Dr Melville. I appreciate your seeing me without an appointment.'

'I liked Ross very much. I shall miss him. Aside from wanting to see him more at peace with himself, I enjoyed our conversations. He was interested in a great many things, and I'd hoped he'd have time to pursue them in the sort of depth he would have, if he'd lived longer. He should have had many more years to sort himself out.'

'Could I ask you one other thing? Would you be willing to give me the name of the solicitor who handled his account here?'

Dr Melville studied Kate for a minute, then wrote a name on a prescription pad, ripped the sheet off and pushed it toward her across the desk. 'His office is in Dunblane.'

Seven

It was a disconcerting day, even then. Tied as it was to a string of choices made on instinct, because of Ross MacNab's death.

When Kate looked back on it later, it made her shiver – the decisions she'd come to without thinking that led her places she never thought she'd go. To the edge of death, finally. In a way that terrified her. That she'd dream about for twenty years.

It was the fact that Ross MacNab killed himself that got her started. Suicide, disturbing her that day the way it had for years. The despair, the suffering, the self-loathing. The fact one sad human being being overcome by anguish, caused *or* imagined. From tragic circumstances, from mental imbalance, from lack of faith in what *can* carry us through. From any, or all, or more.

It made her imagine what that must be like, and wonder if it could've been prevented. And how you'd feel if you were the parent, knowing your son had despaired of the life you'd given him here.

It came too from when Kate was in college after the war. After Graham had been killed. After she'd learned about anguish herself. When she was finishing her degree at Northwestern, and had gone to her doctor in Evanston with a nasty case of bronchitis.

She'd had shakes and a cough and a high fever. And when they'd finally led her to an examining room, it was next to one where a teenage boy who'd just tried to kill himself sat staring at his mother.

The door had been open as she'd walked past, and she'd seen him on the examining table, a tall good-looking kid who was trying to talk but couldn't make his tongue move properly, so that the, 'I'm sorry, Mom, I'm sorry,' he kept repeating was barely understandable. Tears ran down both their faces, and his mother kept saying, 'I love you, Brad. I'm so glad you're OK,' while the doctor worked at comforting them both.

They'd left the door open for several minutes more, for reasons Kate never understood, and she'd heard the whole thing. The doctor saying, 'Now that we've pumped the barbiturates out of your stomach, you're going to be fine, but we'll have to put you in the hospital overnight, and let you talk to the doctors there.'

The boy said, 'I'm sorry, Mom,' another umpteen times, and she repeated, 'I love you so much,' till the doctor interrupted, saying, 'You've got so much to live for, and we have to help you understand this, and figure out how to keep you from feeling so discouraged again. There'll be doctors at the hospital who'll want to discuss . . .'

It had made Kate sick to her stomach. Listening. Not being able to stop, even with her door closed, lying on the table trying to imagine what the boy felt, and what the mother must feel, and how much worse it would've been if nobody'd found him in time.

The thought that this young boy, with so many years ahead of him that *could* be filled with good things, regardless of whatever he'd already lived through – with loving other people, and being loved, and learning whatever interested him, with doing work that accomplished something and made him see that he was useful, with coming to understand why he was here, and the care that lay behind that. The thought that he could throw it away for angst over anything, especially what matters when you're sixteen, when everything then is the end of the world and you can't put much in perspective. The thought of that had made Kate sick.

She'd only just started praying again then, shortly before she'd seen that boy, and she'd prayed for Brad and his family all the years since without ever knowing anything more about how they'd done through the years.

The situation she faced now was almost that distanced. It wasn't as though Kate had known Ross MacNab. It wasn't grief, of the kind that comes when it's someone you actually love.

It came from thinking about what he'd gone through in the war, and how hard it had been for him to come to grips with that. And imagining him working to drag himself out of it – only to be beaten down by an unnamed anguish, one that came without the kind of warning that could have led others to help him.

Kate kept asking what could have happened to make him change that much, that no one else could see, as she drove the narrow twisting roads from Leith House toward Dunblane.

She considered that boy at the doctor's, and that world that stretched beyond her – even there on the Dunblane road – with all the lives she could never know. She thought about Ben, and Jessie's death too, and the work that filled his days. And avoided the question she knew she couldn't answer.

What's making me go on with this, even though it makes no sense?

Because there was no possibility she wouldn't keep trying to understand who Ross had been and why he'd felt driven to kill himself. And what the war had been like for him. And why he would've sent her Graham's eye – *if*, in fact, he had.

The thing I'm dying to know first, of course, is who paid for him to stay at Leith House, and why was the secrecy so important? Was it just a self-effacing altruistic desire to stay anonymous? Or is there something more, with wider implications?

Kate knew she'd keep poking at Ross MacNab's life till she couldn't go any further. Or she found out enough to satisfy her – the curiosity, and whatever else it was – the inexplicable sense she had that that's what she was intended to do.

Half of her was looking forward to it. To chasing after the unknown because it would lead to the unexpected. Which made her ask if her life was too safe. Knowing that life never can be. That one phone call, or one routine test, can change it forever in a second.

The other half of her was back-peddling fast. Thinking about deadlines, and the work she had to do, and the dangers of stirring up trouble.

*   *   *

That day, at least, she accomplished something. She went to the solicitor's office in Dunblane and learned everything Edwin Smith was willing to tell – and more.

He'd been contacted in 1953 by a solicitor in a foreign country and asked to arrange payments to Leith House for the care of Ross MacNab. That he'd never known the identity of the donor. That bank cheques arrived from a UK bank every six months and were forwarded to Leith House by Smith's firm, which stood ready to contact that bank, if, and when, information from Leith House required communication.

Smith wouldn't tell her the name of the bank, but Kate got it by reading the file when Smith was called out of the room.

Kate also found Welsh's house, an obviously empty bungalow on a quiet Dunblane side street. And was told by the neighbor next door that Mr and Mrs Phillip Welsh had moved down to the Borders, where Mrs Welsh had family.

The neighbor couldn't remember the name of the town, but she did know that Mr Welsh had left the hospital without giving as much notice as he would have liked because Mrs Welsh's mother had been taken ill. They'd promised to get in touch when they'd gotten settled. And Kate gave the woman her business card, and asked her to pass on their address.

Then she found a public phone box and wrote down the numbers of every bank in town. She phoned each in turn and, using her best Scottish accent, identified herself as Mrs Phillip Welsh inquiring about an account in the process of being closed.

The first two banks said they had no such account. Kate giggled and said, how silly of her, she was so distracted with the move they'd just made, she'd phoned the wrong bank.

The third bank had a record of her account, and Kate said she'd misplaced the paperwork in the course of their move which indicated the balance they'd left to cover incoming cheques.

The clerk was unable to accommodate Mrs Welsh over the telephone. She would have to present herself in person to receive that sort of information.

Monday, January 8th, 1962

Kate phoned the London bank that had paid MacNab's fees, and learned nothing but the name of the man who'd overseen the account. He'd been quite condescending as well as rude, and Kate had come very close to snapping at him, which she generally tended not to do. Her fits of pique were usually directed at blood relations who'd repeated themselves one too many times, or were trying to tell her what to do.

Another atypical act that would have surprised her family and friends was that Kate looked through her closet for something to wear to the Suspense Writers International banquet with three full weeks to spare.

But the biggest departure from normal behavior was a repetition of an earlier one. She'd phoned Welsh's bank in Dunblane and pretended to be Mrs Welsh, a flustered and fussy Mrs Welsh, saying that the December bank statement had gone astray because of an incorrect address. Would they please read her the address in their records so she could make absolutely certain they had the correct one in their files, and the mistake had been nothing but typographical? Having just recently moved, with the second account in a new bank, and all the details of changing addresses and trying to keep track of what bills were outstanding from the previous account, she wanted to make doubly sure no more mail would be delayed.

It was disconcerting how easy it had been to lie like that. Which Kate told herself to think about later, while she wrote down the Welshes' new address in the Borders not too far north of Northumberland, England.

Wednesday, January 10th, 1962

The Welshes' cottage was a mile and a half past Traquair House, tucked into the same woods. And there Kate parked, behind a red Morris Minor, to the right of a small, whitewashed cottage.

She sat for a minute, and took a deep breath, staring at the moss-covered slate roof, before she started up the stone path toward the dark wooden door.

It was opened before she got to it by a salt-and-peppery man who stared at Kate coolly but correctly, with large watery-looking grey eyes magnified by the lenses in round black plastic frames.

'Mr Welsh? I'm Kate Lindsay. I wonder if I might talk with you for a moment.'

'Have we met?'

'No. I had an appointment to see Ross MacNab two days after he died. I'm interested in his life at Leith House, and I wonder if I could ask you one or two questions.'

'I shouldn't have thought myself the most appropriate person.' He was considering it visibly. Weighing the pros and cons. Deciding finally to organize his face, as well as his own options – when he opened the door wider and asked her into the room.

Kate sat in a wooden rocker close to a flickering coal fire, as Phillip Welsh asked if she'd care for a cup of tea. He'd taken the cozy off a brown porcelain pot, and was swirling the tea that was left.

Kate thanked him, but said no, that having dropped in un-announced, she didn't want to impose any further.

'How did you manage to find me?'

'You left a change of address with the postal service.' Kate was rummaging in her bag, hiding her eyes from her own prevarication, looking for a pad and pencil.

'I'm surprised they would have passed it along. What is it you wish to know?' He crossed one solid-looking leg over another and finished the tea in his cup.

Kate explained about the eye, and how she'd tracked MacNab down, hoping to ask about her husband's last days. 'When I learned he'd killed himself, I began to think it might've been because of me. Because as I understand it, he never had any other visitors, and how could anyone be sure how he'd react? You were there when he arrived, back in 1953, and you must have an impression of him. Would you have thought my coming to see him would've caused him to kill himself?'

Phillip Welsh was staring at the fire, his undistinguished face carefully closed and shuttered. 'I didn't know MacNab a-tall well. Dr Melville could tell you far more. I would've expected you'd question him.'

'I have, but I'm trying to talk to others as well. Sometimes people on the periphery can see more than those up close.

Had you noticed any worsening of Ross' condition before you left?'

'No, I hadn't. Except for the days of really inclement weather when he seemed a bit more restless. Wanting to get to his blind, and having to make do with reading and music.'

'Do you know anything about his benefactor? That's just idle curiosity on my part. The thought of someone who would do such kindness for a stranger makes you want to know more about them.'

'I know nothing a-tall about the person who paid his expenses, and I've made it rather a point not to speculate. One must set an example for staff in such cases.'

'Yes, I know what you mean. Why did you decide to retire? I'm sorry.' Kate smiled a warm, interested smile, as she swept the sides of her shiny dark hair back behind her ears. 'I'm a fiction writer. I have this uncontrollable curiosity about all sorts of unsuitable things, as well as everybody I meet, and I even embarrass *myself* occasionally.' She laughed and leaned back again, making the rocker rock.

'My wife's mother precipitated events. She lives in Galashiels, which is quite close, and she had a severe stroke a few weeks ago. That spurred us to make the move as quickly as we were able.' He seemed to be easier now, more relaxed and settled, as though this were ground he didn't mind covering. Unlike Ross MacNab.

'Do you think you'll be bored not working? You don't look old enough to be retiring.'

'I shall be working a few hours a week. My wife's family owns a modest hotel in Galashiels, and they're hoping for a bit of help in upgrading staff and adding a bit of polish.'

'That should keep you interested.'

'I hope so, yes.'

A pause followed. Coal burned. Tea was poured by Phillip Welsh. Ankles were crossed by Kate Lindsay, who waited a minute before asking Welsh if he knew who had brought MacNab to Leith House when he'd first arrived.

'I don't, no. A physician I think. It is normally a physician. Ross came from a military hospital, and that would've been usual.'

'His benefactor didn't come with him? Or appear any time after that?'

'No. No, we've never seen hide or hair of whoever the benefactor may be. Ah, Patricia. This is my wife. May I introduce Kate Lindsay?'

Kate shook hands with a thin, short, pleasant looking woman who spoke quietly and a little shyly in a stronger Scottish accent than her husband's.

They talked then about the cottage and the land. And Mrs Welsh told her of Traquair House and its Catholic family, who'd smuggled priests and supported the Jacobites, locking a gate to one of its long drives after Bonnie Prince Charlie rode out, swearing not to open it again till a Stewart sat on the Scottish throne. 'They've kept it locked ever after, for two hundred years and more. And visitors come all year round to see the house and grounds.'

Kate said she'd never heard anything about Traquair, as Phillip Welsh walked to the front door and laid a hand on the handle.

'Did you offer the young lady tea, Phillip?'

'I did, but she declined.'

'No, I have to go. I've already imposed enough.'

'She was asking about Ross MacNab. She knew him during the war.'

'Not well. He was a medic with my husband's Airborne Rangers. I only just located Ross, and I'd been looking forward to talking to him.'

'It was terribly sad, him taking his own life. I know Phillip was quite surprised.'

'Well . . .' Kate looked at the door Phillip Welsh was holding open and saw no other option but to smile and walk through it.

Fifteen minutes later, Phillip Welsh kissed his wife on the forehead, told her not to rush, to feel free to stay and give her mother lunch.

The second she'd driven away, he picked up the phone in the study and asked the trunk operator to connect him to Claridge's Hotel in London.

Phillip Welsh stared out the study window, after he'd finished the call, smiling to himself, and tapping a foot to a Tommy Dorsey tune playing on the turntable in the sitting room.

He was congratulating himself, in a modest way, on a bit of business well played, while also reminding himself to keep well away from any suggestion of greed. For that would prove foolhardy in the extreme with a man like Mr Wagner.

Phillip walked through to the sitting room, where he shoveled a scoop of coal on the fire, and stared at the blue and orange flames.

All those years since Ross first arrived, passing my observations on, proving my own reliability, while Wagner held my feet to the fire in his own gentlemanly fashion. It really is quite gratifying now to have my worth acknowledged with his offer of a trip to Cornwall.

It also precluded any further need to mention his own past services. The extracts of Ross' letters. The descriptions of the first few tentative talks, once Ross had begun to say something more than 'yes' and 'no' when spoken to. The intelligence to read between the lines and recognize what Mr Wagner wished to hear in a timely and regular fashion.

It was the Lindsay woman who changed the tide, of course, as soon as she'd rung Leith House and said she intended to call. A visitor who knew Ross during the war offered a first opportunity for the sort of conversation Ross's benefactor wished to avoid.

Deference. That's the approach. Never unctuous. Never obvious. Dependable and courteous. Never the first word implying that what I know could be dangerous to our American benefactor.

The vital question concerned Patricia. For would she balk at a holiday in Cornwall with her mother lying ill?

Not if I tell her it's a present from me, given in honor of her birthday. I should think she'd find that persuasive.

I do so hope it was the right decision, telling Mr Wagner from the first that Patricia would never learn of his largesse. For Wagner mustn't see her as any sort of threat. Kept in the dark on every particular, she shouldn't warrant a moment's uneasiness. Not from our Mr Wagner.

Assuming I've judged him correctly. For if I haven't, a very great deal could be said to be at stake. He's not a harmless personage, is he? Ross MacNab is well and truly dead. And I must err on the side of caution.

Phillip Welsh stared at the fire, his hands thrust in his pockets, without noticing that the turntable arm was stuck in a groove on the record.

Perhaps there's more I still ought to do to safeguard Patricia's future.

Eight

Friday, January 12th, 1962

The sun was bright, when it burned out from under thick drifts of cloud, as Kate drove south from Loch Rannoch to Fortingall, on the north side of the River Lyon.

It was a tiny village – a short string of stone cottages stretched along the banks of a narrow, flashing river, one small, old coaching inn quietly crumbling into damp and decay, one unassuming parish church, unlocked in the afternoon sun, frequently visited for its churchyard, for the three-thousand-year-old yew tree growing close to its western end.

Visitors also came out of curiosity. For Fortingall is said to be the birthplace of Pontius Pilate, the son of a Roman legionnaire and a nameless Celtic wife. Kate was doubting that such a thing could be substantiated one way or another, and wondering what evidence there could actually be, as she parked her car by the second cottage and looked for the black Lab.

He was behind the house when she knocked on the front door, and he ambled around a corner, lumbering over to sniff her hand – just as the door was opened by a tall, blond man with a scar on his neck and a crooked-toothed smile on an easy everyday face. 'Mrs Lindsay, is it?'

'Kate, yes. Thank you for letting me visit.'

'It's a very great pleasure. I knew your husband by reputation, and whatever I can do to be of service will be an honor indeed. Would you care for a cup of tea? Or would you rather walk awhile along the river?'

'I'd rather walk, if it's all right with you.'

'That's grand. It's my half-day today, as I mentioned when you rang, and I usually take Robbie for a run.'

Robbie the Labrador was looking up anxiously, afraid of

disappointment, gripping a red rubber ball in perfectly straight white teeth.

They walked down to the river and wandered along the grassy brown banks, watching Robbie chase the ball and drop it at George Gunn's feet.

'So you work in Aberfeldy as a motor mechanic?'

'Aye, and have done ever since the war. You said there was more you wished to ask about Ross.'

'Yes.' Kate explained about the eye in the bottle. The desire to hear about Graham's last days. The curiosity now about Ross as a person, and why he would've killed himself right when he did. Her fear that her own visit might have been related. 'There's something about it too I can't quite explain that makes it hard for me to let it go. I write novels, suspense novels, some of them, so I've probably got an overly active imagination, but the secrecy about Ross' benefactor seems odd to me. Tantalizing too, being the way I am. I keep wanting to find out who it was.'

'I rather thought Ross enjoyed the secrecy. The excitement of it possibly, of knowing a secret and keeping it. Or the satisfaction of proving himself trustworthy, by not revealing the benefactor's name.'

'We do like knowing something other people don't. I think it makes us feel powerful, like we're part of an inside clique. What *I* keep asking myself is why the benefactor went to such extremes to keep from being found out. I can see wanting to be anonymous, when you're doing an act of charity. But this seems more excessive than that, and it makes me want to know why.'

'I don't know anything that could help you there.'

'Could you tell me what you do know about Ross?' They were trudging through tall grass, coats and scarves blowing around them, watching sunlight glitter on the water, birds skittering and skimming across it, Robbie barking ahead of them at something lying on the ground.

'There's not a great deal to tell really. Ross was an only child.' George Gunn reached up under his heavy woolen sweater and pulled a pack of Players out of the pocket of his shirt. He lit one with his back to the wind, and blew out a long stream of smoke. 'His father worked in an indemnity firm in the outskirts of Edinburgh, though they lived in Falkirk near me. I never knew Ross well. His parents were a great deal older than mine, and not terribly sociable, and Ross was a quiet sort of bide-at-home bloke. Pleasant. A good lad. But not one of the group, if you take my meaning.'

'Yes, I think I do. I was like that too. We sometimes come into our own much later in life.' Kate smiled at George Gunn, as she pushed her hands in her coat pockets.

He laughed and said, 'You don't remind me of Ross MacNab a-tall. Poor wee lad. He wasn't cut out for being a medic. Not by a long chalk. I spent very little time with him when we were in combat. We were attached to different groups after Arnhem. I only saw him once, right before he broke down and was sent off to hospital, like I told you when you rang. Robbie stay down!'

Robbie had jumped up on Kate in an excess of exuberance, and Kate leaned over to pet him, as soon as he'd gotten down. 'So you wrote to him in the hospital?'

'Aye, about a year or so after the war. I found the hospital he was in, and began sending him a Christmas card, and a letter or two each year. I never got a response, and after some little while I phoned the military hospital and spoke to his doctor. He suggested I keep on with it. Ross' father had died, and his mother was poorly by that time, and mine was nearly the only word Ross heard from the outside world. The doctor thought it was good for Ross to get the odd card and letter, even if he couldn't respond.'

'But he did eventually?'

'Aye, he wrote me after he'd gone to Leith House. Christmas 1953. He told me he'd changed residences, and thanked me for writing. So I kept on with it. Once a year or so I'd get a reply. Longer replies over time. I asked him about his bene-factor, but he never said a word. Not till this last Christmas. He mentioned something in passing about his benefactor having been the only person he'd risked his life to save. In the war, I took him to mean. But that's all Ross ever would say. I'm sorry the poor bugger went and killed himself. It's a rotten shame. I thought he'd gotten better.'

They'd turned back toward the small stone cottages, the wind to their backs and gusting hard, when Kate asked Gunn about Arnhem.

'I was with the engineers, but even I could see it was a

frightful blunder, Arnhem. Terrible. Market Garden, the Allies called it. It very possibly could've been avoided, if Monty had listened to the Belgian underground when they told him there were Panzer divisions all across the area.'

'Yes, I've read that somewhere too.'

'That's war, though, isn't it?' They were standing in Gunn's front yard, gazing over at the yew tree growing against the church. 'I haven't been much help, have I? But if I can be of use in the future, I hope you'll ring me straightaway.'

'I will. Thank you. If you think of anything else about Ross that might be important, please phone me right away and I'll reimburse you for the call.'

'Aye, I will indeed.'

It was looking hopeless, Kate thought, as she turned north toward Loch Rannoch. Nothing new learned about Graham. No one else she knew to talk to about Ross. No hint of why he would've killed himself. Or why his benefactor had worked so hard to keep his identity hidden.

Then accept that that's the way it is, and get back to what you should be doing.

And what is that would you say? Living alone. With a father-in-law who's failing. Working alone in your empty little room. Writing about people who've never existed with problems only you can fix. Keeping yourself neatly protected from the outside world. Where you can't control the variables, and the pain you feel is your own.

I'm doing what I'm meant to be doing. The last fifteen years haven't been wasted. But that doesn't mean you're not hiding. Or that you haven't been afraid to look at your life for a very long time.

And what about Ross MacNab? You thought you were supposed to look for his benefactor, and yet that's withering away to nothing. So maybe all it was was me, doing what I wanted to do on my own.

You can't expect to learn much about Ross in less than fifteen seconds. And patience isn't your long suit. No, and never will be. Not without divine intervention.

George Gunn sat in a wooden chair by the coal fire in his sitting room waiting for the phone to ring. His wife was standing next to him, leaning over a small table, pulling a photograph out of cardboard photo holders glued on a page in an album.

The phone rang five minutes later. And the trunk operator told him she had his party on the line.

'Mrs Lindsay? . . . It's George Gunn here. My wife's thought of something that might be a bit of help from when Ross patched me up in the war. I hadn't thought to mention it when we spoke before . . .

'Right. There was a Yank there, you see, when I saw Ross. He'd been shot, and he'd fallen in the river, the Saar River it was, in Germany. He was on a stretcher, and Ross had bandaged his wounds . . .

'When I first walked up, the Yank said something about Ross having saved his life. Having pulled him out of the river, after he'd been shot . . . He told Ross that if he hadn't gotten him out of the river, it would've been the end of him. He'd been unconscious, you see, in the water, though how it happened I don't know . . . It's made me wonder if he might have been the one who became Ross' benefactor. The one Ross said he'd risked his life to save . . .

'Aye, but there's more to tell as well, for you see, I persuaded a Yank photographer to take a picture of us, me and Ross, and mail it off to my wife. She's remembered all about it, soon as we started talking tonight, about me telling her about Ross, and the American he pulled from the river. It was the only photo she had of me, and she'd put it away in a photograph album . . .

'The American's there, you see, in the photo as well, with his leg wound and his bandaged hand, and another Yank who was very bad at the time . . . No, we wouldn't mind a-tall. Not if you return it after you've made the copies . . . Tomorrow then. That's grand . . . No trouble a-tall . . .

'It's Emmie you should thank. I doubt I would've remembered.'

Saturday, January 13th, 1962

The cliffs of Cornwall, the north coast, on the Bristol Channel, had been whipped by wind and rain most of the day, and all the night before. But that morning, the rain had stopped an hour or so before dawn.

Even so, the sun stayed hidden behind heavy grey clouds, blown across the channel by north-west winds, lightening only a thin grey strip where swells of black water touched the sky beyond the rugged shore.

It was a coast that appealed to trekkers and climbers far more than the sedentary. Though regular tourists came in summer, intent on Tintagel, looking for signs of Merlin and Arthur, for hints of a past worth believing in. But in January, after days of rain and worse, the cliffs on the coast between Port Isaac and Tintagel are almost always deserted. And that morning was no exception.

Except for a tall man, in a waxed khaki rain jacket and black knitted stocking cap, who sat in a rented Austin on a patch of gravelly ground, hidden from the road by a copse of trees, a quarter of a mile from the cliffs. He'd parked before dawn and sat with the engine off, swallowing chunks of bread and cheese, drinking strong black coffee, listening to the wind on the headland.

He yawned, and blew his nose, and looked at his watch at twenty to six. Then packed away his breakfast, and climbed out of the car.

He walked up and down a hundred foot section of headland for the next twenty-five minutes, scanning the path with binoculars as the sky lightened, staring over the edge of the cliffs, studying the rocks jutting out of the sea. They were huge there, sharply irregular, jigsaw puzzles of interlocking corners, a hundred feet below a cliff top rough with scrabbly loose stone.

He stopped above the roughest stretch, where rocks shot up out of crashing white water in jagged spiked edges, studying the paths along the cliffs that stretched in both directions.

Good, nobody out and about. And there won't be, most likely, all day today. Not this early, anyway. On a morning as cold as this.

It was raining again. Blowing in gusts off the channel, cutting through cloth, drilling into skin and bone.

Water rats wouldn't want to be out, precisely as I'd hoped. But he'll be here. By six fifteen. Dependable as always.

If I hadn't been soft, one time, Welsh could've lived to be a hundred. But if Phillip's told me the truth, this is where it will end.

*It's not what I intended. I didn't want the risk to begin with,
even back in '46. Ross could've told a doctor then, or anytime
since, and the doctor could've called army records and made
my life a living hell.*

Then why did I risk it when I knew better?

Same answer as always. He dragged me out of the Saar.

He glanced at his watch, and wiped the rain from his eyes,
then rubbed his hands together in their thin leather gloves,
before pulling binoculars from his pocket. He focused them
toward Port Isaac and smiled a second later.

There. Climbing the next to the last rise.

He looked north and studied the cliffs, and scanned the
coast road too, till he saw what he wanted to see. That there
were two men on that stretch of the Cornwall coast – himself,
pulling up the collar on his waxed khaki coat, standing on the
edge of the rock face cliff. Another climbing toward him,
threading his way on a narrow path littered with rubble and
sheep droppings, gripping his shiny black mackintosh against
the wind, holding a cap on his head.

The man in the khaki coat was taller and broad shouldered.
The one in the cap was slighter and grey haired – and it was
he who stretched out his hand first to the man who'd watched
him on the path.

They talked for a few minutes. Looking military and
proscribed, like soldiers on the same side consulting. Nodding
in agreement, finally. And then almost smiling, as though
they'd begun talking about less important things.

They turned to stare at the sea – to point to clouds and
landmarks in the distance, and down toward the waves
breaking on the rocks – standing right on the edge of the
cliff.

The taller one glanced at both sides of the coast, as he
reached for his wallet in his pants pocket. He smiled while
he opened it and pulled something out, then pointed out to
sea again as though he'd seen something unexpected.

The shorter man turned to look where he'd pointed. And
the taller man shoved him, fast and hard from behind, watching
him flail in mid air, watching him land on the rocks below,
jagged rocks a hundred feet down, watching him lie without
moving long enough to be sure he wouldn't.

Wednesday, January 24th, 1962

Ben Reese stuck his arm out the window and signaled a left-hand turn, then took a rag off the worn seat of his gunmetal grey 1947 Plymouth and wiped the inside of the windshield.

Having a defroster that worked might be nice. Just once before I die.

He was back from Dayton, where he'd set-up a test of his nylon-paper preservation process with a friend at the Dayton Museum, and also had lunch with a donor who'd handed him a big metal box, and said, 'Here, take my collection.'

Why would Roy Bossert, the Born Explainer, suddenly give Alderton the coins he's collected all his life, and then not want to talk about it?

He didn't look well. And he's almost ninety. Maybe he doesn't want the coins left in his estate.

If he'd wanted to tell you he would have, and speculating won't get you anywhere.

It was after six when Ben drove up his driveway, and decided to take a quick look at the coins, then lock them away in his closet, and go out and brush Max.

He carried the heavy, pea-green one-and-a-half-foot metal cube in through the back door and set it on the counter in the kitchen.

Then he walked into the dining room, and on, through the corner of the big, white living room, to the square white foyer, to get his mail from the porch. There was an oversized airmail letter from Kate, and he opened it and started reading before he closed the front door.

January 15, 1962

Dear Ben,

Quite a bit has happened since we last spoke. I met with George Gunn, and learned that the day Ross MacNab went over the brink in Germany he'd hauled an unconscious injured American out of the Saar River. Ross told Gunn in a letter that there was only one time he'd consciously risked his life and saved someone, and Gunn thinks it *might* be that Yank. Or that it sounds like a good possibility.

Gunn's wife remembered a photograph too that he'd had sent to her from Germany of himself and Ross and two Americans. The one Ross pulled out of the river is on the left in the copy I've enclosed.

Also, I talked to Nellie Ferguson (who's been a nurse at Leith House longer than MacNab was a patient), and she *thinks* she saw the benefactor when MacNab first arrived. She's always *assumed*, at least, that the benefactor was the American who brought MacNab; someone she saw talking to Welsh in the Leith House car park.

She heard the American tell Welsh to get in touch with him at his vacation home in Europe (she can't remember where), or back in the States later, after a certain date. She doesn't recall the place in the States, but it made her think of an animal the way Texas makes her think of cattle and cowboys and rattlesnakes.

The American told Welsh to keep him informed, to let him know if MacNab: (1) needed extra money, (2) started talking about the war, or (3) had any visitors. He also said that if Ross did start talking more, he (the American) would see it as a sign of real improvement.

This wasn't the Scottish doctor who picked MacNab up at the military hospital. Nellie knew him (and saw him in the car when the American and Welsh were talking). The doctor took MacNab inside Leith House and handed him over. She remembers the American in the car park as being tall and dark-haired and somewhat good-looking.

So now we know Welsh talked to this person. It may <u>not</u> have been the benefactor, but it *could've* been, based on the conversation she heard. If it was, Welsh lied to me in no uncertain terms. It also could've been someone paid by the benefactor to take MacNab to Leith House. She had no way of knowing which.

And (you may be as surprised to hear this as I was) Welsh died last Saturday, the 13th. I heard it from Nellie Ferguson. He fell off a cliff on the north coast of Cornwall. He and his wife had gone there for the weekend, and he was walking the cliffs alone, and apparently slipped and

fell. Does that seem odd to you? MacNab, and then Welsh?
This close together? And if so, do you have any theo-
ries?

   Hope all Alderton troubles are now a thing of the past.
   Thanks for all the help.
   Kate

Ben sat down on the steps that led up to his bedroom, and
laid the letter on one of them, before he slid two taped-together
sheets of cardboard out of the manila envelope.

He broke the tape and pulled out a three-by-five black-and-
white print. And when he looked at the picture of Ross MacNab
and George Gunn, and the two American soldiers on stretchers
on the ground, Ben said, 'It can't be!' and leapt off the stairs.

His eyes were outraged, and his lips looked bloodless, tensed
and tight against his teeth, the bones of his face even sharper
than usual, as he shook his head and said, 'Mitchell!'

It is.

Ted Mitchell.

Look at him!

*The butcher and traitor I should've stopped when I had the
chance!*

Ben stepped into his study, found the magnifying glass in
his desk and studied the face in the photograph partly hidden
by an upraised hand.

He looked at his watch then, and picked up the phone.

'This is Ben Reese, is Chief Hansen still there, please? . . .
Thanks . . . Hey, Chester, it's Ben . . . What's the fastest way
to trace somebody who was in the military during the Second
World War? Call the military records place in St. Louis? . . .
The problem is that I don't know if this guy *was* technically in
the military. He was one of those scientist types they sent
in behind the front line troops . . .

'Right, but most of that technical squad stuff is still classified . . . They *would* probably answer you faster than they
would me. Since you're a real live Chief of Police . . .

'The name's Ted Mitchell. Theodore Mitchell, or Edward
Mitchell, I don't know which. They gave him the rank of
colonel, even though he wasn't trained, or actually part of the
Army. I ran into him in January of '45 and took him into
Germany . . . It's too long a story to go into on the phone, but

I'll tell you sometime. I'd like to hear what you think . . . No, but there're several very good reasons why I have to track him down . . . Oh, would you also try to find out where Mitchell was from? The family address listed in his papers? Thanks. Now go home and see your wife . . . Yeah, you too.'

Ben dropped the receiver in the cradle and stared out across his side yard past the cluster of blue spruce, seeing Ted Mitchell in 1945 leaning against a tree in a German forest, adrenaline buzzing in his eyes, an army-issue Colt hanging from his hand.

Nine

B en Reese had just tied his blanket roll on top of his beat-up musette bag, when a GI pulled the tent flap back and said, 'Company Commander wants to see you, Sergeant.'

'Thanks, I'm on my way.'

Ben slung the bag over his shoulder, grabbed his Springfield, and shoved his helmet on his head.

Captain Fields was leaning over a folding table signing papers when Ben walked into the CP tent and saluted the top of Field's head.

'Got a Jeep waiting for you, Sergeant, to get you to the replacement center closer to Monschau. These are your transportation orders for picking up transport there, plus maps and disposition papers that just came through from regimental. Good luck down there. Sounds like it's heatin' up.'

Ben thanked him as he took the packet. And then went to look for his Jeep.

Five minutes later, he was being driven west through camp, when he saw Ted Mitchell, fifty feet in front of him, watching his driver put two metal boxes into the back of his Jeep.

Ben refused to salute Mitchell. He stared into his face instead, as his own Jeep passed Mitchell's, and flipped his cigarette at Mitchell's feet.

Ben was in the replacement center at 0800 hours, snaking his way through the chaos and the crowds, shaking his head at the pink necks and the new boots and the freshly painted helmets, at the squeamish eyes and the nervous-looking lips. Ben's uniform had parts of France, Holland, Belgium and Germany ground into it, and he hadn't shaved in a week, or showered in too many more.

But he told himself to back off anyway, because these kids had been shoved into cattle cars, and packed fast into troop trucks, with no information about where they were going, or what to expect when they got there, and it had to be hitting them hard.

He also asked himself if he'd ever been that green, while he scratched the back of his neck. *They look like ten-year-old kids. And how long are they gonna last anyway? You put them in the woods around Bastogne with as little training as they get now, and I'd be amazed if—*

'Sergeant!'

Ben could hear it all right there in the voice, and he told himself to shut his mouth. He'd been busted down to private twice for saying exactly what he thought, when life and death had been at stake. But it made no sense to go through it again for anything picayune.

The voice belonged to a second lieutenant (clean and perfectly pressed, insignias bright and shiny) who glared at Ben before he snapped, 'You're out of uniform, soldier, and you got yourself unauthorized equipment!'

'Yessir. I'm just in from the line, sir, and I'm under special orders now to report to the front down south as fast as I can get there. I'm to pick up transportation here—'

'Show me your orders.'

'Sir.' Ben had already started pulling them out of the breast pocket of his battle jacket.

'There's a four by four over there on its way to—'

'I think you'll see, sir, if you read on, that I'm instructed to find individual transportation. They're moving a bunch of scouts south fast, and my other orders, under that page, instruct me to—'

'Carry on, Sergeant.'

'Thank you, sir.' Ben saluted and took back his orders as the second lieutenant marched away.

Ben closed his eyes and sighed, before he walked on toward the motor pool.

It took Ben all day and night, plus all the next day and half that second night to get where he was going – to drive down the eastern border of Belgium, down the length of Luxembourg, down past Trier, Germany, which lay east across the Saar River.

They drove past bombed and burned villages, around piles of brick and craters in the earth that were all that was left of too many. Past pastureland too, and mountainous ravines, that made Ben want to stop and stare.

They could've made it faster, if God *or* man had co-operated. It was snow and ice and terrain. It was hospital trucks and supply convoys and tanks blocking the roads.

It did give Ben time to read his maps and disposition papers. And study the Saar valley around the town of Trier, and the large evergreen Saarbrücken Forest that stretched away on the south. Which is not to say he thought he knew enough. The intelligence was old and sketchy – too spotty and too simple, the way it looked to him.

He still hadn't been told why they were bringing scouts in from all over. It could've been some kind of search-and-destroy, to clean out something nasty before they sent troops in. Or it could've been wide-ranging recon to set up a big advance.

He also knew it could all have changed by the time he got where he was going. The front as fluid as it was right then, there could easily be good reason to send every scout packing again and scatter them ten other places.

But Ben got to sleep, in the cold and snow, using his blanket as a poncho. And he walked too, to get blood to his toes, when the Jeep was down to a crawl. He drove and let his driver snore through most of the Luxembourg mountains.

And he didn't have reason to shoot a single round. Not one in two and a half days on the road.

But awake, or sleeping, or drifting in between, Ben Reese brooded on Mitchell. On his hidden Luger, and the ice in his eyes. On Baylor's first words, and Baylor's last, and the ones he couldn't get out before bullets in the back tore his soul away.

Ben wondered where Mitchell was, and who else he was doing what to. And he tried to come up with something he could do to put pressure on Colonel Mitchell.

He also asked himself why OSS would send the techs in right at that time, saddling scouts and front-line troops with even more responsibility. They were making a critical push right then, after a couple of really tough months. *You'd think the techs could've come in later, farther behind the front line.*

It's not like there's not enough to do, or plenty of strain to go around.

Ben was making up limericks about Mitchell, when the Jeep got to the pick-up spot on the west side of the Saar. It had turned the 21st by then, 0300 hours. And there was snow driving into Ben's face out of a pitch-black night.

His driver had radioed ahead a couple of hours earlier, and the flat-bottomed square-fronted standard metal assault boat was there waiting to pick Ben up, manned by three guys from a front-line unit hunkered down on the German side.

They rowed Ben across without any trouble, then walked him four miles into camp, reported their return at company CP, and found Ben a spot in a foxhole that looked drier than most.

He spent the rest of the night there dreaming about Mitchell, seeing him do unspeakable things, waking up to the clink of a Zippo being lit by another GI.

Ben had been the third scout to show up, and he'd been debriefed by S2 as soon as he reported in that morning. Intelligence was trying to get a comprehensive picture of the western border of Germany, and they'd be questioning every scout as soon as they made it in.

It had been foggy and badly overcast or snowing hard since the 14th, grounding all observation planes, which meant S2 was running blind – blinder, certainly, than they wanted to be inside the German border.

They had *some* first-hand information, but they wanted Ben to scout their eastern perimeter and report back before noon. Another scout would be assigned to him. They'd send him to Ben when he'd been debriefed. And they'd pass on then what they knew about the front.

Ben wanted to ask why they were bringing in so many scouts, but he knew better than to try it then. And he told the two S2 officers he'd be waiting in the mess tent, and went off to find coffee and K-rations.

He'd finished a fair amount of both, when a shiny new second lieutenant walked up with a scout Ben would remember for ever by not much more than the name Gene, and a vague idea that they would've been friends if they'd ever had time to talk.

Ben asked the kid lieutenant how it looked in front. Meaning, 'What does Intelligence say is out there?' Which he saw later as a very large mistake made by Ben Reese. He'd been on the line so long himself, he'd expected too much of somebody new.

He'd assumed the kid understood what he meant, and had been sent with info from S2. Only to learn very painfully later that the kid hadn't had a clue – that his answer to Ben of, 'Nothing to worry about,' should've been probed hard.

He should've asked what S2 said was east of them, and, 'Who brought the word in, and how old is it now?' Because then he would've talked to Intelligence, when he saw the kid didn't know anything.

Instead, he walked out in a khaki uniform in three feet of clean white snow and got himself trapped between the lines.

It was grey and cold and spitting snow. And Ben had stopped – Springfield in his right hand, .45 under that arm, hatchet hanging on his left hip – listening to a soft white world that muffled and distorted sound.

He froze where he was, absolutely still, half a mile east of American lines behind a tall dark fir that, unlike the trees left standing around Foy, still had lower limbs.

Combat instinct kept him there, every body part on high alert – listening hard, controlling his breathing, holding back the adrenaline – as he stared around the thick needled boughs down a straight stretch of powdery snow between two rows of planted trees.

Gene was on Ben's left, twelve or fifteen feet away now, straining to hear the same way Ben was, trying to figure out what it could've been.

Ben had heard something close-up a second ago, off on his left beyond Gene, and he'd signaled Gene to wait and listen when Gene hadn't stopped on his own.

Ben hadn't heard anything else in that direction, and it might've been something small and furry scurrying away from the sound of men – from him, from Gene, from what was worse rumbling their way in the distance, sounding large and ominous deeper inside Germany.

It was rolling land there, higher behind them and higher up ahead. And there was a narrow roadway off on their right that cut east-west between tree rows, but looked to Ben like it curved to the north fifty yards or so in front.

It was lower ground where they stood. Marshy too on the left beyond Gene, where there were swaths of low trees and thick clumps of wild shrub tangled with tall grass and weeds. Everything marshy was frozen solid and covered by new snow, and there were strangely shaped drifts everywhere they looked, blown along between trees.

Gene shrugged at Ben in a I'm-not-hearing-anything-near-here-now kind of way, and looked like he might step out from behind his tree. But Ben waved Gene back and pointed up ahead.

Ben knew what they were by then, even though he couldn't see them. Tiger tanks, more than one, coming from the north on the track through the woods, from the left as Ben looked east through forest, straining to catch the first glimpse.

He was about to motion to Gene to set up his bazooka, when he saw Gene swinging it up, getting ready to set it on his shoulder.

The first Tiger cranked out of a thick stand of trees running left to right as Ben saw it, then turned the curve in the road heading west straight toward them, one tree row over on Ben's right, fifty yards up ahead.

Ben was trying to see how many were behind it, to decide whether to try to stop it, or melt away fast and scout another day – when a machine gun opened fire sixty feet away on Gene's left.

It was where Ben had heard the soft sound earlier, from the marshy ground covered with bushes and weeds, which he realized now, entirely too late, was a well dug-in machine-gun nest manned by at least two men – two very experienced men who dropped Gene with their first burst, with a thirty caliber round to the brain.

Ben crawled across to what was left of him, machine-gun bullets spraying the air above Ben too, before and after he grabbed the bazooka and crawled and rolled to the next tree east.

He'd put himself on the safer side of a large fallen tree trunk, but the machine gun kept him well pinned down while he watched the Tiger roll west – two tree rows south now, and roughly five rows east.

Ben lay on his stomach, wishing he could crouch to fire the bazooka but having to shoulder it prone, watching the gun turret of the Tiger swivel toward him, holding his breath as he aimed the bazooka at the seam between the turret and the tank.

Ben had just watched the Tiger blow apart, when a second tank turned the corner in the road, its front machine gunner starting to strafe him, while the machine gun behind Ben whittled away at the log.

Something hit the watch on Ben's left wrist (his dad's watch from the First World War) without doing damage to him. Though nine rounds did right after that, slamming into him in rapid succession – some from the gunner on the Tiger tank, some from the nest behind him.

Ben lay on a snow drift the rest of that day, packing snow in his wounds to slow the blood flow, while entirely too many Tigers rolled west through the Saarbrücken Forest, and American guns answered back.

The machine-gun nest was silenced fairly soon by something lobbed from the American lines, but Ben was long past knowing or caring what had taken it out. He was down and damaged in the middle of a firefight. A sitting duck for friendly fire as much as enemy attack.

He never did have a clear idea of what it was that fought that day, or how broad the front was sweeping south beyond him. The German troops were new to the area, that much he understood – a tank unit (or regiment, or division) G2 knew nothing about. There was American artillery, obviously, 75s probably. And a whole lot more than that that Ben couldn't see, or wasn't conscious enough to notice, that beat back the tanks and stopped their attempt to break through.

Ben never knew how long he lay there. Sometimes he thought it must've been three hours, sometimes he thought it was more like five or six, while he packed snow into all those holes and watched himself die.

He had died. He'd seen it happen. He'd felt it happen in a way he couldn't have described. He looked down, from somewhere up above himself, and saw his own body, twisted and torn, lying dead on blood-soaked snow – and knew somehow, in the next instant, that he was being sent back by someone with thoughts and intentions and purposes. Larger thoughts, and deeper, than any in the minds of men.

Ben wouldn't have said that he'd heard a voice, but the message got communicated. There was something more for him to do. Something that was still required. *That* came down to him loud and clear. And there was conscious purpose in that, which he had to choose to take up.

It hung there in front of him – the chance to do good or the chance to do ill in the time that lay before him. And his whole soul and his battered body and the mind that couldn't run anything right then ached to be able to help – to heal harm and ease hurt. To keep people like Ted Mitchell from shattering those around them.

Then he was back, lying on a cold white drift, licking flakes of snow off his lips, while he tried to move his right leg.

Ben thought he heard someone call to him, sometime in the afternoon, the medic behind the lines maybe, saying, 'Hold on, buddy, hold on, we'll get you out of this soon!' But hours went by before anyone could.

He passed out and swam back to the surface off and on all afternoon, while the air exploded around him, as both sides threw what they had across him, as trees shattered in brain-splitting shrieks, as the world slid from grey to black (bitter and colder than ice), without him being hit again, which he knew made no good rational sense with the odds that stacked against it.

His teeth chattered. His feet felt frostbitten. He couldn't begin to raise his head long before the firefight ended. He wondered once about the sound he'd heard, coming from the machine-gun nest, if it had been the cocking mechanism being carefully set in place.

A medic did come, when the shells had almost stopped. He shoved a syrette of morphine in Ben's thigh and tied a strip of gauze around his waist to tell the world he was still alive and needed medical transport.

Friday, January 26th, 1962

'I hope Maggie made that.' Chester Hansen, Hillsdale, Ohio's Chief of Police, was leaning back in a director's chair at Ben's kitchen table in a neatly pressed tan uniform, adjusting the braided beige wire behind his left ear that wound down under his clothes to the hearing aid control in his shirt pocket. 'Maggie cooks even better than the wife.'

'Would I serve you something *I* made?' Ben was ladling chicken and vegetable stew and smiling at Chester over his shoulder. 'Would you mind shoving a log in the stove?'

Chester threw two in the Franklin stove, then sat back down by the window again, one patch of soft grey hair still sticking straight up on the top of his head from the way he'd yanked his hat off. 'So'd you buy this horse you been talkin' about?'

'Last week. I really like him. He's a great mover, and he's smart and well meaning, and he seems sensible too.' Ben set the chicken stew on the butcher-block table, with tossed salad, and cheese and crackers, and then sat down across from Chester.

'Well, when you gonna tell me 'bout this Mitchell guy? I've been patient.'

'Yes, you have, and now is probably as good a time as any.' Ben ate a spoonful of chicken and cut himself a slice of cheddar cheese. 'I met him in January of 1945. I'd been scouting across Belgium, and across the German border, in and around the Bulge, and they pulled me out—'

'Who pulled you out?'

'Army Intelligence. Sending orders down through regimental headquarters. I was never attached to a specific army, like First Army, or whatever. I always worked directly for Intelligence. Anyway, they sent me north from down near St Vith, to just over the German border.

'The front line was right there. They'd moved in that day, and set up camp, and brought in these three technical guys. I had to take them behind the lines to some German installation. Industrial, not military. That's what they told me it'd be, and I could see that myself when we got there.'

Ben told Chester everything he knew, clearly and precisely but without any extra detail, saying next to nothing about what he did, or how he led. Just that he'd guarded the buildings and the courtyard while the tech team went in. That he had no idea what Mitchell found in the labs, except what he'd seen himself when he'd swept them before he let Mitchell in. Which wasn't much. Electrical and chemical paraphernalia. Glass-making and metal-working equipment.

That, and the metal boxes. Which he'd recognized, finally, a year or two later, when reel-to-reel tape recorders came on the market, as what must have been early prototypes.

He described the deaths and his suspicions. And the Luger hidden by Mitchell. And about being sent out an hour later without seeing Mitchell again.

'So where'd you go from there?' Chester Hansen had just finished his chicken stew, and was using a toothpick and sucking at something between his teeth.

'They sent me south to meet up with a bunch of other scouts, down through Luxembourg to the Saarbrücken Forest. I was attached to an outfit south of Trier.'

'That where you got shot up?'

Ben nodded, and ate his last carrot.

'How'd you get home?'

Ben drank half a glass of milk while he thought about whether to answer him. He didn't talk about that firefight or what happened after. Some with Richard West. Now dead. His friend since before the war. More with Jessie. Dead longer. His wife and his best friend and whatever it is that's bigger than both. A little with Kate, in the last half-year. But never with Chester. Nothing specific about the war. And he studied Chester's open, calm, uncomplicated face over the rim of his milk glass, his own face still and cool and considering. 'Men I didn't know at all went out of their way to give me a chance.'

'Yeah? How'd they do that?'

'They strapped me on a stretcher under a Piper Cub artillery spotter that—'

'Under the *outside* of the plane?'

'Right, and flew me out, under ack-ack fire, through the treetops in an evergreen forest, to a railhead in—'

'Man, how cold would thatta been?'

'Cold. But them doing that, getting me into France fast, on to a train to Paris, into an American hospital there, that's what saved my life. That, and an army doctor there flying me back to the States.'

'You musta been shot up pretty bad.'

Ben didn't say anything, as he reached for an apple.

And Chester changed the subject. 'So you never heard nothin' 'bout Mitchell again?'

'Not till the hospital in Michigan. A few weeks after I got there, a letter arrived from a guy I knew in Intelligence, way up the chain of command from me, who'd been told about me asking for information. He said Mitchell was a mechanical engineer, and he had a decent enough record on paper, but that there'd been several people killed in his team. And that was pretty unusual with the T-Forces, the way they usually went in. Following the front-line troops, with transport and a fair amount of back up.

'Anyway, Intelligence said there were rumors about him. That his men didn't trust him. That he was secretive, even with his team. Keeping them from knowing what they were looking for as much as he could, and not explaining what they'd found. There was plenty of that kind of leadership feedback about him, but all of that's subjective. It could just be style, and nothing more. It wasn't anything you could do something about. Nothing that pointed to him doing anything under-handed, much less murdering anybody.'

Chester Hansen hooked his thumbs over his belt and cocked his head to the left. 'But you think he killed Baylor?'

'I do. And probably Mills as well. Maybe other people too, before *or* after that. Though there's no way for me to know.'

'So what'd you do about him after the war?'

'Nothing.' Ben ate a Triscuit with cheddar cheese before he looked at Chester. 'There was nothing I could do for awhile. I was in hospital for a year and a half. I married Jessie six months after I got back, after the first couple of operations, when I was reasonably certain I could be enough of a husband to rope her into it. But the—'

'You met her here, after you got hurt?'

'No, when I was being trained as a scout. I got sent to a university to study languages for six months, and I met her at a dance the first week. We got engaged before I got shipped out. But the first year we were married, I was in hospitals most of the time, getting operated on, getting nerve therapy done, doing rehabilitation of one kind or another. Anyway, I decided to turn my back on Ted Mitchell. I chose not to make myself nuts over it till there was something concrete I could do.'

'Why wouldn't you? With what you'd been through. With the war and all and everything. With trying to recuperate too. Nerve therapy, that's real bad, from what I've heard.'

'The war being over was part of it. I think we all wanted to pick up our own lives again.'

'Sure did. Me too, just being in England in the military police.'

'But if Mitchell's done what I think he's done since, I shouldn't have dropped it the way I did. Especially since it might've been me talking to Baylor, before we went out that night, which might've made Mitchell see reason to kill him. Thinking I was asking him questions Mitchell didn't want answered.'

'You don't know that.'

'No, but—'

'Haven't I heard you asking somebody else the same thing? When they looked back on something they couldn't't've known?'

'Maybe.'

'So?'

'OK, Chester, I get the picture.'

'Good.' Chester was rubbing the places on his nose where his glasses sat, looking like he was trying not to smile. 'And what could you have done then anyway?'

'I don't know. Something.'

'Sounds real unlikely to me. So whatta you figure he was up to during the war? When he was goin' to the labs and all?'

'Stealing science for himself. Picking technologies that he thought he could use. Bringing back the papers and plans. To pass it off as his own work, probably. Maybe he used whatever he'd found to sell, or start some business of his own.'

'The way he made a point of searching the labs alone, it points in that direction, don't it? Some guy, Mitchell. Just the kind of fella you want your daughter to marry.'

'Exactly.'

'And you figure it was electronics they were working on in that plant you went into?'

'Yeah. Different kinds. There was vacuum tube work going on. That was what they manufactured. But then as things turned out, that technology was knocked out after the war by the development of transistors in the fifties, so the benefits of that would've been fairly short-lived, if that's what Mitchell had stolen.'

'Right. But would he have known that was gonna happen?'

'Maybe. Maybe not. There was work being done here he could've known about. Whether there was transistor work being done there, in that lab then in Germany, I didn't know enough to know. But it's fairly obvious to me now that what was really new there, and what he was taking with him, were magnetic tapes, different kinds of coatings being laid on different surfaces, and the tape recorders themselves. Here in the US, from what I've been able to learn, we'd worked on both in the twenties and thirties, but thought there wasn't much market potential. We didn't perfect *or* sell magnetic tape recorders till a couple of years after the war. GE didn't even see the uses for tape recorders. And it's probably just hindsight that makes it look inevitable.'

'Maybe. Though it's kinda hard to believe.'

'From what I've been able to find out, the really breakthrough work on magnetic recording was done first in Germany, starting in the thirties. And was then used for military purposes there during the war, while lab work still went on.'

'Well, that would give you somethin' to look into. Who came out with it here, and when. I figure we oughta hear back from army records tomorrow, or Monday, either one. So why'd you get interested in Mitchell all of a sudden?'

'Ah. That's another story I'll tell you while I fix the grapefruit.'

Ten

'What's the matter, Maxie?' Ben was riding Max across Walter Buchanan's farm, and he'd come through the oak and fir woods out on to the edge of a winter wheat field into bright morning sun. Max had tossed his head, and turned it away from the light, the same way he had the first time that morning when they'd walked out of that section of woods. 'Is the light bothering you? It's bright shining off the snow.'

Max had done it between trees too, turning his head away from the sun, craning it off to his right.

'Let's go home and look at your eyes.'

There'd been a soft, deep, powdery snowfall the day before, and under that lay a sandy trail Ben knew well. So he shortened his reins, and put Max on the bit, then softened his hands slightly and sent him forward. They trotted for a quarter of a mile or so, and Ben said, 'Good, Max, that was really nice. Let's do it one more time.'

What Ben found, back in the barn, when he'd put the halter on Max in the crossties, was that Max's left eye looked slightly swollen. There was a streak through the center of it too. A cloudy spot, that didn't look normal. But different, Ben thought, than the scar he'd seen when he'd first looked Max over.

The owner had been perfectly honest about it. Max had punctured his eye on something in the paddock in Illinois where she'd had him before she'd come to Hillsdale on sabbatical. It had healed fine, though, and her vet *and* Ben's had said the eye looked normal except for the inevitable scar.

But it didn't now. And Ben put Max in his stall, fed him two apples, and went into the house to call the vet, and borrow a flashlight from June Buchannon.

She came out with Ben to look at Max. She was a nurse at the local hospital, liked horses in general, and was particularly fond of Max. So she held his halter and talked to him softly while Ben aimed the flashlight in his eye.

'The eyeball looks a little swollen to me, and you can see he doesn't like the light.' Every time Ben aimed it at Max's left eye, Max tossed his head, or strained to turn away from it. He didn't with his right eye. Then he just blinked and looked patient.

'I can see the old puncture wound through the cornea.' June Buchannon was standing on her tiptoes stroking Max's chin, carefully studying his left eye. 'How long ago did he do that to himself?'

'Six months is what I was told.'

'But both the vets said it was OK?' June's face was close to Max's cheek, and she kissed him before she let go of him.

'Martin thought it had healed fine. And what's-her-name had a written statement from her vet in Illinois that said the same thing.'

'Cynthia Black. PhD. Geologist.' June smiled and patted Max's neck, then pulled her beret down to cover her ears. 'How soon will Martin be here?'

'Sometime before lunch.'

'Then you don't have time to go home. So why don't you come in and eat an early lunch with me? Walter took the boys over to his brother's, and I want to hear what you were up to down south.'

'You don't have to give me lunch.'

'No, I don't, but I want to.'

Dr Jack Martin put chartreuse dye in Max's eye so he could see more clearly if there were active ulcers (cuts, punctures or abrasions) – but didn't find any. He drew blood to send to a lab, to look for leptospirosis, or other systemic disease.

He started Max on antibiotics to see if that helped (injections *and* crushed pills), while he waited for results from the path lab. He couldn't say one way or the other, as to whether the inflammation came from the old puncture wound. A reaction like this, that much later, was certainly highly unusual, but he wasn't willing to eliminate anything until he knew more.

Martin put Max on atropine drops to dilate the pupil and help the eye drain from the anterior chamber, in an attempt to relieve the pressure and make the eye less painful. He told Ben atropine would also help keep the back of the iris from attaching itself to the front of the lens because of the swelling – *if* the atropine worked. Martin left a tube of hypertonic saline ointment, plus powdered steroids to add to his feed.

When Max wasn't in a dark stall, they'd have to put a patch on the eye, which Martin gave Ben, before he wrote out detailed directions for all the pills and drops and powders and ointments. He told Ben there were other things to try as time went on, if these approaches didn't work. And he'd be back to see Max the next day.

Ben got home about two in the afternoon and found a note on his kitchen table written by Maggie Parsons telling him to phone Chief Hansen at home.

'Hey, Chester . . . Fine. So you've . . . Mitchell's *dead*? They're absolutely certain? . . . Hunh . . . So he died in March of 1945, right after that picture was taken? . . . Well, I guess that's some kind of justice . . . Yeah. Thanks for taking the trouble . . .

'Oh, one other thing. Where was he from? What was his father's name and address? . . . Yeah, I've got a pen . . . Thanks, Chester. You've really been a big help . . . Right, he had nothing to do with Ross MacNab's death . . . Thanks, Chester. I'll talk to you later.'

Ben stood in his study with his hands in the back pockets of his Levis, staring out past the evergreen trees at his neighbor's plowed field – before he picked up the phone and dialed the long distance operator.

There was no Dr Theodore Augustus Mitchell listed in Falmouth, Massachusetts. So he asked the operator for any other Mitchells in that part of Cape Cod.

He wrote down four numbers.

And phoned them all.

And didn't hear anything that helped.

Then he got the number of Falmouth Library and called there, asking for a local history librarian, or a research librarian, either one – and was told to wait for the director.

He did, with his jaw set off to the left absently tapping his teeth together, till it was time to explain who he was to a brisk, elderly sounding Massachusetts native by the name of Eloise Coffin.

'I'm trying to trace the family of someone named Ted Mitchell who used to live in Falmouth. His father was Dr Theodore Augustus Mitchell, and his mother's name was . . . Marietta, yes. So you knew them?'

The librarian was acquainted with Mrs Mitchell *and* her elder daughter, who now lived in Woodstock, New York. Ben told her he'd known Ted in the army, and would she be willing to give him their addresses.

Ben wrote both down. And thanked her. Then walked into the kitchen, thinking that that was only one of the advantages of small rural towns. *At least for someone like me. Someone pathologically nosey who can't let anything go.*

He grabbed himself an apple and a glass of water, and walked back to the study, where he picked up the phone and called June Buchannon to ask if she'd mind giving Max his medications, if he left town for three or four days during semester break.

Ben then placed a person-to-person call to Kate in Scotland. He waited, eating his apple, trying to decipher a page from John Finlay's frontier diary, *Travels with the Indians, 1823*, while he waited for the operator to call him back.

He told Kate that according to army records Ted Mitchell had died in Germany in March of '45. That he was leaving the following day to talk to Mitchell's family in Woodstock, New York, to make sure the records had the right Ted Mitchell.

Kate invited Ben to her awards banquet in New York City that Wednesday, since her editor had had a family emergency and had to go out of town. Ben hesitated, and then said yes. He'd do some work at the Brooklyn Museum and kill two birds with one stone.

Monday, January 29th, 1962

Ben had pulled in past two mailboxes nailed on top of a tree trunk, on to a dirt and gravel drive, rutted and slick with ice and snow. He slid on between stubbled corn fields to the bottom of a high hill, where he'd been told to park by an old wood-sided station wagon.

It was less than ten degrees, and a little more than a mile from the car to Mrs Mitchell's house, but Ben was dressed for it, and the sun was out. And the view from the pasture on top of her hill turned out to be worth the climb.

There were sheep there between Ben and a frozen creek, nosing tufts of grass up from under the snow, not too far away from a long-haired dog that was running toward Ben from a path in the woods on his right. The dog barked fifty feet away, then sniffed when he got to Ben. And Ben talked to him and patted his broad brown head, as they walked on toward the trail.

Ben kept to the path past a chicken house, past geese and ducks pecking and squawking, toward a weathered Cape Cod salt box that looked two hundred years old.

Vines covered parts of the house, and there were gardens clustered around it, following a string of arbors too, that led down to other gardens carved in the hill below.

Ben smiled as he sniffed the wood smoke trailing from the house's three chimneys, then walked past a perpendicular wing, following the dog and people prints to a low-roofed entryway with a shallow front porch between that wing and the house.

He wiped his boots on the doormat, and rubbed the dog's cold floppy ears, before he rang the big iron bell.

He heard a door open somewhere inside and firm quick steps cross uncarpeted floor. The door opened abruptly, and a very thin woman with tiny gold glasses on the end of her nose and an artist's paint brush in her left hand, stared at Ben above the frames. 'Yes?'

'I'm Ben Reese. I talked to your daughter Saturday—'

'You may leave your boots by the door. Ruben, you stay out.' Her face had changed when she heard Ben's name, stiffening behind the bones, under wrinkles and furrows on a hard framed face, sunken and slackened with time.

'It's nice to see so many animals.'

She didn't speak, or even look at Ben, as she smoothed a section of fine white hair, sweeping it toward the chignon fastened at the nape of her neck.

Ben left his work boots inside the door, then stood in his socks in the brick-floored entry, waiting for Marietta Mitchell to do something other than gaze out the window and pull at the collar of her dress.

She turned without a word, and stepped into the west wing, the hem of her dark wool skirt swinging against her ankles.

There was a fire in the broad brick fireplace at the left end of the long room, and candles lit on all the tables, even though there were also floor lamps lighting an oil painting of dried hydrangeas propped on an easel in the center.

'I'll clean my brushes and be with you in a moment.'

'I'm sorry to interrupt.'

'You asked if you might visit, and I agreed. There's no need to apologize.'

'I paint as a hobby. I do work everyday that takes concentration. I don't like interfering with somebody else's work.'

Marietta Mitchell's faded blue eyes looked at Ben for a second, then shifted back to her brushes. She cleaned them meticulously, then blew out the candles, and led Ben through the entryway into the parlor of the house.

He asked how old the house was, mostly to make conversation. And watched her smile a gratified smile.

'I built it in 1949.'

'It looks as though it's been here for ever.'

'Perhaps that was the intention. Which would you prefer, coffee or tea?'

'Whatever you're having is fine.'

'If I hadn't wished to know your preference, I assure you I wouldn't have asked.' She stepped from the parlor into the kitchen, took the lid off a burner in a huge cast-iron cookstove, then began feeding kindling into the bowels beneath.

'Tea sounds good.' The house, the candles, the kerosene lamps, the cookstove, the shawl, the ankle-length dress – it was life a hundred years before. And made Ben wonder why. 'Did your daughter tell you I knew Ted during the war?'

'Yes.' She poured hot water from a kettle already simmering on the stove into a navy blue teapot, swirled it around for several seconds, then poured it into a watering can waiting in a large stone sink.

'I didn't know him well. I took him to one of the scientific businesses where he had to gather information. What did Ted do before the war?'

Mrs Mitchell poured boiling water into the teapot, added loose tea, and set the lid on the pot. The delicate scent of jasmine flowers had already wafted across to Ben by the time

Mrs Mitchell spoke. 'Ted studied at MIT. He was also employed by Pratt & Whitney some months before he graduated.'

'What kind of work did he do?'

'Metallurgy. Aircraft engine applications. The machining of the metal itself.' She strained the tea into two china cups and carried the tray with cups and teapot into her small square parlor, where she seated herself in a high-backed chair. 'Ted volunteered very little, and I never wished to pry.'

'I guess a lot of aircraft technology was classified then anyway.'

'Yes, so I've been led to understand.' Mrs Mitchell said it ironically with a small condescending smile.

'Do you have a photograph of Ted you wouldn't mind me seeing? To make sure the Ted Mitchell *I* knew is actually your son, and army records and I are talking about the same guy?'

She took a sip of tea, staring at Ben's wool socks. 'You may look at what I have, yes.'

She walked across the sitting room into a narrow back hall, where she opened a door on the right into a small yellow bedroom stuffed with stuffed animals, and puppets, and toys. There was an unusually large collection of photographs and drawings, and paintings too of a baby, and a boy, and a young man – the same young man Ben had known as Colonel Ted Mitchell.

His mother stood silent in the doorway, crossing her black shawl across the brown bodice of her shirtwaist dress, looking as though she were holding her breath, as she watched Ben pick up a black and white photograph of her son at MIT.

'It *is* the Ted Mitchell I knew.'

'You may join me in the studio when you're through.' She walked quickly down the hall, the sturdy stacked heels of her lace-up shoes clacking on wide pine boards.

Ben had picked up a book with a watercolor painting of Ted as a small boy centered on the cardboard cover, and was skimming the handwritten story about Ted and his adventures. There were drawings of him on every page. There were more than a dozen other Ted books too, written and illustrated by his mother.

When Ben got to the studio, a teapot, three cups and a plate of cookies sat waiting on a table, and Marietta Mitchell stood staring intently at her painting.

'I understand you're a book illustrator.'

'I'm primarily painting flowers at the moment for magazines and gardening books. Prints are made and sold as well. One has become a postage stamp. A photographer is working on a book of my gardens here at Haycroft, and will—'

'Mother?'

'You may join us in the studio.'

A tall big-boned woman walked in, in her stocking feet, carrying a pie smelling of apples and cinnamon, which she set on a sideboard by the door. 'I'll put it in the kitchen before I go. I let Ruben in for a while. It's too cold to leave him out.'

'I'm Ben Reese. I think I spoke to you on Saturday.'

'Yes, I'm Francie, Ted's older sister. I live up the lane from Mother.'

'It's a great piece of land.'

'Even when the winter's indescribably brutal, I wouldn't live anywhere else. Jenny's coming home tonight, Mother. She's off on semester break, and she'll stop in, I imagine, on her way up the hill to us. So was *our* Ted the Ted you knew?'

'He was.'

Francie bit into an oatmeal cookie, then brushed a crumb from her corduroy collar. 'How did you know him in the army?'

Ben explained again, and then said, 'The paintings your mother painted of him were very much like him.'

'Yes, Ted was quite the favorite.'

Mrs Mitchell looked at Francie as though she didn't appreciate the remark, but wasn't going to argue in front of a stranger. She got up out of her wingback chair, and put more wood on the fire, then carried her painting to the French doors to study it in natural light.

'Ted was the baby, and he was ill a great deal when he was little. He almost died in 1918 when he was three, in the influenza epidemic, and then he got rheumatic fever a year or so after that. He had to stay in bed for a year, and Mother did all kinds of things to help keep him amused.'

'As I did with you too, *and* the rest as well, whenever you were ill.'

'Yes. Though . . .' Francie raised her eyebrows at Ben and glanced at her mother's back. 'What are you working on now, Mother?'

'An article on hydrangeas for *House & Garden*.' She set the painting on the easel. And then sat back in her chair.

Francie ate the last of another cookie while watching her mother gather up her needlepoint from a stool beside her chair. 'It's good tea.'

'Thank you, dear.' Mrs Mitchell hadn't looked at her daughter since Francie and Ben had sat down.

Ben could feel the eddies and undercurrents. The words being left out. The long-standing assessments being swallowed. The burning irritations being banked again instead of spewed out.

'Care for a cookie? I brought them to Mother last night, and they need to be finished off.' Francie was holding the plate toward Ben, and he reached for the one closest. 'Were you stationed in Europe long?'

'The night before D-Day to the end of January 1945.'

She was looking at the scar on Ben's left wrist and the index finger that didn't bend, and she said, 'It must have been good to get home. My husband did chemical research for the Navy during the war. Most of it's still classified.'

'That must've been interesting.'

'I don't know. Maybe.' She laughed then and glanced at her mother, who hadn't looked up from her needlework. 'So what made you suddenly decide to find out about Ted?'

'A friend of mine in Scotland and I were talking about friends of ours from the war who'd died, and I got to wondering what had happened to Ted, and decided to try to track him down.'

'I expect Ted was appropriately brave. He wasn't the kind to run from conflict.'

'No. Ted had plenty of nerve.'

Francie laughed and said, 'You can say *that* again,' before she looked at her mother, who'd glanced at Francie coolly before turning back to her work.

'Well. I need to run into town. Anything you want, Mother?'

'No, thank you. I have everything I need at the moment.'

'I ought to be going too, Mrs Mitchell. Thank you for seeing me, and giving me tea as well.'

'You're welcome. Tell Jenny I need her to help me eat the pie, Francie. You know I won't eat it on my own.'

'She always comes to see you.'

'She didn't last time.'

'Yes she did, with her friends from—'

'I'm not criticizing your daughter's behavior, Frances. The pie is my concern. I don't wish to waste food.'

The last word.

The last look.

The last time Ben wanted to see it.

'She has electricity, but doesn't use it except to paint?' Ben was following Francie on the path to the sheep pasture, smiling at three young goats that were standing with their front legs on the fence bleating and watching every move he made with worldly mischievous eyes.

'She likes candlelight and oil lamps better. She's done a great deal of study on New England life in the mid-1800s, and she's chosen to live in that style. It wasn't that way when we were children on the Cape. It's been a gradual . . . I suppose you could call it, "retreat" into that time period. She has a phone hidden away, she has central heating she can use if she wants to, and she does have a refrigerator camouflaged by a wooden door. Though why she uses the cookstove, with all the work involved, I don't understand. You noticed she tends to avoid talking about Ted.'

'I didn't know whether it was because I was there, or—'

'Once in awhile she'll talk about him with my daughter, who was born about the time Ted died. No, Mother was completely and utterly devoted to Ted. When he was sick as a child, the other four of us ceased to exist. She wrote books for, and about, him. She made puppets and wrote plays in which he starred. She made elaborate costumes for him to play pretend in bed. She's tremendously creative, as you must have seen for yourself.'

'Yes.'

'My father was the only doctor in Falmouth, and he worked round the clock then with house calls, getting paid in chickens and fish and kielbasa, and worrying about keeping a roof over our heads. Yet even *he* could see how enamored Mother was of Teddy. He knew Ted was spoiled rotten, and he tried to make her see it, but she couldn't. She wouldn't, anyway. Why, I don't know.'

'Strange how that happens. Favoritism in families. Jealousy

with, or without it. It goes back to Cain and Abel, and it doesn't skip generations.'

'I think there must've been something about Teddy that made it easier for her to be childlike herself. To laugh and relax the way she couldn't with the rest of us. Though she *had* been playful with Daddy too, in a different way, when we were young. And I may not be seeing it clearly. Though why I'm boring *you* with it, I don't know.'

'How often *do* we see our parents clearly? The way it is when we aren't there, at least. Anyway, I'm glad you're talking. I'd like to know more about Ted. How did your mother react when he died?'

'Well, when Ted went to war, she was beside herself. And when he died, she went to pieces. Stoically, you understand. No sobbing. No histrionics. More work. Less talk. Less attention to everyone else. Father loved her very much. And they rubbed along, both of them in silent pain, I suspect, until he died of a stroke. Then she moved here. And retreated to the 1850s.'

'I hope I didn't upset her by coming.'

'I don't imagine so. I don't mean to imply that she's unstable. She won't have a breakdown and be unable to work. She creates the world she wants around her, and pays very little attention to anything else. Perhaps we all do in our different ways. Though—'

'Did you come here to be near her?'

'No, my husband and I already lived here. We bought two hundred acres in 1946, and offered her twenty if she wanted to move near us after Daddy died. She decided she did. And became possessed by her gardens.'

'How did Ted feel about her?'

'My brother Teddy was a cold, heartless, self-centered, highly intelligent manipulator who wanted to make a splash in the world. And Mother never would see it.'

'That's more or less what I saw.'

'Yes, somehow I thought you had. You made no laudatory comments, which most people do if somebody's dead. Watch your step on the stairs.'

They were dirt steps, covered with snow, cut into the hill by the drive to make the up-and-down easier.

Yet it wasn't until they were standing by their cars that

Francie spoke again. 'Ted enjoyed the adoration when he was small, but by the time he was in high school, he didn't care to be bothered with Mother. Her attentions were an irritation. An embarrassment, at the very least. She never admitted that she saw that, but she must have. He hardly ever came home from MIT, and listening to her make excuses used to drive me to distraction.'

'At least you didn't have a family business. I've seen that tear families apart. Thanks for persuading her to see me.'

'It was partially curiosity. I wanted to see if Mother would ask you what Ted had been like in the war. I didn't think she would. Even though she was probably dying to know. Better not to disturb the memories. Better to remember him as a small boy than the snotty college kid who mocked and avoided her. Why did you want to find out about him? If you saw what sort of person he was, why would you care?'

'I've been wondering what he's been up to since the war, and who he might've hurt.'

'You really *did* get to know him, didn't you?'

'I have a copy of a photograph of Ted that was taken after he was injured. I could get a copy made for her. Should I do that, and send it to your mom? Or leave well enough alone?'

'I don't know. Let me ask her. Maybe she'll give me an answer.' Francie turned and smiled cryptically at Ben as she opened the door to her station wagon. 'Well, I'm off to Kingston. You know how to get back to Woodstock?'

Ben nodded and opened his car door, then waved as she drove away.

Eleven

B en read room numbers down a long narrow hall in the old Algonquin Hotel in New York, trying to remember what little he knew about the publishing lunches that had made the place famous, while he tucked the back of his tie under his collar and picked a piece of lint off his navy blue suit.

Kate opened her door as soon as he knocked, then stepped back looking ill at ease. But striking, Ben thought. Without being entirely sure why.

She watched his eyes self-consciously, before she asked if her jacket looked too weird. It was long and straight with a Mandarin collar, a dark-blue and black Chinese silk embroidered with gold and silver thread, and she wore it over a black silk camisole and long, narrow, black skirt.

Her chin-length hair was tucked behind her ears, so that the big African-looking gold disc earrings gleamed against its dark gloss, as well as the creaminess of her skin. But she still said, 'You think it's OK? I don't like typical little cocktail dresses, but I don't want to look too extreme.'

'You look fine. Believe me. The jacket's great.'

'I didn't mean to fish for compliments.'

'That's not the way I took it.'

'Good.' She picked up a small black satin purse and started fiddling with the clasp, saying she thought she'd already put the tickets in it, but probably ought to check.

'Where'd you find the jacket?'

'My sister-in-law sent me the silk last summer from Chinatown in San Francisco, and I found a seamstress who could . . . I'm sorry. I'm blabbing uncontrollably. And we both know what Mr Bennett said. "No discussions of finery."'

'Right. Because Jane Austen didn't miss much.'
'Where could I have put my coat?'

There was a cocktail party at the Plaza Hotel for the nominees and their guests, and Kate and Ben stood off to one side gazing around the room.

Kate said hello to two or three people in the first twenty minutes, looking like she'd rather be anywhere else in the world. And when the two of them talked, it was strained too, because neither of them did well with crowds.

When they looked at the room – at the hot swirling faces, drinking and eating canapés, laughing unnaturally and looking panicked periodically over whether they (or their friends, or family) were about to win a Wilkie Collins Award – it made both of them want to run.

Kate kept moving her evening bag from one hand to the next, holding her breath and catching herself letting it out in small short sighs, before *and* after, she heard herself say, 'It's not like I really care.'

'No.'

'I never expected to be nominated, and I know it doesn't matter, but it's the waiting to find out.'

'I know.'

'It makes me relive all those petty miserable class elections when I was a kid. When I felt like an isolated little prig who had no idea what any other person my age thought, *or* did, and was about to have that made public again, since no one would vote for me.'

'That's what it was like for—'

'But it's not just that.'

'No?' Ben was smiling at her, his eyes crinkling at the edges, his eyebrows managing to look amused.

'I don't do well in big groups of people. They make me feel like I'm twelve, and bored stiff, and totally boxed in.'

'It's the small talk too, for me. Not knowing what to say, and feeling the need to try, and rarely hearing anything that's worth remembering five seconds later.'

'And after that gets *really* irritating, *I* get controversial and pick a fight with the next person I see. Although—'

'Ladies and Gentlemen, if I could have your attention please.

Those who have been nominated need to gather at the far end
of the room for a group picture . . .'

Ben had watched Kate pick at her food from thick hotel soup
to gooey chocolate dessert, as the tension tightened in the
Plaza's ballroom, the talk getting sharper and more insistent,
like violin strings being tuned too high, painful and threatening to snap.

It was way too hot too. And too noisy to keep shouting
across the table. And halfway through, after yelling at the PR
person from Kate's publisher, and two other editors from the
same firm who didn't work with Kate, Kate and Ben had
given up and concentrated on each other.

They both forgot about where they were, which was the
best that could've been expected, as they talked about books
and writers, and the hassles at Alderton, and Max's eye, and
the novel Kate was working on.

And then Ben remembered what he'd wanted to tell her. 'I
read something that reminded me of the eye you were sent,
and I thought it might be something you could use in a book.
It's grisly, but it's true.'

'Oh, good, I can hardly wait!'

'No?'

'I'm kidding. Go ahead.'

'Well, a French woman, living in the Deep South, late in
the 1800s, had her husband stuffed after he died and set in a
chair in a glass case inside her front door.'

'Ooooh.' Kate's eyes and mouth both crumpled as though
she'd touched something slimy.

'It wasn't till a year or so later, after she'd gone to Europe
and come back with a husband she'd met there, that she had
her first husband buried. It makes me wonder what the guy
thought when he stepped inside the front door.' Ben smiled
and looked at Kate.

And then they both laughed.

Someone announced that the program would start soon, and
anyone wanting to visit the restrooms, or buy a last drink,
ought to do so soon. Cigarettes were lit all around the room
again. And Kate got quiet and looked strained.

Ben started searching for something to ask her, and settled
on the first thing that occurred to him. 'Tell me the name of

your perfume. I don't care for many, but yours I really like. It makes me think of gardenias.'

'It's called Fracas. And it's odd that you should ask, because I just read an article about perfume on the plane flying over. It was written by an American visiting Paris whose boyfriend had just decamped, so she went to this small perfumery, where they blend and sell perfumes, wanting a new perfume as a pick-me-up to—'

'That's just what *I'd* do, if somebody dumped me.'

Kate laughed and said, 'Do you want to hear this or not?'

'Of course. I'm hanging on your every word.'

'Yeah, I know when I'm being mocked. *Anyway*, when a clerk came out, the customer told her she'd only worn two perfumes in her whole life, but very much needed a new one. The clerk nodded knowingly, and asked her what scents she'd worn.

'The customer smelled a bunch of perfumes, but nothing seemed right. Till the clerk brought out one last scent, which the customer liked more than anything she'd ever smelled. She bought two big bottles without asking how much it cost.'

'*That* sounds dangerous.'

'Yes, but *then* the clerk told her that the same perfumer who'd created both the other scents she'd worn had created this fragrance for his wife. He'd never allowed it to be sold to anyone, and his wife had worn it for forty years. The husband had died five years before, and it was just this year that his wife decided to let it be sold to the public.'

'It's a great sales pitch anyway.'

Kate laughed and poked Ben's shoulder. 'Don't be such a cynic!'

'Ladies and gentlemen. If I may have your attention . . .'

'I'm sorry you didn't win.'

'Don't be. It doesn't matter. I would've liked to, of course. Vanity being what it is. And because it would've helped sell books. But it happened the way it was supposed to. You know what CS Lewis said when asked about his literary career?'

'"Too little thought can't be given to it."'

'Right. So what *I* need to tell myself is to concentrate on the work.' They were walking south on Sixth Avenue toward the Algonquin Hotel, having finally given up every last hope of finding an empty cab. 'Anyway, tell me what you think about Mitchell.'

'What *can* you think? At least he's not here doing something horrible to someone new.'

'True, but it makes me feel worse about Ross MacNab. It's sadder, in a way, than being murdered.'

'It still doesn't seem finished to me, Kate, and I don't know why. I don't even know what I mean by that. Are you too cold? You want my coat?'

'No, I'm fine. Except for my feet. Why do we do it? Wear high-heels with pointy toes? We're like lemmings. Letting ourselves get manipulated by greedy sadistic designers. When are you planning to leave tomorrow?'

'Seven or so. I want to get home to see Max's eye.'

'I can't imagine what a swollen eyeball looks like. Course, I try not to think about eyes at the moment. Severed or swollen, either one.' Kate's own eyes were smiling ironically, though her mouth looked less detached.

'You seem to be handling the package in the mail really well.'

'I think looking for Ross MacNab ended up helping me get over it.'

They were in the elevator heading toward Kate's floor, catching each other in the mirrored walls – looking, then looking away.

'Thank you for doing this. For driving down from Woodstock. It was really good of you to bother.'

'It was no bother at all, Kit.'

'Me being nervous, and blabbing about perfume for twenty minutes, that must've been *really* interesting.'

'It was. I don't know anything about it. Would you want to have breakfast together? I probably ought to eat about six, so that may be too early for you.' Ben wasn't looking at her when he asked. His eyes were on the floor numbers above the door, and his mouth wasn't giving much away.

'I'd like to. I'm still on Scottish time, so I'm sure I'll be up.' Kate was fitting her key in the lock.

And Ben said, 'I'll meet you here then, a little before six.'

'Good.' Kate held the door open, looking sideways at Ben.

He reached over and touched her hair, wanting to wrap his arms around her, and trace the shape of her ear with his tongue, and lick the hollow between her collarbones – but telling himself not to. Not until he had a much better idea of where they ought to end up.

Kate was saying, 'What's all this?' as she stepped inside the room.

There was a bouquet of cream-colored roses sitting on the desk by an iced bottle of very good champagne.

She read the card on the blotter. And seemed to have trouble looking straight at Ben. 'It's from a friend in Scotland. I thought it was from my parents, but it's not.'

'No. I can see that.' Ben said it in a low neutral voice. 'The roses are really beautiful.'

'Yes, they are, but—'

'I better go. I have to finish packing. And you know, Kate, now that I think about it, with rush hour here being what it is, I probably ought to get out of the city earlier than six, and stop for breakfast on the road.'

'Ben—' She was walking toward him, still holding the card in her hand.

'Good night, Kate. I hope you have a good flight back.'

'Do you need anybody? Ever? Do you ever let anybody in?'

Ben stood and stared at her. Before he said, 'Do you?'

'I'm sorry. It's none of my business. I just—'

'I let Jessie in. I let Richard West in.' Ben's jaw was set, his eyes were cold *and* hot, and his lips were tight together. 'He talked me through Jessie's death. If it hadn't been for a friend like him, I don't know how long it would've taken me to take on the outside world again. I loved her. I needed her. I needed him later. And they knew it.'

'Ben—'

'Goodbye, Kate. I'm sorry we hit a dead end with Ross.'

Kate locked the door and leaned against it and said, 'Damn,' three times in rapid succession.

Thursday, February 1st, 1962

It was after eleven when Ben got to the Buchannons, but a light was still on in the barn, as he slid the door open and walked in.

June Buchannon was standing by Max's stall studying his left eye. 'Walter told me you were coming out.'

'You didn't have to stay up.'

'I didn't. I was working the three-to-eleven shift.'

'How's he doing?'

'Not great. I'd say it's gotten quite a bit worse.'

Max's eyeball was much more swollen, the top lid stretched and puffy looking too, matter stuck to both lines of lashes, eye-drop trails caking the side of his nose. His ears were drooping and pathetic looking. And his head hung listlessly over the half-door of his stall.

'He's been real good about everything. He's getting shots all the time, and an ointment that he hates, but he's putting up with it anyway.'

'I'm sorry you had to bother with it. I never should've left him.'

'It's easy for me. You couldn't have done anything different than I did, and you had things you had to do this week.'

'No, I didn't as it turned out. It was a complete waste of time and money.' He was scratching Max's chin, staring hard at his eye. 'My car broke down too, on the way home. And I'm going to have to make myself go out and buy another.'

'That's too bad.' June looked at Ben without saying anything for a minute, then handed him the vet's instructions.

Ben thanked her again, and said he'd be out early in the morning to take care of Max. Then he fed him three large apples, and talked to him for half an hour.

Ben's next two weeks revolved around Max – medicating him morning and evening, meeting with the vet, watching one thing not work after another, seeing Max in progressively more pain, watching him brood in a dark stall with the patch on all the time, seeing the eye get sorer no matter what they did.

There were days at work when Ben felt like he was suffocating. When he wrote the letters he had to make himself write (his normal daily percentage of the 3000 letters he wrote every year to alumni, students and faculty who needed an archivist's help). There were days spent doing PR for Alderton, taking visitors on tours of the library and the archives, or talking to them on the phone. When he would rather have worked on the coins or mentored his apprentice, or finished his own paper preservation research.

There were days of being watched by Roger Simms, the

bureaucrat born in a button-down collar with a burning desire to please the powers-that-be. President Frederick Harper, at *that* moment. Who had *not* forgotten Ben's role in bringing the Harrison will to the attention of the board.

Ben's decisions were challenged daily. His agreement to help evaluate a collection of rare books for the city library was opposed. His request to leave for Tuscany one day early for spring break in March (in order to give a talk in Florence on the paper preservation method) was turned down without explanation.

Which made no sense at all. The reputation of the university had always been thought to benefit from faculty members speaking at international forums. And it wasn't as though Ben had students whose schedules would be disrupted. He had no midterms to oversee or grade. He had one apprentice working on an on-going project. Ben had always worked far more hours every week than anyone had a right to expect. And yet his request was turned down by Simms in consultation with Harper.

It was a cold two weeks, those first two in February. Inside *and* out. The hunt for Mitchell was over. The search for the sender of Kate's package had ended with Ross MacNab's death. The contact between Kate and Ben had atrophied to nothing.

She'd sent him a thank-you note for meeting her in New York. But Ben hadn't seen any reason to respond.

He'd spent a lot of time trying to learn about T-Forces and related groups in Europe during the war. And the several waves of scientists too, called by various names, usually answering to different authorities, that had been sent to occupied Europe later. He contacted military and government archives, searched industrial journals, got a librarian friend to help him find what there was.

Most information was still classified. Military applications weren't discussed. Though there was a certain amount available on the technology taken after the war that went to American industry.

Some saw both as completely justified – the only war reparations the US would ever get from Germany for the millions of dollars America had spent fighting the war and rebuilding Europe. Others took the opposite view, that nothing could justify the taking of science from any German, or anyone else, even if it was partly done to defend ourselves against Stalin, who'd kidnapped many eminent scientists and stolen armaments as well.

He read whatever he could find (about the magnetic tape recording industry too, making notes on the early manufacturers, and when their patents were issued), and compiled a series of files – all the time asking himself why he was doing it. Telling himself Ted Mitchell was dead, and there was no good reason to spend any time on that kind of research.

Which meant – all of that, taken together – that when he got a call from Everett Adams asking if he'd come to Lexington to help his sister figure out how to repair the murals in a farmhouse she and her husband were restoring, Ben agreed in less than a second.

Jane Buchannon offered to take care of Max.

And Ben began planning what he'd take to Lexington.

January 21st, 1945

Transport was what saved Ben. Medics and GIs he didn't know at all taking him out on a litter lashed on the hood of a Jeep. Driving him fast across a big empty field to an old Piper Cub. Strapping his stretcher on to the outside, under the battered undercarriage.

Ben tried to laugh, when he realized what they were doing. But a medic did something to him, gave him another hit of morphine probably, and stepped away from the plane.

Taxiing across a rutted field made his bones grind in ways he couldn't have described, and the lift-off was excruciating, like the flight to France underneath the ack-ack fire, so cold his ribs seemed to crack inside him, under skin that felt like it had grown a sheet of ice.

The landing knocked him out, after he'd heard himself screaming, and couldn't make himself stop.

He never remembered anything after that till he felt a needle hit his arm, and heard a woman's voice close up against his cheek. 'Have they given you penicillin, soldier?'

'Me . . . ? I don't know . . .'

'I'll inject a full dose now, and you remember if anybody

asks. There's a tourniquet below your left shoulder. Be careful you don't bump it, OK? You're getting a blood transfusion in your right arm too, so you gotta keep it real still.'

She floated away somewhere, more or less the way he did, into watery dreams and shivering half-light – before he realized, from bits and pieces that came and went without warning, that he was lying on a litter, swaying with the clatter of a lurching train, in nothing but a hospital gown and socks that weren't his.

That got what there was of his attention. Because everything that kept him alive was gone.

His wires and gadgets that he'd kept in his pockets. His Olympic rifle and his Bowie knife. His old Colt and the hatchet his dad made with the big heavy pick.

They'd stripped him naked. And left him defenseless.

And taken his souvenirs. Jackboots. Gloves. The Luger in his musette bag. The German wristwatch that had been a work of art, pried off an SS Colonel. Somebody else was using them now, or planning to make a few bucks off them.

Ben understood that they'd had to strip him. That they had to be able to work on his wounds. But it felt like part of what made him who he was had been ripped out right through his skin. Both times he'd been wounded before, they'd kept his equipment with him when they'd patched him up, and sent him back to the line.

So this time they must know he wasn't going back.

And what that meant began working its way in.

He'd never have to worry again about what was hiding in a hedgerow. Or waiting behind a half-closed door. Or watching him up the road.

He'd never take on another Tiger tank. Or an 88. Or a sniper hidden in a burned-out town waiting to pick him off. No more, ever again, of anything getting zeroed in on him.

No more mines. No machine-gun nests. No lice. No frostbite. No night-after-night-after-night without sleep.

He'd never scout another command post and slaughter the men inside. Or lay his life on a sharp, slippery line on somebody's lousy intelligence. He'd never walk up on another Malmedy and be the one to find the bodies of all those American POWs machine-gunned by the SS.

If he didn't have to go back. *If* that was true.

Ben tried to smile, while he held his breath, a shallow breath that still hurt – letting it out again very slowly, feeling himself sink deeper into canvas, before he closed his eyes.

He saw six stretchers on both sides of the car, when he opened them the next time. And one nurse making the rounds of men silent and screaming.

Some died, and got carried out when the train stopped at the stations. Other litters got squeezed in. New nurses checked wounds and IVs, while Ben wove in and out.

The door to the car slammed shut behind him, shaking him awake with a start, as another stretcher was carried through – Ted Mitchell staring at Ben as his litter was carried past.

'Stop him!' Ben struggled to sit up, yelling, 'He murdered his own men!' A nurse pushed him down again, and when he could look around her, he saw it wasn't Mitchell.

He tried to tell the soldier he was sorry, that he'd thought he was someone else, before he closed his eyes once more and dreamt something worse about Mitchell, something weirder and gorier he couldn't remember when he woke.

He never knew when he got to Paris. It was dark, he could see that. And he remembered a nurse telling him he was going to Sainte Coeur, the biggest American hospital there.

He couldn't have said when it was they deloused him. Before they took him to surgery he thought, some time in the night. But he couldn't be sure of that anymore than anything else.

They stitched his left arm, starting with the tip of his index finger, sewing up to, and around, his shoulder – and then they put the arm in a cast (after they'd cleaned out the dirt and debris and tried to do something useful with what was left of the bones). Thirty caliber rounds slam through bone and beef like butter, especially at the range they'd hit Ben, so there weren't bullets left to dig out, just shreds of bone and cloth.

They tried to clean his internal parts (his stomach and gut and left lung) and sew them together so they'd stay, before they stitched the outside holes – and put him to bed in a large, packed ward with every imaginable wound.

When he'd stopped retching from the ether (and how long that took, that and all the surgery, he never had any idea), he found a wheelchair beside his bed, and no nurse in the room.

He'd been dreaming about Mitchell, watching him slit

Gene's throat this time, without being able to get to Gene to help. And then he woke, and listened hard to all the misery in the room.

Ben told himself to think about something else, and started with the men by Trier who hadn't known him from a hole in the wall, but did everything that could've been done to help him stay alive. He compared that to Mitchell murdering the men he led – and that made Ben even more incensed.

He told himself to think about something good – like Jessie, and going home, and starting college in Indiana again – when it hit him suddenly that he was in Paris with free time on his hands.

His father had been in Paris during the First World War, and he'd told Ben stories that made him think it was time he saw it too. He stared at the wheelchair, threw back his covers, and took a look at his legs.

The right didn't look too bad (one flesh wound, stitched together). The left was heavily bandaged (lower leg and upper), with blood seeping through. That led him to roll on his right side and push himself to sit up, which turned out to be intensely painful, because of the crater in his stomach.

He had to sit there and hold on to the bed for a minute.

But he was in the wheelchair five minutes later, wheeling himself down a long hall using his right hand and foot. The Champs-Elysées, that was where he was going, then on to the Louvre another day when he wasn't feeling so queasy.

He'd almost gotten to the hospital's front door when a nurse came flying around a corner. She turned him around and pushed him back toward his ward, asking exactly what First Sergeant Reese thought he might be doing.

'Heading toward the Champs-Elysées.'

'How old are you, soldier?'

'What's today?'

'January twenty-third.'

'I'll be twenty-two next week. Why do you want to know?'

'You were waking up from the ether, talking about taking kids into combat, and I figured you had to be older than you looked.' She smiled when she said it. And then went on to point out that Ben was at least old enough to notice that he was all but naked, which might disturb the Parisian population. 'Winter's still with us too, you know, and wheelchair travel can be risky.'

He was back in bed two minutes later, without his hospital gown this time, to discourage further attempts at departure, the wheelchair having been swept away to an undisclosed destination.

He slept for a while, then sipped something fizzy, before he looked at the room.

There was everything in that ward – shell and shrapnel mutilations, single and multiple limb amputations, burn cases among the worst (tankers and pilots usually, whose faces and body parts had been seared off), men whose colons had impacted horribly, which nurses had to scrape out.

The GI in the bed on Ben's right was one of those, and when Ben's neurosurgeon, Dr Willard Jones, wheeled Ben off to an examination room, Ben was mildly ashamed of himself, but profoundly glad to get out.

He wasn't without difficulties himself. His left leg was badly shot up. There was a serious wound in his abdomen, and another somewhat less severe on the upper left side of his back. He couldn't move his left arm, and had no feeling in it anywhere below the top of his shoulder.

Several depressing facts about bone grafts and nerve damage were presented by Dr Jones, before he started his summing up. 'I still don't know if I can save your arm, or how much use it'll be if I do. Your left leg should respond pretty well, since the slugs didn't shatter the bone. Your abdominal wound is a concern, as I'm sure you know from the ones you saw in combat, and the wound on your back is nothing to take lightly. You've got a substantial amount of surgery and nerve stimulation ahead, especially on your arm, and most of it will be experimental. So what that means is it's too soon to call. It could've been a lot worse, though, as I'm sure you already know.'

He asked Ben about his interests, and what he'd done in the war, while he probed the nerves in two parts of Ben's arm.

Jones stared at Ben for half a minute without saying a word. Then asked the last question Ben expected. 'How much do you weigh?'

'I don't know. One-seventy-two at the end of basic.'

'You're a good bit thinner than that now, for being six feet tall.'

Dr Jones and a tiny nurse (who looked like she was twelve

years old) hoisted Ben up on a big metal scale and held him there till he was balanced.

'A hundred and forty-nine, including the plaster cast. That's good, Sergeant. That means you get to go home.'

'What?'

'I want you back in the States right away. A medical flight's leaving tonight, and I can add a hundred and fifty pounds, but not an ounce more. That OK with you?'

Ben Reese swallowed as he stared at Dr Jones. Something funny was happening in his throat, and he nodded at Jones instead of trying to talk.

Twelve

B en had had one of his dreams and gotten up at three, sweating and staring at the corners. He stood naked for a while in the dark by a window, looking out past the tops of bare trees. Seeing the evergreen forest by Trier. Seeing his own dead body lying on blood-soaked snow the way he had in real life.

He went in the bathroom and splashed water on his face, then stared at his scars in the mirror. The skinned over holes splattered across his body. The rips in his stomach. The slices in his left leg. The jagged tear and bone graft cuts in his right. The long white incisions, stretched and puckered-looking, snaking up his left arm, and across his shoulders, and down along his back.

He turned the light off and asked himself why he'd bothered, as he pushed his wet hair back from his face, when he didn't normally notice unless bone or metal started moving, making it hard to ignore.

He washed sweat off his stomach, and rubbed his hair with a towel. Then pulled on his robe, and went down to the kitchen for the Camels he kept in the freezer from one of his dreams to the next.

He opened a window in the bedroom and smoked two in the dark, sitting at Jessie's desk, staring out at the night. Seeing hospital wards. Seeing bedridden men. Much worse off than he'd ever been. Still there. Still paralyzed. Still brainless. Legless. Gutless. Still pieces of what they'd once been.

There's a VA hospital an hour from here, and you ought to be doing something useful. Not what you and Jessie did. Writing the newsletter. Bringing in animals from the zoo. Taking the guys for picnics where no one would stare. You're

*an outsider now, and it won't be the same. But it's time you
started doing something. Even if you have more dreams.*

But what do I do right now?

He couldn't go back to bed. And he didn't want to work
on the coins. And he found himself reading Jessie's last letter.
Written when he'd been out of town, three weeks before their
baby was born, when his wife and son died together.

He told himself to go to Lexington as he put the letter in
the drawer. To shower and eat breakfast and leave before five,
and give himself time to do something but work – to tour one
of the horse farms, or see something historic.

Ben was driving through high hills, a little after eight, thirty
miles north of Lexington, glancing at a white-fenced paddock,
when it came to him suddenly and made him laugh.

*Texas is longhorns and rattlesnakes. Lexington's thor-
oughbred horses. Even the Queen of England's come here to
the breeders' sales.*

*But what can you do when you don't have a name to work
with?*

*The Lexington newspaper makes the most sense. Even
though it's a long shot of more than mythic proportions.*

*I can't let it go, can I? I can't believe Ted Mitchell's dead
no matter how hard I try. Not with Ross MacNab dead. Not
with Phillip Welsh dead. Not with Mitchell on a stretcher in
a picture next to Ross MacNab.*

Nellie Ferguson had made Ben think of it. The nurse who'd
told Kate that the place Ross MacNab's benefactor came from
reminded her of an animal, the way cattle made her think of
Texas.

*If it was Ross MacNab's benefactor that she overheard.
That's still an assumption, you'll remember. And one you can't
overlook. Still, there's no place in America more identified
with an animal than Lexington, Kentucky is with horses. And
if Mitchell is alive he can't be using his own name. Not with
the army thinking he's dead.*

*If by some miracle Mitchell does live in Lexington, the
paper might have a picture.*

*You're grasping at straws, you know that. Waste time if you
want to, but don't be telling yourself lies.*

* * *

Ben walked into the library at *The Lexington Herald Leader* and introduced himself to the woman behind the desk. He asked to see their photograph files, telling her he was looking for someone he'd known in World War II whose name he wasn't sure of, who might be living in Lexington.

She told him their prints were organized as news, sports, or entertainment, with alphabetical topic files under each. They did keep back copies of the last year's papers, but every year before that was now filed on microfiche.

Ben said he'd start with the back issues. And she took him to a table in an alcove, showed him the stacks of papers on the shelves, and walked back to her desk.

There were conversations going on between her and another librarian, and reporters coming and going, machine noises too (typewriters, teletypes, adding machines) – all of which Ben tried to ignore, as he spent the next hour flipping through hundreds of pages without finding a face that made him think of Mitchell.

Then he started the painful process of scrolling through the microfiche, beginning with 1952.

That choice was arbitrary. MacNab went to Leith House in 1953. But if Ben didn't find a photograph from 1952 on, he'd go back earlier, probably to '48.

He used the magnifying glass from his key ring as he rolled past the text, scanning every photo, straining his eyes and cramping his neck, till he got to 1955.

He passed it, and had to scroll back – a large photograph taken at Keeneland Racecourse during a race that spring. A medium-range shot of a tall dark-haired man, standing behind a millionaire from Maryland who owned the winning horse.

The dark-haired man had raised a hand, half hiding his face from the camera, but Ben could still see him well enough to think he looked like Ted Mitchell.

Ben was west of Lexington, driving-up Rose Hill in Versailles (which Kentuckians pronouce 'Vur-SAILS'), when he turned off sharply to the left on to McCowans Ferry Pike.

There were hills covered with horses, with classic old houses, with history everywhere he looked. And Ben told himself to drive home through Midway and look at the horse farms there too, the big old famous ones he hadn't seen in years.

He found it two miles out of town, at the bottom of the first steep hill – the driveway to Mount Prospect between two dry stone walls.

He turned right, in his new used car, his blue '57 Chevy Bel Air, which had the smallest fins he could find that year, and an engine with 30,000 miles on it.

He was on a narrow gravel drive that cut through the middle of a long hill with the high ground on his right and a ravine on his left, where a creek ran parallel to the drive. Pastures and plowed fields swept above the creek on the left-hand rise, up to, and around, a stately old white farmhouse shielded by clustered trees.

There were six or eight pregnant mares close by on Ben's right who watched him pass toward the dark wooden barn between their paddock and a large-muscled stallion licking salt in his own field.

The drive dipped quickly just beyond him and crossed a narrow stream before splitting into two drives, both lined with walnut trees that looked a hundred years old. Ben took the right lane that climbed up to a cattle guard in the right side of a high hedge, then led him on to a large front lawn, where he parked in the circle drive and stared at Mount Prospect.

It was a long, metal-roofed, two-storied red-brick house with black shutters, and white doors and windows, and several tall brick chimneys. The front-porch roof rested on narrow columns topped with ionic capitals, but the house wasn't grand or pretentious – it looked like an eighteenth-century farm-house, long lived in and loved.

Ben got out and stretched, gazing up at the huge old trees growing around the house – just as two Great Danes appeared on either side of him. There was no barking or growling. Just one solid black dog and one white one with black spots, whose heads stood as high as Ben's waist.

'It's a good thing you're friendly, huh?'

They were standing right up against him, letting him pat their heads, sniffing his coat and gazing up at his face with curious pink-edged eyes.

'They're harmless.' A good-looking woman in wool pants and sweater under a sheepskin coat had walked around the right end of the house carrying a stack of kindling. 'Let me dump this by the kitchen, and I'll meet you at the front door.'

'Thanks. I'm Ben.'
'Hey, Ben. I'm Jo.'

They stood in the foyer looking at the mural that covered the walls above the chair rail and climbed the staircase to the upper hall.

Ben was using a flashlight to study the painted surface – the dark greens and browns and blues that were speckled and mottled and splotched with mold and lost paint. 'It looks like oil paint on plaster to me.'

'All we know for sure is it was painted by someone named Alfred Cohen, who came here from France in 1820.'

'You've lost a fair amount of paint. Unfortunately. But I really like the simplicity of it. The big trees, and the rivers and the hills. The frontier cabins and the farmhouse.'

'There's a ruined castle and a steamboat in the parlor, and the incongruity's kind of fun.'

'There's been quite a bit of water damage too.'

'Oh, there has. The house stood empty a good long time before we bought it, and started in on the repairs. We had to tear down the kitchen wing and start that over from scratch.'

'May I look at the murals in the living room?'

'Please.'

Ben did. For some time.

Jo watched for a while. Then went off to the kitchen.

He went to work in the upstairs hall, where the light streamed down from the front second-floor window into the U-shaped stairs.

He worked on the painted surface first, starting with the fungus, dabbing a cotton ball soaked in a very dilute solution of Clorox on to a small spot of sky in a corner, blotting it with non-toxic blotting paper, examining the residue on the cotton ball, looking at the changes in the fungus on the paint.

He dabbed a mild solution of green Phisohex soap on another small spot of grass hill below it, blotting that carefully and comparing the two, looking at both for unintended fading through a battery-powered magnifying glass with a light inside the frame.

He dried both spots with a hairdryer, then switched the applications (green soap solution on the sky patch, diluted bleach on the hill spot), before blotting and drying them again. He stood for a minute and studied a ten-inch patch of exposed plaster, deciding it was probably oyster shell based, because of the intensity of the whiteness, instead of made with limestone.

Ben squeezed eight or ten shades of watercolor on to his palette, and mixed them carefully with a palette knife. He painted stripes of dark green-blue like the sky of the mural, and a brownish grey-green like most of the hills, on a foot-square plaster tablet he'd made and brought from home – then dried them with his hairdryer and compared them to areas on the wall.

He remixed, repainted and dried each version, till he'd blended colors that matched the cleaned spots on the mural. Next he outlined two irregular shapes of exposed plaster adjoining the places he'd cleaned with very fine lines of brown paint. He dried the lines with the hairdryer, and painted inside them with the sky and ground colors that came the closest to the cleaned paint. He dried them with the drier, dropped his brushes in a bottle of water and wiped his palette with paper towels.

He stood up, rolling his shoulders in circles, then stepped back to look at the corner and bumped into Jo Austin. 'I'm sorry. I didn't know you were there.'

'I snuck up on you from a guest room, after coming up the back stairs. I wanted to watch without disturbing you. What do you think so far?'

'It can be done, but it's a big job. Bigger than I can tackle myself anytime soon. If all you had was the downstairs hall, I could probably get to that this summer. The problem is that I'm not sure right now that I'll have the whole summer off. I'm not an expert conservator either. I'm a jack-of-all-trades-master-of-none kind of archivist with some training in conservation.'

'Looks to me like you know what you're doin'.'

'There're a *whole* lot of people better at it than I am, but it also depends on what will satisfy you too. If you don't expect perfection, the restoration's worth doing. If you don't mind the occasional patch of discoloration, and crack lines left in the plaster. If you want it to end-up looking old and authentic, not new and slick and just painted.'

'I'd like it to look old, but I don't want the mustiness and the scratchy-looking bare spots.' She was holding her thick reddish brown hair back from her forehead without seeming to notice, staring carefully at the bit of mural Ben had treated and painted. 'That looks good.'

'It's a start, at least.'

'Why did you paint the line around it?'

'I'm using watercolors instead of oils because they can be removed. The thin brown ring tells the next restorer what's inside this area is new paint.'

'I see.'

'It'll be hard to get new oils to dry to match the old pigments, even after you clean the walls. And to pay someone who has the experience and the technique to do that really well, on this scale, might be extremely expensive.'

'I don't know if Ev told you, but we did contact an art museum, and got the names of two professional conservators. When we sent them photographs and dimensions of the murals, the price they quoted made my jaw drop.'

'That's what I was afraid of.'

'We had to spend much more than we intended saving this house, and there's nothing left now to go to some New York conservator. We're leasing the land to a stud farm, and I'm running cattle myself to help out, but—'

'That's what happened to me. I restored an abandoned farmhouse, and had to turn most of the second floor into an apartment to help pay the mortgage.'

'So what alternatives do we have with the murals?'

'What *I* would do, if *I* were you, is contact the Cincinnati Art Museum, and see if you could get them to send students down here to do the work. See if they'll arrange for an instructor to get them started. And then you give the students room and board, and let them do it for the experience. If Cincinnati's not willing, we'll find some other students somewhere. If you wanted to consult me on the approach they were taking, whether to use acrylic or watercolor, that kind of thing, I could give you my opinion at least, so you didn't feel like you were in this completely on your own.'

'Students wouldn't have occurred to me.'

Ben was packing up his equipment, arranging his cleaning supplies in one fishing-tackle box, his paints and brushes in another.

'May I carry something for you?'

'If you wouldn't mind taking the dryer and unplugging the cord in the dining room.'

'I b'lieve I can manage that, yes.'

Jo Austin was coiling the cord, waiting at the bottom of the stairs, when Ben came down with his tackle boxes.

'Did you see the stain here on the stairs? The fourth step up from the bottom?'

'Nope.' Ben carried his camp stools down the staircase and set them on the floor by his boxes, then looked at the dark brown lopsided circle four or five inches in diameter.

'*That* is a fatal bloodstain over a hundred years old.'

'Any idea whose?'

'We know for a fact. Mount Prospect was built by Colonel William Henry Stanley Field, this original portion of the house here, in 1796, when—'

'Did he come with an army land grant, after the revolution?'

'He did, yes, from Virginia, to claim his thousand acres, bringing his wife with him, his cousin, Sally Field.'

'Ah.'

'Apparently, the Colonel had a reputation for drinking more whiskey than was good for him on occasion, and one night, a servant woke him up and told him his wife had been killed. The general assumption seemed to be that he'd killed his wife in a drunken temper. Not because he was violent, or relations were bad between them, but from lack of evidence that it could've been anyone else.'

'Did the Colonel deny it?'

'He did. Said he had nothin' whatever to do with it, and Henry Clay defended him. That's Henry Clay's mother's house next door, the big white house you see when you drive in. But Colonel Field was found guilty anyway, and put to death soon after.'

'Why do I have the feeling the story isn't over?'

'You surely are right about that. For a week or two later, the house servants got to talking, and it turned out that a slave woman had let slip to someone when she was drinkin' that she'd been the one who'd stabbed Mrs Field. The other slaves gave evidence against her, and she did admit it finally before she was executed.'

'That's a very sad story.'

'It still gives me the shivers. No matter how hard everyone who's lived in this house has tried to clean away that blood, it never will fade the least little bit. Do you hear a car?'

Both Great Danes were rushing down the hall toward the front door, as Jo said, 'I reckon it must be Everett. He's coming to spend the afternoon with you, and stay on to dinner. His wife's in Louisville for a week with their daughter seeing to a brand new grandbaby.'

She let the Great Danes out, then waved at her brother, where he stood petting the dogs. 'Ev appears to be carrying something that looks like a velvet box.'

Thirteen

Ben was sitting with a photograph album in his lap in Jo's library, when Everett Adams came through the door from the parlor.

'This is the old travelers' room, you know.' Ev was carrying two mugs of coffee, and he set them on the trunk in front of Ben.

'I could see the fireplace was really old.'

'Yep, this room was originally built with no door to the house to protect the family, and yet allow them to shelter travelers. What book are you looking at there?'

'It's a scrapbook. One of Jo's husband's. There're more horses in it than people.'

'Course there are, you're in Woodford County.'

'By the way,' Ben pulled the print the newspaper had made for him out of a manila envelope and handed it to Everett Adams. 'Any chance you know this guy?'

'Hold on a minute.' Ev put on his reading glasses and held the photo under the floor lamp beside his chair.

'*The Herald Leader* took it at Keeneland in June of 1955. There were names for everyone else in the shot on the back, except for him.'

'His name's John Wharton. If you keep turning the pages in that album, you'll see this photograph there too. I've met him many times, but I wouldn't say I know him.'

'Does he live around here now?'

'In a manner of speaking. He married a widow woman from Versailles not too long after the war, and he lives here a portion of the time. His business is down in Knoxville, and his primary residence is there too.'

'What do you know about him?'

'Well, his wife has passed away now, but when she was alive, he was here a good bit more, especially in the early fifties when he had a research facility here. I believe he came up four days a week. John was an orphan, and Ruth believed he enjoyed having her family around him. Her family has been here in Woodford County for a hundred and fifty years. She'd inherited her first husband's house on the other side of Versailles, so she and John split their time between that house and a big old farmhouse they fixed up down near Knoxville.'

'Did they have any children?'

'Ruth had a daughter from her first marriage, and when Jenny was little they both went down to Knoxville a good bit. Once she got to going to school, they spent more time up here.'

'How did John's wife die?'

'Cancer. In 1956. Her daughter's being raised here by Ruth's sister, Alma. She was ten years older than Ruth, and had never married. Jenny's father died in 1947, when she was a year or two old.'

Ben was staring at the photograph again, using the magnifying glass on his key ring, studying it under the lamp.

'Why are you so interested?'

'He looks like someone I knew during the war. Someone who died in 1945, according to army records. His name wasn't Wharton, but it looks like the same guy. And it sure looks to me like he doesn't want his picture taken.'

'I s'ppose it could've been his double you knew. They say doppelgängers do exist.'

'Yeah, maybe, but in this case I doubt it.'

'I do remember hearing that John did behave kind of peculiarly about that picture. They say he went to the newspaper office and asked them not to run the photograph. There was a visitor in it from out of town, that fella in front of him, someone important to racing they needed a shot of, and the paper went right on and printed it. They probably weren't going to let themselves get told what to do by an outsider either.'

'I've seen another picture of this guy trying to cover his face exactly the same way. Why's the picture in Jo's scrapbook?'

Everett raised his eyebrows and looked at Ben over the match flame he was sucking down to the tobacco in his pipe.

'The horse owner from out of town was a good friend to Jo's husband Tom's daddy.'

'Whatever you can tell me about Wharton will help. It's very important, but I can't tell you why right now. I promise I will when I can.'

'I don't know a great deal about him. His wife was Ruth Bodley Hunt. The Bodleys are an old family, and she married into another. Her husband, Win – Winthrop was his given name . . . Win was a fine man, eight or ten years older than she. An engineer who built himself up a business in Lexington that manufactured generators. I believe that's how she met John Wharton. She was up north arranging the sale of her husband's firm after his death, and mutual friends, or business associates of some sort, introduced the two of them. She did right well for herself when she sold the business.'

'So she was wealthy when John married her?'

'Her own family had lost its money years ago, but I s'ppose she was then, after the sale. Ruth had a good mind for business. She told me herself that she loaned John a good bit of money when he was expanding his business in Knoxville, but she always kept her money separate from his, and he paid her back at the proper time. She felt like it was her daughter's inheritance more than it was hers, and it behooved her to look after it. Ruth started up a group around here too to help folks fix up the old houses falling down on the farms.'

'What about John?'

'He talked her into marrying him pretty quick. That's what it looked like to folks. She married him a year and a half or so after Win died. Jenny must've been close to three at the time, and that may've been why. Perhaps Ruth didn't want to wait so long that it'd get harder for Jenny to accept John.' Everett Adams got up from his chair and threw another log on the fire.

'Who are you two talking about?' Jo was standing in the parlor doorway sipping a mug of tea.

'John Wharton. Ben knew someone in the war who looked a good deal like him.'

Jo raised an eyebrow and quietly considered Ben.

'Do you know him? I'll explain why I'm asking later, but I do have a good reason.'

'I don't know him well.' Jo curled up in a deep chair covered in brown and white cowhide, and tucked her feet underneath her.

'Does Jenny get along with John?'

'Pretty well. Wouldn't you say, Ev? John was good to Ruth, from what anyone could tell. He's kind to Jenny, but he's very preoccupied with his work. *I* never felt like it was the close marriage that Ruth had had with Win. I don't think she blamed John for that. She didn't want to move down to Knoxville, with her family, and her restoration work here. So I b'lieve she thought she was doing the best she could for her marriage, and giving Jenny a secure life too. Giving her the Bodley and the Hunt families here, the family Jenny'd always known, and a stepfather who treated her well too.'

'What kind of person is John?'

'I don't know him well enough to say. He's intelligent. He's personable. He's interesting to talk to and all, but you feel like you never get past the surface. I presume he's a competent businessman.'

Everett nodded, then drank the last of his coffee. 'John started a business before he met Ruth that was founded on new ways of heat-treating metal. I believe the first application that really got him going was working on broaching the "Christmas trees" that are part of the rotor blades in jet engines. They were terribly hard to produce when they were first designing jet engines before the war, and not too long after it too, when they were trying to get jets into production.'

'So that's a type of jet engine metallurgy?'

'Yes. Wharton's developed all sorts of fancy heat-treat techniques that are used in aircraft and other specialized jobs, working with rare and expensive alloys. He manufactures the machines that machine the parts for difficult applications.'

Ben set his coffee down and said he knew nothing about that.

'Well, there's a lot to it. Years ago, in the late thirties and early forties, when they were first working on the jet engine, they used carbon tetrachloride to do the machining on those Christmas tree pieces. But carbon tet is toxic, and if you take a drink of alcohol with carbon tet in your blood stream, the problem can become severe.'

'I don't know anything about it.'

'Not many do. They say John's machines, using his approach

to heat-treating, were head and shoulders above anything else on the market after the Second World War. I've heard he may be doing work for Oak Ridge, the government research people there. But I don't know it for a fact.'

Jo nodded while she sipped her tea. 'One thing I *have* noticed is he doesn't do much socializing. Certainly not when he's here in Versailles. Not the charity balls, and all.'

'Where his picture might get taken.' Ben smiled and closed the album.

'I s'ppose so.' Jo looked at Ben consideringly.

And he said, 'When I *can* explain, I promise I will. What do people think of him here?'

'Nobody feels like they know him very well.' Jo set her mug on the floor and stretched her arms over her head. 'Course they don't find fault with the way he treats Jenny. Lots of folks around here send their teenagers away to boarding school, but when Jenny didn't want to go, John arranged to have a tutor from the university work with her some, to add to what she gets in school. She's very busy with her horses too. She's breeding her mother's broodmares and raisin' up the babies.'

'John takes her to Italy with him occasionally too, to his house there, and she really enjoys that.' Ev was knocking the tobacco out of his pipe into a large brass ashtray.

'You know where in Italy?'

Jo looked at Everett, before she said, 'Tuscany. Close to one of those hilltop cities. Cortona? I can't be sure. I will say John has been very kind to Ruth's sister, Alma. Ruth asked Alma to raise Jenny, and paid her a salary out of the will, asking her to live in Ruth's house here in Versailles where Jenny was used to living.'

'John accepted those arrangements with very good grace. Though I suppose he had to. He never did adopt Jenny.'

'And he is good to Alma. Who *can* be a little trying.' Jo smiled, and then shook her head. 'Alma stews and dithers, and John Wharton never does. Course, she has relieved him of a large measure of responsibility for Jenny, and that might've been welcome. Ev, did I tell you Jenny's going to Italy in March to take a course?'

'Don't recall that you did.'

'There's a group going from the University of Kentucky

for a two-week seminar on Italian art, and the person leading the tour is Tess Johns.' Jo looked from Everett to Ben and said, 'She was one of Ruth's best friends. Jenny's just seventeen, but they'll be going during spring break, and Tess has talked Alma into letting Jenny go, even though she'll have to take an extra few days from school.'

'Ben will be in Italy in March, to find the owners of that jewelry Mark brought back from the war, and give a lecture in Florence. We need to talk about that trip, Ben, in a lot more detail.'

Jo asked if the jewelry had been in the box Ev had brought. And he said, 'Yes, I—'

'By the way, I just got a call from Brad a little while ago.' Jo looked at Ben and explained that Brad was her son, and he and his wife were driving home to Louisville from North Carolina, and had called and said they could spend the night. 'So we'll wait, and have dinner with them.'

Ben asked if she had enough room for all of them. 'Because I can go on home tonight if that would—'

'No, we'll do just fine. I'll put them in the old log cabin on the south end of the property, and you can stay here in the—'

'Why don't you put me in the cabin and let them stay in the house?'

'Well, I . . .'

'I don't mind at all. I really don't.'

'If you're sure. Then that would be fine. Everett, maybe you could take Ben over there before dinner, and give him a chance to settle in.'

Ben said, 'I might like to meet Jenny and her aunt sometime. Not today. I need to check on some things first. But maybe another time. I really will tell you what this is about when I can. And please don't mention me to John, or Jenny, or Alma the aunt. Please. Don't mention my name at all. I'll explain why as soon as I can.'

Everett Adams and his sister Jo raised very similar dark brown eyebrows, glanced at each other, and agreed not to say a word.

Ben didn't want to. And he told himself he was being childish, as he walked the drive before dinner. He'd run up and down it five times, and now he was heading south from the big house toward the old weathered cabin. Fields and barns stretched between the two, and Ben stopped on that high ground, next to Jo's herd of cows and calves, and watched the clouds change beyond the clustering hills. He walked on, between paddocks of horses, thinking about it while he watched. Knowing he ought to go and call Kate and tell her what he knew about Wharton.

But I still don't want to. And it looks like pride and ego. Did you think you were the only man she knew, and didn't like finding out you weren't? How ridiculous would that be?

Or maybe you're using the flowers as an excuse not to get involved yourself.

So was she was getting too close for comfort? Was the thought that someone might have a hold on you too painful to contemplate? Or was it her asking if you'd ever needed anyone? Maybe she's not allowed to question Ben Reese. The self-sufficient, independent man of many parts.

Or was it you getting too close to her? Is that what this is about? Wanting to talk to her, and see her, and touch her, because she's Kit Lindsay. A specific her. Who might be able to prick a hole in your own impenetrable skin.

All wives don't die young. All women won't want you tied-and-gagged. Jessie didn't, needless to say. And there's no reason to think Kate would. You saw how good she was with Graham.

Or is it that I like being alone? Doing what I want to do, when I want to do it. It's fairly pathetic, anyway you look at it. So be a man and get a move on.

Ben was standing with his hands in the pockets of his pea jacket, the sun cold now, sinking below the trees beyond the old log cabin.

It was just the kind he could've lived in. The original part small and square and roofed in cedar shakes. A tail section built on to the back (on the right of the cabin, as he walked toward that side of it), with a wide foyer with French doors connecting old and new.

He went in that way, through the shed-roofed porch, turning left in the entryway, stepping up one wooden stair to the pioneer cabin's largest room.

There he stood by the big fieldstone fireplace and placed a call to Scotland, charging it to his home number.

*   *   *

Kate had just come into the house from her small cottage studio and was standing in the library door listening for sounds of David Lindsay. It was silent, except for Joshua's breathing, and the crackle of the library fire.

David must've gone to bed, but put more wood on for me.

Kate stepped into the study, with Joshua (the big yellow Labrador-mutt Ben had rescued and given her the summer before) walking right on her heels, wondering what to do to help David get stronger. His glaucoma had gotten worse, and he was less steady on his feet because he couldn't see well enough to walk the woods the way he always had.

She hadn't come up with anything useful when the phone rang on the desk behind the sofa, and Kate sat and picked it up before it could ring again.

'Hello . . . Speaking . . . Really! Then you think John Wharton could be Ted Mitchell? . . . With a house in Italy too, yeah. Sounds like the American Nellie Ferguson saw . . .

'Once you look up his patents, how can you find out what kind of work was being done on jet rotors in Germany during the war? Or heat treating, or whatever it is? . . . No, but there *is* something I wanted to tell you. You know the man who sent me the flowers in New York? He's a professor at Aberdeen who knew David when he taught there, and went to university with Graham. He's a friend, but there's no other interest there at all, except that . . . Well, I only thought that you might . . . OK. Sure! Why would I have thought that? Whatever you say, Ben!'

Kate hung up. Then stood up in front of the fire and kicked a wicker waste-paper basket two feet across the room, which panicked Joshua, who leapt-up in the air and hid behind a chair. She knelt beside him and stroked his ears until she got him to lie back down.

Then she said, 'What *is* the matter with him?' *Why would he act so . . . ?*

The phone rang again, and Kate looked at it. She told herself not to let it wake David, and stepped across and picked it up. 'Hello? . . . I'll wait . . . No, I guess I *don't* understand it, and it doesn't seem very fair . . . Wait a minute, *that's* not fair! When I want to enjoy being irritated, you're not allowed to make me laugh!'

She did laugh, as she sat down and scratched Joshua's back.

'I know. Me too. It's been a long time for both of us, and we're probably out of practice . . . No, I understand . . . OK, I'll talk to you then. I'm glad you called back.'

Kate smiled and kissed Joshua's head, then stretched out on the sofa and picked *Persuasion* up from the end table, where she'd left it that afternoon.

Sunday, February 18th, 1962

'So you know for a fact that Alma and Jenny are gone?' Ben turned away from the curving hills and the creek on McCracken Pike and looked at Everett Adams, who was driving Ben in his big black Chrysler at a relaxed and dignified pace.

'Jo called last night.' Everett had rolled his window down and was now adjusting his mirror. 'They've gone to church and Sunday school, then on to a family brunch. Jo has a key, for emergencies and all, and she told Alma that a friend of mine was in town who's interested in antebellum architecture, and asked if I could bring you along to see it before you left this morning. Alma was pleased as she could be. She enjoys showing folks the family antiques.'

'Look at the dry stone walls along here. Can you imagine how hard it would be to do that day after day?'

'The man who built them is a fine old colored gentleman by the name of Lee-Franc Tibbitz.'

'Lee-Franc is a real artist.'

'He truly is. He moved back here as a young man, after living in another county for several years, and he appeared at the door of a very good friend of mine over near Midway. He introduced himself, very early one morning, and he said, 'Mr Sawyer, you don't know me, but my people were slaves on your family's farm. And when I was coming down Spring Station Road at the back of your farm this mornin', I seen 'bout ninety foot of that old stone fence had fallin' right down. I can fix it for you if you want me to.' Lee-Franc didn't mention that he'd picked up every single stone out of that road already.'

'Humbling, isn't it?'

'Yes, it is. And when he finished repairing that wall, he only charged a dollar a foot. Mr Sawyer paid Lee-Franc a good deal more, but that's the sort of fella Lee-Franc is. He was

the deacon in his church for many, many years that folks went
to for every sort of advice. He's away up in his nineties now.
And white and colored both, we all hold Lee-Franc in the
highest regard.'

They'd just passed a gate on their right to a large, elegant,
stud farm, and Everett began to brake to make the turn to the
next gravel drive, three hundred yards beyond.

The big lumbering Chrysler rumbled slowly up a steep high
hill bordered by plum trees and white four-rail fence, where
broodmares beyond both were peacefully cropping grass, or
dozing in the sun.

The drive curved to the left at the top of the hill, around a
cluster of bare branched trees, ending in a circle by a two-
story brick farmhouse with a peak-roofed porch in the center.

Everett unlocked the white double doors. And they stepped
into a wide hall with a staircase on the left, just beyond the
arch to the dining room.

'The drawing room's here on the right.'

Ben followed Everett into a peach-colored square room with
two tall matching windows on either side, a fireplace on the
far wall, and family pictures on the tables.

Ben looked at all of them, but didn't find one of Wharton.
'Ruth is the good looking woman in her thirties?'

'Yes.'

'And the teenage girl with the blonde hair, that's Jenny
Hunt?'

'Yep.' Everett walked through the doorway to the right of
the fireplace and stepped down two steep steps. 'This was
Ruth and John's room. John still uses it when he's here.'

There were two photos of Ruth on the bedside table, one
with a dog, and another with a mare and foal.

Ben opened the drawer below them without asking Adams
if he minded. And there he found a picture of Wharton with
an arm around Ruth's waist. 'There.' Ben handed it to Everett.
'The man I knew in Germany.'

Ben pulled his tiny black Rolex camera out of the inside
of his waistband and unclipped the chain from his belt.

He slid the photograph out of the frame, laid it down on
the desk, took the shade off a floor lamp, pulled it near the
photo, shot the photograph with three different exposures –
and put it back in the drawer.

When he looked up, Everett was back in the living room.

'Now, behind the dining room – ' Everett was halfway across the hall by then, heading straight for the dining room – 'is the study that John used to use as an office. Whether he does now, I don't know.' Everett stepped down the three steep steps from the center of the dining room's back wall into a smaller room with a window on either side, and a door to the kitchen in the back left corner next to the fireplace that faced the steps.

'That's John's desk there.' It was in the corner just to the left of the dining-room stairs. And one small photograph sat on the top.

It was a black-and-white picture of a broaching machine.

And Ben carried it to the window, and looked at it carefully with his magnifying glass. 'Wharton Machinery, is that right? The logo's a large red "W", with the left-hand leg made to look like a cutting tool?'

Everett Adams nodded and said, 'I won't object if you go through the drawers.'

Ben smiled and pulled out the center one, and the two on the sides as well, then wrote something else in his notebook, before he looked at Everett. 'How do you know I'm not up to no good?'

'The stand you took on the Harrison will. That's all I need to know.'

They were on their way back to Versailles, taking the curves slowly, gazing across rows of soft rounded hilltops as far away as the horizon, when Ben told Ev he was having trouble arranging his Italian trip. 'I think it's because of the Harrison will. The library director's making it tough, along with our illustrious president. Who is none too pleased with me at the moment.'

'Yes.'

'They're refusing permission for me to leave a day early. I want to have time to research the jewelry for you, and I've got to deliver the paper. And if, by any chance, Jenny will be there while I am, I'd like to try to get to know her, and see if I can find out what she knows about Wharton. That may not work out. For all I know, *he* may be in Italy with Jenny the whole time. But if you could find out when she'll be there, and where she'll be staying, and whatever you can about the studying she's doing, that would be a big help.'

'I'll look into it right away. You can't see your way clear to explain this to me?'

Ben looked at Everett for what seemed like half a minute. Then finally swore him to secrecy, making him promise not to even tell Jo, explaining about Mitchell, and MacNab and Welsh's deaths.

'Good gracious!' Everett looked at Ben, then back at the curving road. 'I believe you took my breath away.'

Neither of them said anything till they'd turned into the drive to Mount Prospect.

'You've got me to thinking, Ben. There's something else you could do for me in Italy, that might persuade Harper to give you some leeway with your schedule. I believe I've told you I've collected a handful of old books over the years?'

'Yes.'

'I have a manuscript on vellum of *The Dialogi* by Seneca, which is pretty hard to decipher, with the script being as elaborate as it is. I would like you to locate and buy a copy of the first Aldine printing of the same work. I've checked in this country through the book dealers I've dealt with before, and they're tellin' me I'd have more luck in Europe. You bring it back to me, and I'll keep it till June, and then donate both the Latin manuscript *and* the Aldine Latin edition to Alderton University during commencement weekend. The two together would be a very useful gift. Students could compare the two, and learn a great many things.'

'You're sure you want to do that? They're both—'

'I might want to borrow them from time to time, but yes. I don't have a volume of the *Naturales Quaestiones*. I have the other essays, *The Consolations* and the rest.'

'Ah.'

'If I had my druthers, I'd like the Aldine to be in a signed binding. An edition bound by a really fine Italian bookbinder for a particular person. Someone historically interesting, if you can find it. Who had a fancy cover tooled and stamped and signed by the binder.'

'You don't want much, do you?'

Ev laughed and said, 'Perhaps that's why I couldn't find

one here. But it does make good sense for you to do that for me in Italy.'

'Boy, Ev, I don't know, that'll be awfully hard work. And boring too. I don't know if I could stand it.' Ben was grinning, looking sideways at Everett.

'Yes, I thought you might enjoy it. And since you have to go to Tuscany to talk on a specific date, it's logical that you would do the search while you're there. Mark and I will pay your expenses together, in recompense for your work. Shall I call Harper and get him to authorize the extension of the trip? Or would you rather talk to him about it yourself?'

'Whichever you think. I really appreciate this, Ev.'

'You're doing me a service.' Everett Adams smiled at Ben as he climbed out of the car and patted the heads of the two Great Danes leaning on either side of him. 'I believe I'd like the pleasure of talking to Fred Harper myself.'

'One other thing.' They were just outside the side door of Mount Prospect that led into the kitchen wing. 'I know I already said this, but it's *really* important that nobody here even hears my name mentioned. Wharton, if he *is* Mitchell, would recognize it right away. And I need to keep him completely unaware of me, and my interest in him.'

'I won't say a word to anyone. I'll remind Jo too, about not mentioning who I took to Jenny's house, though Jo's very good at keeping secrets.'

They'd walked into the kitchen, which was huge and filled with light, with a raised brick fireplace opposite the archway to the hall, and a great old English worktable sitting right in the center.

'Jo's catered since the boys were little, and she's never had a big enough kitchen before this. She's left a note on the table for you.'

Everett picked it up and handed it on to Ben.

Jenny – Cortona, March 12th through 25th. Lectures at Museum there. Trips all over. J.W has a house two or three miles north of Cortona. She'll be staying there with housekeeper. Will get address later.

'Jo doesn't waste much time, does she?'

'Never has. You should've seen her tearing down walls, and

scraping bricks, and helping to rip off the roof. Jo doesn't sit and wait for inspiration to strike.'

'One thing I do need Jo to find out, if she *can* without raising any eyebrows, is where John Wharton will be when Jenny's in Cortona. Knowing that will make me feel easier about talking to Jenny there. Especially if I find out what I *think* I'm going to find in the meantime.

Fourteen

'No Roger, I'll take it as a day of vacation. I have to haul my horse to Ohio State to get his eye removed . . . I called you last night as soon as I found out, but you didn't answer the . . . Oh, so you, as Alderton's Library Director, don't think my job performance is quite at the level you'd like? . . . Ah, that's what I thought. I'll talk to you when I get back.'

Ben dropped the receiver in the cradle, took a deep breath and held it for a second, then walked out the Buchannons' back door and went to get Max from the barn.

'I know, kiddo, I know your eye feels miserable, but I've got to put the patch on again. That's good. That's a good boy. Here, I brought you an apple.'

Max was in the cross ties, his head hanging to the left, his good eye looking worried, as he took the apple without much caring, before Ben snapped the lead rope on his halter.

He unlatched the cross ties and led Max out of the barn straight toward the ramp of Walter's horse trailer, feeling Max stiffen as soon as he'd seen it. Ben could also feel Max thinking about resisting. Because Max didn't want to walk up that ramp and ride anywhere in that metal box, where he'd have to stand trapped in a tight dark space.

But Ben kept talking to him, walking steadily straight ahead. And he could feel the moment when Max decided not to fight him, but to follow him up the rubber-covered ramp.

Max walked into that trailer without hesitating at all when Ben brought him home three days later with his eyelids sewn shut across the empty socket, with his head drooping listlessly to his left, with his ribs showing through his thick winter coat, and his good eye looking anxious.

He was spooky when Ben tried to take the halter off in his stall, wheeling away from Ben in too small a space and knocking him into a wall. When Ben tried later that evening to give him his antibiotics and his anti-inflammatory paste, Max fought getting his halter put on as though he were afraid it would hurt. He managed to spit out the anti-inflammatory twice, and tossed his head in every direction, which made it hard to get a needle in his neck.

Max had to stay in his stall the next day, but he seemed marginally quieter. Though he still fought getting his halter put on, which told Ben something about how much the eye socket hurt.

The following morning, Ben walked Max inside his usual paddock, then took off the halter and turned him loose. He watched Max walk around the perimeter, then amble into his run-in shed. He came out a second later, bucking and kicking across snow and ice, till Ben was afraid he'd go down.

But he didn't. Max was nothing if not good on his feet. And after four or five minutes of impressive pyrotechnics, he walked over to Ben and snuffled his hand for a treat.

Saturday, March 3rd, 1962

> Dear Kate,
>
> Max is doing much better. His stitches came out day before yesterday, and he's eating better and acting more like himself. The pathology lab never could figure out what caused the uveitous, but they all say it's nothing that'll spread to the other eye. Max is tough, and well meaning, and I'm really glad I've got him.
>
> I know for sure that this John Wharton I've run across was injured in the skirmish in which Ted Mitchell was 'killed'. Wharton (the *real* John Wharton) was a technical guy sent over to bring back science from the Germans, just like Mitchell. Army records show he (Mitchell using Wharton's name) was shot in the leg and suffered a minor head wound, and was dragged out of the Saar River near Beckingen after he'd been shot. This Wharton (Mitchell) was released from a US military hospital in May of 1945. (Confusing, huh?)

The *real* Wharton was an orphan raised in an orphanage in Bloomington, Indiana. He had a high school physics teacher who encouraged him to go to college and helped him get a scholarship to Purdue. Wharton studied all kinds of engineering. It sounds like he was unusually intelligent and hard working, and he finally settled on electrical engineering, working largely in radio development.

He had no next of kin, so he listed that high school physics teacher to be notified in case of injury or death. Chester got his name for me from army records, and I've sent him a copy of the photograph you sent me of Ross MacNab and the two injured Americans, asking him to identify John Wharton, but there hasn't been time to hear back. This teacher never heard from Wharton after the war, which was a real surprise and disappointment to him, and he doesn't know what became of him.

So what does that all mean?

There's reason to ask a few pointed questions. For instance, if Ted Mitchell (who was apparently working with Wharton at that time, and could've known he was an orphan) wanted to come back and use the science he'd stolen over there (including the magnetic tape recording stuff I think he found at the place I took him), if he wanted an identity that gave him no awkward questions from relatives (like 'Where did you get this magnetic recording invention when you've never worked with anything like that?') would it have behooved Mitchell, seeing Wharton die, to take on his identity? And *if* anyone ever wondered why Mitchell's team died like flies, a dead Mitchell couldn't be investigated. (*My* assumption being that he eliminated the others so his stealing wouldn't be detected.)

All Mitchell would've had to do was switch dog tags. He wouldn't have had much of a chance of running into someone he knew. He wasn't in an outfit the way regular army would've been. And if he did, in a hospital somewhere, he could just say someone else mixed up the dog tags somewhere along the line, and he hadn't been able to get it sorted out.

So that could be Wharton in the photograph. Wharton could've died right then, when the picture was taken. And Mitchell could've seen his chance. That he could come back to the States as Wharton with the plans for the magnetic tape and the tape recorder, translate them into English, redraw everything himself, and have credibility as a Purdue graduate electrical engineer who'd been 'working on his own before the war and had perfected his invention after he got out of the army'. In mid-1946 someone named John Wharton *did* sell his work on magnetic recording for a very substantial sum.

Who knows what else Mitchell could've stolen? I have no way of knowing, except what he based his business on. He could've taken the money from the recording stuff and used it to start this machine-tool business he has now. There was excellent work being done in this field in Germany when he was there, which was way ahead of ours on jet engines, and on heat treating as well, from what I've been able to find out so far. Mitchell certainly could've taken it as his own. He could've improved it himself too. He had a degree in mechanical engineering from MIT, and he'd gone to work for Pratt & Whitney in jet engine metallurgy before the war, so that would be right up his alley. The tape recorder money would've gotten him started.

So did Ted Mitchell switch the dog tags when he and Wharton were injured by the Saar River, when Ross MacNab patched them up? Was Mitchell the person MacNab pulled out of the river, the way George Gunn thinks he did? And did Mitchell act as a benefactor to him partly because of that? Or was it also partly the fact that MacNab suspected he'd switched identities? I suppose that's possible. Maybe he actually saw him switch the dog tags?

He could have, I guess. I think he was beyond understanding, *or* caring what he'd seen, if he did see it that day. You saw him in the photo. You know what Gunn said. You know he was picked up later that same day completely over the edge.

He was silent, for what, a year or more? And he never really talked about the war after that. He didn't have visitors either, though, did he? How could he have told anyone from the outside world?

And then you arranged to visit. (Now, don't feel guilty about that. You meant well, and you had no way of knowing that there might be adverse repercussions.) You know from Nurse Ferguson that Welsh talked to someone, possibly the benefactor, who looked something like Mitchell when MacNab was brought there. (I assume you'll be showing Ferguson the photo?) Whoever that was asked Welsh to report MacNab talking about the war and having visitors. Yet Welsh lied about it to you. What if Welsh was paid to keep in touch with Mitchell? To tell Mitchell how MacNab was doing – particularly whether he was talking about the war, and if he had visitors.

If MacNab saw Ted Mitchell switch dog tags with John Wharton, would Mitchell be so afraid of having his assumed identity discovered that he'd be willing to kill MacNab to keep him from telling anyone else? If Mitchell-Wharton did get information from Welsh, he'd know about your intended visit, and he could easily know what medications MacNab took, and about his blind and his daily habits, and be able to fake MacNab's suicide.

And what about Welsh? Was he silenced too? It wouldn't be hard to shove someone off the edge of the Cornwall cliffs near Port Isaac.

Am I sounding nuts here or what? Am I jumping to ridiculous conclusions? I don't know. But it seems to me to fit remarkably well.

Any chance you could visit Welsh's widow and see if there's anything else you can dig up? It might be worth doing, if you have time.

I'm leaving for Italy on the 6th. Everett talked to Harper about wanting to give an Aldine first edition of Seneca to Alderton, and needing me to find one, which means what could Harper say? So I'll work on that for Everett, and do my talk, and try to get to know Jenny Hunt, once she gets to Italy.

The burning question I'm dying to ask her is, 'Where was your stepfather, John Wharton, on New Year's Eve when Ross MacNab died?' I tried Wharton's secretary, using a phoney name, and trumped-up excuse, and got absolutely nowhere. He's trained her very well.

I'll be doing work in Florence and Siena, and then I'll be staying with a friend of mine at his family farm, La Fortezza della Felicità, south of Siena near Sinalunga. He was an archivist at the Vatican for years, and I met him a long time ago when I was trying to authenticate the Dante we have at Alderton. Maggie will know where I am at every minute, as will my secretary.

Hope all is well with you.

It was good to talk to you the other night.

Ben

Wednesday, March 7th, 1962

Ben took an early morning train up from Rome to Florence, and then met with curators in one museum and one library. They helped explain what was actually documented and what could only be assumed about Renaissance jewelry and the goldsmiths who made it.

The most significant fact was that not a whole lot *was* known about the jewelry makers then. Some were famous for their sculpture and other art, Cellini and Ghiberti being the foremost examples. A few pieces of jewelry could be attributed without question to a particular artist of that time, yet most attributions seemed to Ben to be based on a fairly high level of assumption.

Still, everyone Ben worked with in Florence was helpful. He was shown photographs of pieces in private collections and museums all over Italy, and jewelry was brought out of display cases and archives so he could examine and photograph the works those institutions owned.

But no one he'd shown his photographs of the brooch and ring knew anything about their background, or could say who the artist had been.

Toward the end of the afternoon, he walked out into warm spring air a block from the Arno River, into streets filled with dazed-looking tourists wandering past lines of leather vendors selling belts, purses, coats, hats, and everything else you can make from leather under multicolored tents. Carpenters and tile masons on flimsy looking scaffolding smoked and argued and pulled buckets of cement up to high windows in ancient stone and brick houses. Tangles of Florentines and first-time visitors ate gelato on the corners of crooked streets.

Ben stopped and watched, standing in the middle of the Piazza della Signoria, then did exactly what he wanted to do – turn his back on his own work to stare at Michelangelo's David, walking slowly around it twice with his mouth hanging open.

He strolled toward the Arno after that, between the long broad columned wings of the great Uffizi Gallery, considering other experts to consult. On another afternoon. When he wasn't walking under water, numb and slow and stupid with jet lag.

Yet he still wasn't ready to go back to his room, and he walked across the crowded Ponte Vecchio – the fourteenth-century stone-arched bridge lined with wood-paneled goldsmith shops – hardly glancing at the jewelry.

He stared instead above the east wall of shops to see what he could of the enclosed upper corridor the Medicis had built so they could walk in private, past their own paintings, from one family palace to another – from the Palazzo Vecchio on the north of the Arno, to the Palazzo Pitti on the south.

Ben wandered the gardens of the Pitti Palace for almost an hour, then crossed the river again to look at the art he loved as much as any in Florence – Ghiberti's baptistry doors, and Fra Angelico's paintings in the monks' cells in the Church of San Marco.

Yet he found himself thinking about Mitchell anyway. About John Wharton's physics teacher. Who'd told him at lunchtime when Ben had phoned, that the John Wharton *he* had taught was the American on the stretcher on the right in the photo.

Which means we know for sure now. Which could've been hard to prove.

Ben was sitting on a bench by San Marco staring at traffic. Listening to noise. Smelling car and bus fumes. Telling himself to get up and move.

When he did, he dragged himself back to his hotel, soaked in a hot tub, found a trattoria one street over, ate an early dinner, went to bed before nine, closed his eyes thinking about how to legally tack Ted Mitchell to a wall and make it stick

– until he suddenly remembered what he must've been trying to forget.

Early the next morning, he, Ben Reese, introvert and silent observer, would be standing in front of a roomful of people trying to string words together without sweating through his shirt.

'As you can see, I'm heating the nylon slowly in a shallow metal pan on an electric hotplate. I use the smallest pan that will fit the particular document I'm preserving.' Ben made himself swallow and told himself to relax his shoulders, while what he'd said was translated.

The Italian took longer than the English, and Ben looked around the lecture room in the Palazzo dei Congressi-Villa Vittoria at the forty or so archivists and conservators who'd been invited by Professor Giovanni Balducci from libraries and museums in Florence, Siena, Lucca and Pisa – wishing he could get it over fast before his mouth got drier.

'The unheated nylon has a very high viscosity, so it has to be heated until it's a thin liquid.' Ben's hands were sweaty, which irritated him considerably, and he wiped them on a towel on the table, as Giovanni translated.

'Wood pulp paper would disintegrate if I dipped it directly in the nylon.' Ben was pulling on surgical gloves, staring hard at the table. 'So I use a nylon substrate to strengthen and support it.' Giovanni translated that, while Ben found his scissors. 'The solution I've come up with may make you laugh, but at my university I need to develop inexpensive techniques. Giovanni doesn't have that problem at the University of Siena.'

Ben smiled at Giovanni, listening to the rich deep voice translate his small attempt at humor. 'So, in the interests of economy . . .' There was much amused laughter as Ben cut the top of a large pair of pantyhose into a letter-size rectangle. He arranged a piece of paper on top, and laid them on the liquid nylon. 'Once the paper is fused to the hosiery, I'll lay it on a window screen and let it drip dry.'

Ben waited for Giovanni to translate, while he propped the screen up on small wooden blocks. 'You'd only use this process for one-sided, everyday documents. Memoirs. Tax rolls. Letters of little historical importance. The second technique I'll demonstrate is designed for linen and rag paper, both single *and* two-sided, but you still wouldn't use it for illuminated manuscripts. Or Aldine first editions. Or Da Vinci's hand-written notebooks.'

Once Giovanni had translated that, a ripple of laughter circled the room.

After Ben's blood pressure had dropped to normal – after he and Giovanni had lunched on the Via Guelfa, and Giovanni had gone off to work of his own – he made his way to the Uffizi Gallery where he had an appointment with a well-respected expert in renaissance sculpture and jewelry.

Ben showed the curator his pictures of Mark Adams' brooch and ring. And both of them read, looked at books, and compared them to pieces of jewelry belonging to the museum. After considerable discussion, they guardedly hazarded a guess, that though the pieces had no identifying marks, the choice of jewels, and the style, and the exceptional quality of the craftsmanship in gold and enamel was reminiscent of Benvenuto Cellini, or possibly Lorenzo Ghiberti – though next to nothing was known about Ghiberti's work as a goldsmith (except that he joined the guild in 1407, and wrote about his designs in his autobiography).

There was also nothing Ben could learn there that gave him direction in finding the owners of the brooch and ring. And all he knew to do next (other than meet the following day with another curator recommended by Armani at the Portrait Gallery in Siena), was to get recommendations of other experts when he was in Siena and Cortona, and wait for word from Interpol, for they still had lists of artworks stolen during World War II that had been compiled by the Allies. The lists included paintings, sculpture, furniture, jewelry – whatever had been taken and reported. And Ben had contacted them as soon as he'd photographed the jewelry in Lexington.

He'd given them Giovanni Balducci's address in Siena and the dates when he'd be there, as well as the address and dates of when he'd be visiting the retired Vatican curator on his farm near Sinalunga.

But that day, as he trotted over to Santa Maria Novella train station to look for Giovanni in the crowd, it didn't feel to Ben as though he'd accomplished anything.

January 23rd, 1945

Only three of the wounded GIs on Ben's plane (Ben being among them) had ever flown before. And no matter what they'd been through in combat, they were scared stiff by the take-off *and* the turbulence, which lasted most of the flight.

A nurse set up two poker games to take their minds off up-lift and gravity, and played in both herself, all the way to the Azores (then on to Bermuda, New York and Dayton, then finally Battle Creek, Michigan). She beat the pants off the bunch of them, but gave back every cent she'd won from whatever GI was carried off at each stop in the States.

Ben had phoned Jessie and his parents from Dayton, and when he got to Percy Jones Hospital in Battle Creek, he snagged a wheelchair and snuck out of his ward to wait for them in the lobby.

Jessie got there first. She was teaching English Literature then, not too far away in Ann Arbor. And Ben got to watch her run through the door, and look for him in the crowded lobby, and see her eyes when she first saw him sitting wounded in a wheelchair.

Then they got to talk, and stare, and touch each other. Though not for more than a handful of minutes, because a large nurse with a frozen face came and rushed Ben back to his second-floor ward.

Dr Jones was waiting for him, which was a complete surprise to Ben, who hadn't known Jones was headed for Battle Creek. He thought then it was the best thing that could have happened. (And came to see it later as a gift he'd been given.)

Jones (together with a very fine orthopedic surgeon) put him through a year and a half of surgery, rehab and nerve stimulation. But Jessie was there from the beginning. She took a leave of absence from the University of Michigan and worked in a restaurant to pay for a room in a boarding house. (She'd teach again at Michigan in the fall, and commute then, whatever days she could.)

Percy Jones Hospital specialized in surgical cases. Its top floor was reserved for commissioned officers (which irritated Ben whenever he thought of it). The fourth floor was a restricted area for facial disfigurement cases, and the elevators didn't stop there. (Ben discovered that, once he'd gotten better, and begun to play hide-and-go-seek on gurneys that he and the rest would commandeer in a feeble attempt to whip up excitement in a bunch of bored combat vets.) The rest of the floors were mostly bone and nerve cases. Ben Reese being both.

The abdominal wound turned out to be complicated. Peritonitis set in right after he got to Percy Jones, and ended up nearly killing Ben, with drains and adhesions and secondary infections taking more out of him later.

He had a very bad time in early March. His left arm wasn't responding well. They'd put in a steel rod, and taken bone out of his lower right leg and screwed it around the rod, but it didn't seem to be healing the way Willard Jones had hoped. He got an infection in his left leg too, that looked like Staphylococcus, but was finally discovered not to be, the same day Ben came down with the first symptoms of a nasty case of a serious form of pneumonia.

He was in an oxygen tent and delirious for three or four days, and Jessie told him later that he raved about Ted Mitchell more than she would've expected.

It was right about then too, March 12th or 13th, that Ben got a letter from Robert Flynn, an intelligence officer he'd known in France not too long after D-Day. The S2 guy Ben had reported to about taking the tech team to Stoltz Electronik had indeed done what Ben had asked. And Ben's request for information about Mitchell had made it to Major Flynn, whom Ben had known in Normandy as a First Lieutenant Company S2.

He was Army G2 now, stationed in England, coordinating intelligence that came from sources all over Europe. He'd remembered Ben right away, and done some extra unofficial digging he said he hoped would help.

From what Flynn had been told Mitchell was a mechanical engineer who had a good record for recognizing and delivering valuable scientific material. He requested scouts to take him behind the lines more than the average tech team, which usually followed the front-line troops and went in with substantial protection. Mitchell's explanation for his approach was that going in after the front-line troops meant too much damage got done before he could secure a site, thereby destroying the information OSS wanted most. Operating the way he did assured valuable data.

Mitchell's handling of his men was said to be less successful. There was nothing concrete that would have persuaded his superiors to interfere, but there appeared to be a consistent lack of trust in his teams. Mitchell communicated very little about what he was looking for, or what he'd found at the sites they were sent to. He had a higher team kill rate than average too, which OSS assumed was a result of his choosing to go behind the lines. It wasn't so high that they'd make him stop using scouts, but high enough to be noticed.

Ben lay in the dark the night he got that letter, out of the oxygen but propped up on pillows – getting thumped on the back, getting shot-up with medication, listening to nurses gossiping in the hall, watching them make their rounds – holding the letter from Flynn in his hand, composing an answer in his head, till breakfast was brought in.

His fever was higher and he was a lot more exhausted all the rest of that day, as he wrestled with what to do about Mitchell, talking about it with Jessie too, the minute she walked in.

He went through it all again the next afternoon, when she stopped by on her break. Circling back, time after time, to what Mitchell did to his men.

'I don't know how to explain it exactly, but when you're out there getting shot at, when you haven't slept in days, when you're covered with vermin, and you're hungry, and filthy, and you don't know from one second to the next if you'll make it through the day with any or all of your body parts intact, the *one* thing you want to count on is that the guys around you can be trusted.

'We all knew why we were fighting. Tojo attacked Pearl Harbor. Hitler took Europe and bombed England into rubble. But that's not what you're thinking about when an .88's aimed at your position. You're trying to get your job done, and protect your own guys, and keep yourself alive.'

'I can't imagine what that must've been like.'

'No, and I, for one, am glad you can't. Anyway, *my* situation was different. I didn't know the guys around me the way a lotta GIs did. I didn't go through basic and stay with the same platoon for three years. I got trained all over the place, and got shuffled around from one army to the next, so I never had buddies around me. When I scouted around Bastogne, I could really see how different my experience was. The paratroopers there, those guys went out of their way everyday to help each other make it. Me, I didn't want to know anybody's name.'

Ben coughed hard, and then couldn't stop. And he looked away from Jessie, till he could wipe his mouth with a handkerchief and begin to catch his breath.

Jessie handed him his water, and rearranged his pillows, before she said, 'Your cough still sounds pretty awful.' Her dark hair was in a pageboy that day, with the sides swept up and pinned, and she pushed a pin in as though she were making herself do something else to keep from fussing over Ben.

'Thanks, Jess.' Ben pushed himself up on his pillows and drank the glass of water. 'The scouts I went out with, even the ones who got attached to me for training, I didn't want to get close to them, and then watch them get killed like the others. With the kind of stuff I had to do, I felt like the only one I could trust was me.

'And then to have some officer, somebody with a sworn duty to take responsibility for the men under him, shoot his own men in the back, and shoot 'em with a Luger to cover it up, I can't tell you what that does to me. It's like swallowing ground glass. It makes me want to make him die a slow and painful death.'

'Hey.' Jessie was standing up by the head of his bed, and she leaned over and smoothed Ben's hair back away from the bones of his face, all sharp corners and edges then, under hot papery skin. 'I haven't lived through it, but if I had, I expect I'd see it the same way. Just the thought of it makes me shudder. But it's not good for you, Ben, to let yourself get upset.'

'I'll live. Believe me. I keep seeing Baylor's face.'

The next afternoon, when Jessie came in, *she* was the one who mentioned Mitchell first. And everything about her when she came through the door – the set mouth, the stiff shoulders, the way she perched on the edge of his bed – told Ben Reese that Jessie Gerrard had something pithy to say.

She kissed him a long time, the way she always did, as though she still couldn't believe how good it was to have him there to hold, and touch, and taste again.

And then she pulled a bed screen over and stood it at the end of his bed. She sat down on the visitor's chair and looked straight at him, her blue eyes taking on his, her long thin hands fiddling with the belt of her dark green dress, her wide soft mouth looking closed in and still. 'You know I always tell you what I think, Ben.'

'Yeah.'

'And I'll keep it up till you tell me not to.'

'Good. I want you to, you know that.'

'Then I'll start by asking a question. Is there anything you know to do that could prove that Mitchell killed those two men?'

'Not that I know of now, no.'

'Would your telling this Major Flynn what you think might've happened to Baylor and the other guy, without you having any proof, lead him to go to Mitchell's bosses at OSS and get them to pull him from the tech group?'

'Probably not. For Flynn to persuade OSS, I'd expect him to have to have some kind of proof, something more than hearsay. But I did write him a letter today, so he can decide for himself whether to pursue it or not. A nurse brought me a typewriter that—'

'Can you think of anything else useful you could do about Mitchell yourself?'

'No. That's what's driving me nuts.'

'Is there anything you could do here, once you get this next bone graft behind you, that would help the men in the ward?'

'I think so. I've been talking with the two guys I told you about before the pneumonia. The guys from the same town in Kentucky who've both lost a leg? They're thinking about trying to start a business when they get out, and we've been talking about photography, and what I did with it to make money in high school, for the real estate companies, and the paper. We've been playing chess too, and planning what we'll do for fun when I can drive the hospital handicap car. And I thought I'd try to get Barnum & Bailey, when they come here in June, to do one circus performance for just the men in here.'

'But while you've been sick, you haven't been able to do much for anybody?'

'Right.'

'So what makes the most sense? Letting Ted Mitchell eat away at you? Or putting all your energy into building yourself up so you can be useful now?'

'I can see what you want me to say, Jess.'

'Is it logical?'

'Yeah, but—'

'Even though it's not all altruism on my part.' Jessie reached over and took Ben's hand and kissed the ends of his fingers.

'No?'

'I want you well, and out of here, and us an old married couple living a life together.'

'Then I guess you better talk to him.' Ben smiled at Jessie and pointed beyond her with his good hand.

Dr Jones stepped out from behind the screen with his hands in the pockets of his long white coat. 'OK, I was eavesdropping. And Jessie's right, Sergeant. *You* need to concentrate on getting yourself well. I told you last week when you and I talked about Mitchell, you can't do anything about him now, and it's going to take a lot of hard work for you to get fit and healed enough to get yourself down that aisle.'

'When's the earliest I could do it, do you think?'

'Depends on both of you. You're likely to be here for a year or more. And you'll only get out on occasional week-ends for a long time to come. There're more surgeries, and months of rehab, and nerve work to be done.'

Ben looked at Jessie before he said, 'We've talked about it already. Being together some of the time's better than both of us being alone.'

'You mind wearing braces on your legs when you're walking down the aisle? Maybe using crutches too?'

Ben and Jessie were watching each other when they both shook their heads.

'What about having a cast on your arm? That's new news, by the way. That's me telling you that it looks like we can save it. If you don't mind a few more months of pain and hard work.'

Ben didn't say anything for a minute. He gazed at the cast

lying on his chest – the dead weight he couldn't have moved if a gun had been put to his head – before he looked at Willard Jones. 'Thank you, Doc. If you hadn't worked at it as hard as you have, there wouldn't have been a chance of saving it. Being as smart as you are helped too. Coming up with all the new techniques.'

'Plenty of physicians would've done what I've done. That's one good thing coming out of this war, new medical procedures that had to be developed overnight.' Jones was reading Ben's chart, looking faintly embarrassed.

'You mind me wearing a cast at the wedding, Jess? Casts don't always smell great.'

Jessie laughed and said, 'I'll take you whatever way I can get you. I told you that a long time ago.'

Dr Jones cleared his throat, and hung the chart on the end of the bed. 'Then *I'd* say you could set the date for middle-to-late August. *If* you'll forget about Mitchell, and get to work on yourself.'

Ben said, 'I'll see what I can do, Doc.'

And then he actually did.

He pushed Mitchell into the past, into the cubbyhole where he kept unfinished business. Filed under 'Futile Pursuits' till new information came in. He made himself eat more. And did four times the recommended rehab. And also began to teach himself to write with his right hand.

Ben read a lot too, in the next weeks – the Koran, the *Upanishads*, the *Bhagavad Gita*, the *Tao te Ching*, the teachings of Confucius, two books on Buddhism. And then he started on the Bible, the Old and New Testaments both.

Someone with a mind had sent him back. And he wanted to know who that was.

He wouldn't set a date for the wedding, though. Not till the end of April, when he'd worked himself hard enough in rehabilitation that he really began to think he could be the kind of husband he wanted to be for them both.

They settled on Saturday, July 28th. And Jessie started making her wedding dress the very same day Drs Wilson and Jones cut into both Ben's arm and leg again, and screwed another piece of bone on to the rod in his forearm.

He came up out of the anesthetic gagging over a metal pan – sweating, sick and shivering.

But what bothered Ben was having seen Mitchell in a strange confused dream back Jessie up against a dark paneled corner in a loud crowded cocktail party, then lean down and whisper in her ear and take her face in his hands – all the time smirking at Ben across the top of her head.

Fifteen

They took the train to Siena late that afternoon, drove to Giovanni's home, deposited Ben's luggage, spoke to Giovanni's wife and daughter (who were spending the evening at a school program), then went out to walk the town.

Giovanni's house was inside the walled medieval city on the Viale Curtatone, and they walked past the church of Santa Domenico down a hill on the Via della Sapienza, a narrow, steep, curving cobbled street past medieval brick buildings turned into town houses and apartments, into greengrocers and jewelry stores and bookstores selling maps to tourists.

They walked for more than an hour, down one of the three hills and up the next, around and then toward the Piazza del Campo – the shell-shaped, brick-paved, amphitheater-like 'square' – surrounded by terracotta brick buildings roofed with rounded pantiles, like most of old Siena.

The Torre del Mangia stretched above the square too, the tallest bell tower in Siena, the tone of it shaking your bones and your blood whenever it struck the hour. It rang as they stepped down on to the top of the long curving stairs, and Ben stood still, looking down into the Campo, feeling the sounds reverberate in his chest, trying to imagine what it must have been like to have seen that shell-shaped piazza six hundred years before.

The Campo is where the Palio is run each summer – the bareback horse races with riders in medieval costumes. And Ben asked Giovanni to explain the history, once they'd started down the steps.

People were roaming everywhere across the Campo – taking exercise before supper, drinking coffee and wine in cafés or on the steps, promenading slowly with their families, chatting with friends and acquaintances, buying bread or prosciuto or fruit on their way home.

Ben and Giovanni talked about Italy while they watched – its history, its future, the work they both did (Giovanni at the University of Siena, where he was a professor of Medieval Art). Though most of the time Ben asked questions about what he was seeing in stone and brick, as well as the habits and the customs of the people. Giovanni gave him the context, and the history, and the perspective Ben didn't have.

They climbed a steep cobbled street out of the Campo, and walked around the thirteenth-century Gothic Duomo, the black-and-white horizontal-striped marble cathedral on the top of one of the Sienese hills, while Giovanni told Ben about the history of the Duomo – till they drifted down a side street Ben couldn't find on his map.

They considered the cheese in more than one shop. They eyed the antiques in others. They looked in the windows of the leather and paper shops. Then started back toward Santa Domenico through spider-web streets and back passages.

They climbed past St Catherine of Siena's family home, under narrow brick arches attached to buildings on both sides. And there Giovanni turned left suddenly, up three-foot-wide stone stairs hedged closely by old brick walls.

The wall on the left fell away abruptly, where the stairs ended in a steep narrow street, opening out into a view of hills bristling with pantiled houses. Yet, before they'd walked ten feet farther, Giovanni stopped and stared down through a wide arched window on his right.

He said, '*Bene, bene*, it-tis not in the least crowded yet. Please, if you will descend here,' and held the heavy wooden door for Ben, who stepped down into a wren-sized restaurant, turning his feet sideways on the narrow stairs.

They were seated in a tiny irregular-shaped niche with the street window high above it, plants trailing from the ceiling, four empty tables pressed close around them.

Ben asked Giovanni to order for both of them. And as they talked about work and family and mutual friends, they ate fried eggplant, and marinated shrimp, and peasant bread dipped in herbed oil. They ate veal shanks with roasted garlic, with mushroom risotto and *insalata*, then finished with pears and pecorino. They drank good red wine and strong black coffee and talked about Italy since the war.

Ben told Giovanni again in considerably more detail about the jewelry he was trying to identify for Everett and Mark Adams. And Giovanni lit his second cigarette, watching the smoke curl, his dark eyes under black brows interested and intelligent, his lips parted in his well-cut face, shadowed now with stubble. 'You have photographs, do you?'

'Yes.' Ben laid the photographs in front of Giovanni, then watched a couple on the other side of the room. He turned to Giovanni when he heard him laugh.

Giovanni swept both hands through his thick black hair, then picked up the pictures and pushed them toward Ben. 'I think we may make some progress, you and I. I have gone through files at the university – ones passed on to my predecessor from a former curator in the museum here in Siena. There was a letter describing jewels stolen during the war by a Nazi soldier. The description of the jewels fits quite closely these photographs of yours.'

'Really?' Ben's elbows were on the table and his chin was resting in the palms of his hand when he looked at Giovanni with an expression of real surprise.

'Si.' Giovanni laughed and blew out a match.

'It sounds too good to be true.'

'No, no. No, such letters were sent by this family, and many other families as well, to universities and museums all over Italy in an attempt to regain whatever had been stolen. My predecessors filed these letters and kept them for future reference. You would do the same, as would I.'

'Yes, but—'

'But!' Giovanni raised a forefinger and smiled a secretive and significant smile. 'I have also learned that the owners were a family not unknown to my mother's relations.'

'How could—?'

'My mother's family is from the countryside in Chianti, not too many kilometers from here, where there are many fine-wine growing estates. One of them, a small remnant of what was once a large holding, belongs to a distant friend of my mother's family, a Signora Varini, a woman now in her seventies who lives in quiet repose.

'It was this woman's *madre* who sent the letter to the

museums. She and her daughter, they are Riscasoli by descent. Not directly descended from the Iron Baron, who owned Castello di Brolio many, many years ago, he who gave the world the formula for Chianti Classico. No, but Riscasoli nevertheless.'

'It sounds like too much of a coincidence.'

'Perhaps. Though you must try to remember that Tuscany is a small place, my friend. With many ancient family ties. It is not like your United States. Where Boston is closer to England than it-tis to San Francisco. Where families move from one year to the next, from one state to another. Whether this letter describes the same jewels I do not know. Certainly they are jewels very much like these. Strikingly so, from the description. And I shall arrange it tomorrow for you, shall I? A trip to Linari to see the signora, and show her the photographs you bring?'

'You're sure you have the time, Giovanni?'

'I should like a day away. *A piccolo vacanza*. We shall buy provisions for a . . . how do you call it? A picanic? As we walk home this evening.'

'Let's try to get her to describe the jewels herself, or show us a photograph, before I show her the pictures I've brought.'

'We will plan what to do before we arrive.'

When they got back to Giovanni's home, there were several letters for Ben, among them a manila envelope from the Interpol address in Switzerland. It was after ten, and jet lag was coming down on him, so he left the Interpol mail till later, and took the rest into the sitting room where Giovanni had said it would be 'agreeable' for them to sit, while he translated Ben's letters.

'I know you can read Italian well enough to manage, but you have had a long day, my friend, and I shall make quick work of these.'

They were letters from rare book dealers Ben had written to in Florence, Venice, Siena and Rome. The Seneca edition he was looking for was not to be found in Siena or Venice. Though there was a vaguely worded letter from one of the two Roman dealers Ben had written to implying that he *might* have a first edition Aldine Seneca of the sort being sought, but the wording didn't inspire confidence in Ben *or* Giovanni.

The dealer who wrote from Florence (who hadn't answered that morning when Ben had phoned) had no such work to offer. However, the Florentine gentleman had consulted a colleague in Cortona. This highly esteemed dealer *did* possess such a volume, and would hold it for Ben's perusal. The name and address were duly provided. And Ben smiled as he folded the letter and put it away in his briefcase.

Ben said goodnight to Giovanni, then climbed the marble steps to the guest room that faced the back garden. He opened the wide windows and looked out at the cedars growing close against the house, listening to the birds scrabbling in the branches, who'd stirred as soon as he'd touched the casements.

He sat at the desk, and opened the envelope from Interpol, and looked through the lists of stolen jewelry. There were two descriptions from owners who'd lost both a brooch and ring that sounded like possibilities. One in particular might be worth contacting. A gentleman who lived in Tuscany not too far, apparently, from Florence.

Friday, March 9th, 1962

Giovanni read the signore's name and address at breakfast, while he drank a cup of espresso and ate an apricot-filled sweet roll, saying he'd be more than willing to find the address, if a visit were required.

Then he called Signora Varini, and made arrangements to meet her at her home at eleven o'clock that morning.

Giovanni drove Ben north-east of Siena into the Chianti hills under white-gold sun and high blue sky – threading up and down and around the bare brown vine-covered hills edged with silvery new-leafed olive trees and tall dark spikes of cypress.

He took a tiny precipitous road along the side of Castello di Brolio that led toward the hamlet of Linari, then turned into a cypress-lined drive that curved sharply before it ended in a thick planting of cypress and cedar on a high narrow hill.

A hundred foot wide Cedar of Lebanon grew across the end of the drive, and Ben stared at it for a minute, before he turned to his right and caught a glimpse of a honey-colored house in between spear-shaped cypress.

Large square stone planters of shrub-sized rosemary flanked the front walk, and Ben leaned down and touched a stem of needles, releasing the fragrance as he passed. It was a simple stone house – wide, high, roofed with terracotta pantiles, the windows shuttered in pale grey-green, a heavy arched door painted the same green standing slightly off center.

Giovanni pulled the chain attached to a brass bell. Then pulled it again and waited longer. Before he started down the narrow gravel path past the right side of the house.

They walked in the coolness and the dappled shade made by an allée of young cypress, till Giovanni turned left suddenly in an opening in the trees and trotted down a curved stone stairway that fanned out at the bottom on to a wide stone terrace. There was a wisteria-covered pergola on their left, attached to the end of the house, but beyond that the verandah swept on, running the length of the villa.

It was the view that stopped Ben – down over a deep wide sweep of hill that fell away from the back of the house, past fruit trees and flowers and vegetables planted in terraces cut into the slope, stepping down to meet the vineyard that covered the bottom half, ending in a marshy valley between the folds of several hills.

All the hills, across the valley and on either side, were covered with well-tended grape vines, edged in places by pale silver olives, the fields separated in random-looking places by strips of evergreen woods.

Ben stood and stared for a second, then put on his sunglasses at the bottom of the steps and followed Giovanni across the verandah behind the long stone house.

In the middle of that terrace, by the center set of French doors, an elderly woman stood tall and straight with her hands on her hips looking at a boxwood shrub in a three-foot-high stone pot she'd just finished weeding. There were three other potted boxwoods spaced along the house between the French doors, and she was turning toward the one at the far end when Giovanni called her name.

She didn't hear, and he walked closer, waving tentatively as though afraid of startling her.

She turned and saw Giovanni, then pulled off her gardening

gloves. She straightened her taupe wool sweater set, and walked toward him nodding and smiling and holding out her hand.

Giovanni introduced Ben to Carlotta Maria Varini who smiled softly and waved them to the wicker chairs grouped around a low wooden table facing the gardens.

She and Giovanni talked for several moments, while she smoothed her brown tweed skirt and ran a hand through thick white hair carefully cut in deep waves around her elegant bones. She looked at Ben almost shyly and said, '*Scusa. Una momento*,' quietly, softly, nodding to Ben more directly than Giovanni. She smiled and picked up her gloves, then stepped into the house.

Ben slid down, leaning back against the chair, and stared at the hills and the wet land in the valley, at the tops of olive trees and budding wisteria, at the ant-like men moving along the rows of vines, pruning and tying branches to the wires that ran the length of the rows.

Ben sighed quietly. And shook his head.

And Giovanni laughed and said, 'Ah, to be the country gentleman tending one's own garden. Tying one's vines. Pressing one's olives. Drinking one's own wine.'

'It would *not* be a bad life.'

'No, indeed, it certainly would not.'

Neither of them said another word for at least five minutes. They sat in the sun and felt it soak into their bones, inhaling the fragrance of rosemary and lavender, newly pruned and warmed in the sun, carried on a hint of a breeze.

'I should tell you, my friend, one small thing before the signora returns. She told me she had intended to serve us hot *caffè* and a glass of water, which would be the usual repast at this time of day. But she says she has decided that our visit is an occasion. You are a guest in our country, and it is in your honor that she is bringing us a special . . . how do you say it? Treat. *Vin santo*. A sweet wine. Much like communion wine, and largely made of raisins. This she will serve with *biscotti de Prato*. A small hard biscuit full of chopped almonds. They will be tiny glasses. Thimblefuls, at this time of the day.'

'That's really kind of her, but I—'

'Also, as you and I discussed, I have told her you are an

archivist studying Renaissance jewelry, and when you learned of her letter in my files you were interested to meet with her and ask her about the family jewels.'

'Good, that's true, and it gets the job done.'

'The job done? I do not know what—'

Signora Varini walked through the French doors carrying a lacquer tray with a plate of biscotti and tiny glasses filled with ruby-colored wine.

Ben said, '*Grazi. Grazi, signora*, but we didn't wish to put you to any bother. *Noi non volevamo disturbare.*'

'*Prego, prego.*' Signora Varini said something complicated Ben didn't understand, then shook her head and smiled a sweet otherworldly sort of smile as she sat and handed him a glass.

Giovanni and the signora talked about their families for a few minutes, the friendships with hers on his mother's side, the births and deaths in recent years, as they sipped their wine and ate biscotti.

Then Giovanni explained in his deep musical Italian that Ben had a friend in America, who had found certain artifacts, certain pieces of jewelry, in Italy during the war, and that he wished to return them to the rightful owner. Little was known of the artist who had created these artworks. Nothing was known of the owners. And anything Ben could learn about Italian Renaissance jewelry might prove to be of use.

Did she have, Giovanni asked the signora, any photographs in her possession of her own lost jewels which Ben could study and perhaps compare to what had been found, so that his understanding was broadened? So that he would develop a greater sense of the styles of Renaissance jewelry?

The signora said there were no photographs, but there was a family portrait of an ancestor wearing the jewels long ago. Giovanni asked if it would be permissible to see the portrait before they left.

She said, '*Certo. Certo.*' She rose and smiled, and ushered them through the center set of French doors, leading them to a wide stone staircase and up to the first floor, past the front door and the dining room, into a drawing room filled with family portraits.

Giovanni walked to a painting of a plain plumpish woman with heavy-lidded dark eyes wearing a dress of beautifully painted teal brocade. A jeweled brooch lay suspended on a

gold chain on the rising flesh above her bodice, and a simi-
larly fashioned ring glowed on a plump white hand.

Giovanni said, 'Ah, signora, it-tis a fine painting. Beautifully
executed.'

Ben examined the jewelry in the portrait with the magnifying glass on his key ring, then looked at Giovanni and nodded
almost imperceptibly, while Signora Carlotta Varini spoke to
Giovanni in rapid Italian.

'Signora Varini says the painter is unknown, though it was
painted in the middle of the sixteenth century. This is not the
woman for whom the jewelry was made. The jewels have
been in the family since the late fourteenth-, or very early
fifteenth-, century, and had great emotional and sentimental
value for everyone in her family. They are said to have been
created by the great Ghiberti, commissioned for the much
beloved dying wife of an early Riscasoli. They have passed
down in the family from one generation to the next, along
with certain of the letters that had been written by her loving
husband.

'Alas, she says, the jewels were stolen by a German soldier
during the Second World War, stolen here in the vestibule of
the house, lost now for ever with no hope of recovery.'

Giovanni looked at Ben with a very straight face and shook
his head sadly.

Ben turned to Carlotta Varini and said, '*Grazi, signora,
grazi*, for showing us the portrait and telling us of the history
of the jewelry as well.'

Giovanni translated it into Italian, and then gestured toward
the stairs as if to say, 'Shall we finish our aperitifs?'

Ben had sipped his wine and finished a first biscotti before
he said, 'I wonder, signora, if you would be willing to look
at some photographs I've brought with me?'

Giovanni translated, while Ben reached into the breast
pocket of his corduroy sport coat, and took out a series of
color close-ups and handed them to Signora Varini.

Her face flushed, her hand flew to her throat, clutching the
double strand of heavy pearls, her mouth strained shut, and
tears gathered in her eyes. She pulled a handkerchief from
the sleeve of her sweater, and blotted her eyes, before she
handed the photographs to Ben, and began asking questions.

Giovanni translated, 'How can this be, sir? How can you have photographs of my mother's jewels?'

Ben reached inside the waistband of his khaki slacks and unzipped a small traveling pouch hooked on to a belt loop. 'I believe these are yours, signora.' He handed her the brooch and ring and asked Giovanni to translate his explanation of who had found the jewels, and why he was returning them.

The signora asked questions occasionally, and continued to wipe her eyes. Then she spoke rapidly with rising color and waited for Giovanni to translate.

'She says her mother was wearing those pieces of jewelry fastened to the strap of her slip, because of what they had heard of the Germans ransacking houses nearby. It was when they saw a group of soldiers coming toward the house, that her mother had fastened them to her underclothing.

'She was nearly eighty. Though she was still a formidable woman. She was wearing a wool sweater under a suit . . . how do you say? Jacket? And this German lout, he must have seen the outline of the brooch and ring, and he forced her to remove her sweater in front of all the men. It was a travesty, Signora Varini says. Her mother was a dignified and cultured woman. A private woman. A quiet woman. A woman of great kindness and gentility. And the thought of what was done to her has infuriated Signora Varini all these many years.

'She says she knows that other soldiers committed many worse acts of vileness, but seeing her mother so humiliated, seeing it happen with her very own eyes, made a terribly strong impression on the signora. And now, to know the German was killed, and that a good brave American has wanted to find her family and give the jewelry back, it is a gift of great honor and kindness she says she will never forget. Nor will her children, and her children's children.'

'*Grazi, signora. Grazi.*'

'She says, "May God bless you and your benefactors." And she would ask you to ask this father and this son to visit her home and allow her family to make them welcome.'

'I shall tell them when I return to America.'

Giovanni translated.

And she added, '*Grazi, professore.*' Then said more to Giovanni, and nodded her head at Ben, before folding her hands demurely in her lap.

'She says she is very much grateful that the pig is dead. She will pray to God to thank Him for this death. She will pray continually that this evil German may be tormented for eternity.'

Ben couldn't think of anything to say to that.

It stung like the lash of a whip. This gentle, shy, kind-looking woman praying for the torture of a human soul.

Sixteen

Monday, March 12th, 1962

It was boredom and impatience as much as anything else, and a need to get away from the cold, grey, biting blowing rain that had been lashing Loch Rannoch for two and a half weeks. It was the frost-burned bracken and barren branches, and the snow on the high hills, and the blackness of the Wood of Rannoch staring at her from across the loch whenever she drove east toward the only road that led toward civilization.

It was her own brand of claustrophobia too, in a small house on the edge of her own dark wood where her dead husband's father was becoming less a professor and a poet, and more a man growing old – repeating himself, thinking about his health, not quite catching the drift – and she needed to get away.

She'd felt freer driving south. Seeing signs of life. The sun burning through the greyness. Crocuses splashing color across farmyards. Primroses flowering in villages, and woodlands, and warm spots alongside the road.

There were small lacy leaves on a few shrubs and trees, once she'd gotten as far south as the Borders. And Patricia Welsh's yard, on the edge of Traquair's forest, was sprinkled with small white flowers that Kate stood and stared at, as soon as she'd knocked on the door.

It opened slowly a half minute later, and a thin, haggard face peered tentatively around the edge.

'Mrs Welsh? I don't know if you remember me. I came to see your husband in January to ask about Ross—'

'I do, yes. Come away in.'

Condolences are hard on both sides. Kate felt awkward. Patricia Welsh looked stunned and disconnected. And they sat for a minute and stared past each other afterwards, after Kate had said the things that get said in the aftermath of death.

She added, 'The unexpectedness must've been awful.' And watched Patricia twist her hands in her lap.

'It was horrible, Phillip falling. The rocks and the cliff the way they were. He was such an experienced trekker too. I can't begin to take it in. He walked very difficult footpaths all over Scotland and England, and he kept himself very fit.'

'So you're saying it seems strange that he would've fallen with all the experience he had?'

'Aye. And the bit that makes it terribly sad is that Phillip was so looking forward to being well and truly retired. To the two of us, you see, being together.' Patricia Welsh pulled a crumpled handkerchief out of the pocket of her rust colored sweater and blew her nose twice. 'He'd worked very long hours at Leith House. He'd wanted to make his mark, and give us a better life, but . . .' Patricia Welsh's face flushed, as she bit her bottom lip and stared at the cold hearth.

'My husband was killed in World War Two, and if it's any consolation at all, it did get easier over time.'

'My first husband died in the war as well.'

'Oh. Then you know twice as much about it as I do.'

'I wouldn't wish to say that, no, I—'

'How long were you and Phillip married? I'm sorry, that's none of my business.'

'We met, and married, in 1951.'

There was silence after that. Till a clock struck the half-hour. And birds fluttered at a feeder in the yard. And a cat walked through from another room to jump on the back of the sofa and watch the feeder from a warm strip of sun.

'Would you care to come through to the kitchen? I was making a pot of tea.'

The kitchen table was covered with papers and manila files, and Patricia Welsh moved everything but a chequebook and an unopened envelope on to an old pine hutch.

She set a teapot and oatcakes on the table, then sat and poured out the tea. 'You'll have to forgive me being so wrought up, but I've had a bit of a shock. I've discovered things I . . . I've discovered I didn't know Phillip nearly as well as I thought. Not truly. Not the way I would've wished. I haven't mentioned it to anyone. My mother's illness has the family in a bit of an uproar, and I didn't like to add my troubles to the—'

'*You're* the one who's lost your husband. You ought to be expected to need someone to talk to.'

'Perhaps, and yet . . .' Patricia Welsh shook her greying head and took a sip of tea. 'My family is the sort that . . . well . . .' She turned her palms up in midair as though she knew she'd never find the words that fit. 'My brother is a bit overbearing, and *I'm* not a-tall, and I didn't want to be propelled into a decision I might live to regret.'

'No, I wouldn't either.'

'Moving here as well, you see, without any close neighbors . . .' Patricia Welsh shrugged and pulled her cup and saucer toward her, then stared intently at her tea.

'If you'd like to talk to me, if it's easier because you don't know me very well, I'd be more than happy to listen. Whether I can help, I don't know, but I certainly will if I can.'

'Thank you.' Patricia picked up an oatcake and smiled shyly. 'I haven't felt like eating very much since Phillip . . . had his accident, but I can manage the oatcakes. And I find them a wee bit comforting. It's silly of me I know, but they remind me of nursery tea.'

Kate bit into an oatcake and nodded as though she understood.

'Once Phillip died, you see, I had to learn about paying the accounts, and managing the banking, and it's been a bit overwhelming, with the death duties and the will and all.'

'Yes, I'm sure it would be.'

'So . . . I rather think I should plunge straight in and explain without further ado.' Patricia finished the last of her Earl Grey tea, then folded the napkin by her plate. 'I discovered last week that Phillip had a safety-deposit box in the bank in Peebles, and when I examined the contents on Thursday, it came as a very great shock. That would be to put it very mildly indeed.' Patricia stopped and stirred her tea.

And Kate told herself to wait. To fold her arms across her middle, and not fidget. Or push. Or pry.

'Phillip's indemnity papers were in the deposit drawer, with something more besides. A bankbook and bank statements I hadn't looked for a-tall. Phillip had had a bank account in Dunkeld since 1953. Not Dunblane, where we lived, you see. No, in a bank in Dunkeld, forty or more miles away. The statements had been sent to him at a post-office box I hadn't known existed. So you can see how very deliberate it was, his keeping it from me all those years.'

'Yes, that would be a shock for anybody.'

'I also discovered that there had been regular deposits every six months, which can't be accounted for in any normal way that I'm aware of. He withdrew very little. Funds for a holiday we took to France in 1959. One other withdrawal to pay for our holiday on the Isle of Mann.'

Patricia pushed herself out of her chair, added fresh tea leaves and water to the pot, then sat down opposite Kate again. 'I find it quite distressing, to say the very least.'

'Anyone would.' Kate had been watching Patricia Welsh over the rim of her cup – the sad, worried, jumpy look of a small defenseless animal waiting for another blow. 'It would make me wonder if he was hiding something . . . I don't know quite how to say it. Something underhanded, I guess, might be the best way to put it.'

'You've hit it in one, haven't you?' Mrs Welsh picked up a crumb of oatcake and dropped it on to her plate. 'Phillip wasn't what you'd call a talkative person, and he was terribly unwilling to speak about his past. I knew he was in the Ministry of Ag during the war, and that he worked as an administrator of a military hospital once the war ended. I knew he'd been unhappily married and divorced some-time in the thirties, but any more than that . . .' She gazed at her pink flowered teacup and turned it slowly in its saucer.

Kate waited for her to say something more.

But she didn't.

And after a minute or two, Kate asked why she thought Phillip wouldn't talk about his past.

'I never understood it. Though I have believed for many years that there had been something significant early on, something painful that ate away at him, which he couldn't bear to reveal. You could see it when other people spoke of their lives. A sadness would steal over him. A regret of some kind, I always thought. A defensiveness as well. A very defin-ite antipathy to questioning of any sort. He simply wouldn't answer when I asked about his schooling, or what he'd done before the war. He was terribly good at being evasive, and I'm not the sort of person who finds it easy to pry.'

'No. I can see that.' Kate took a bite from a second oatcake.

Patricia Welsh stared at Kate's cup. 'His parents were both gone by the time we married, and there was no one else I knew to ask.'

'I know people like that. You can be carrying on a perfectly pleasant conversation, and then *wham*, it's like an invisible sheet of question-proof glass comes down as soon as a personal question gets asked.'

'That's very much the way it was.' Patricia reached across the table and picked up the cream-colored envelope she'd left in the center with the checkbook. 'I retrieved this from the safety-deposit box in Dunkeld on Friday, but I haven't yet had the heart to open it. It's addressed to me in Phillip's hand.' She was staring at the strong slant, at the large letters, at the straight line under her name with flourishes at either end.

'Would it be easier for you if I'm here?' Kate made herself stare at her hands, telling herself not to rush her, and not to seem overly interested.

'It-tis unnerving.' Patricia Welsh turned it over and stared at the back before sliding a knife blade underneath the flap. 'It feels a bit like hearing a voice speaking from beyond the grave.' She sighed slowly and pulled out a letter, laying the envelope on the table. 'It's dated the tenth of January. Three days before Phillip had his accident.'

Two tears slid toward Patricia Welsh's mouth as she looked over at Kate. 'I've been so afraid since I found the letter that he may have taken his own life. I don't believe I could bear that, the thought that his life had become such a trial he simply couldn't go on.'

'It may not be that at all. It may be something completely unrelated.'

'Aye.' Patricia Welsh nodded slowly, then reached for the letter written in black ink with a wide-nibbed fountain pen.

It was several pages long, and it seemed to Kate to take her for ever to finish it.

But finally she'd laid it on the table and was sliding it over to Kate. 'Please. You read it. I hardly know what to make of it.'

10 January 1962

My dearest Patricia,

You will have learned by now of the safety-deposit drawer in Peebles, and as a result of its contents of the account and bank drawer in Dunkeld. You will also have become a widow, my dear. An uncongenial thought, I assure you. Though how I will have died, I, for one, cannot imagine.

First of all, I want you to know without any doubt whatsoever that my actions at Leith House were in no way illegal or dishonorable. I shall try to be succinct, but there is much that needs to be told you, and I have little time to review the letter and rewrite it at length.

Before Ross MacNab was brought to Leith House, I was approached by the anonymous American donor who has paid his fees all these years. The donor said he wished to find a suitable home for a patient whose care he wished to fund where he, the donor, would be kept informed of every particular of the patient's progress. He would also insist that his anonymity be preserved absolutely, and arrangements to ensure that eventuality had been established through a London bank.

He wished to be informed of Ross' physical and emotional progress. He wished to be told if Ross had visitors, as well as who they were, and when they would arrive, if advance notice were given. He wished to be alerted if, and when, Ross began to speak about the war.

The donor said MacNab had saved his life during the war, and he wished to repay the debt without being seen to do so. He also told me he had investigated my background and had subsequently concluded that, as the administrative director of Leith House, I was a suitable choice with whom to reach an agreement.

It was a veiled threat, my dear, made in the most polite terms. He was referring to an incident in my past of which you know nothing; an incident I have kept from you to safeguard your feelings, as well as our marriage. I have no choice but to tell you now. For I fear there may be implications which may affect your welfare in the future.

I took a degree in history, and was employed as a

schoolmaster at a respectable preparatory school in England where I taught happily for several years. It was during that period that I married my first wife. Hers was a more affluent family. Her father was something rather grand in the City, and our social milieu, as well as my income, became matters of strain between us. I was abjectly besotted with her, and when I was promoted to deputy headmaster with an increase in salary, I hoped matters would improve. I was given responsibility for overseeing the school's accounts, for purchasing supplies, for superintending repairs and expansions, in addition to duties of an academic nature.

Sylvia, however, over time, became increasingly dissatisfied with our circumstances, and I began to spend money I never hoped to have in an attempt to regain her affection. I arranged for us to take weekends away. I allowed her to purchase furniture. I bought her a necklace I could in no way afford. And, then, when my creditors began to insist upon payment, I borrowed funds from the school.

I never intended to steal such funds, though that is, in fact, what I had done. I promised myself I would gradually reimburse the school, and meant to, I assure you, even though I very well knew I had no prospects for raising the needed sums.

Sylvia left me despite my attempts to placate her, and I was sacked summarily from the school. They chose not to prosecute, thank God. For I managed to convince them I would pay them back, which I did, my dear, even though it took me more than ten years. Still, my career as a teacher was at an end. And it was only through the good offices of a friend of my youth that I found a place in the Min of Ag in 1939 after I was shown to be unfit for service.

A friend there spoke for me after the war and helped me secure the job in a military hospital in Yorkshire, where I worked very hard and very faithfully, as I had earlier at the Ministry, and did later at Leith House. I knew only too well how fortunate I was to be employed in *any* capacity, particularly one with administrative authority. A word about my past in the wrong ear, and I would not have been kept on.

That was precisely what the American was telling me when he alluded to my past. It was a case of the oft quoted 'carrot and stick'. I would be paid handsomely for my diligence on his behalf; I would be penalized soundly if I failed to fulfill my obligations.

Although I questioned his purposes in my own mind from time to time, I generally chose to see them as entirely benign. I believed him to be a demanding American millionaire who was accustomed to seizing control of whatever he undertook, but who had no malign intent. Perhaps I saw what I wished to see in order to excuse my own part in his schemes.

In any event, I believed him to be genuinely interested in Ross MacNab's welfare. He wished to know of any change in Ross' emotional state; the medications he was given; the routines he set for himself. He seemed very pleased when Ross began to paint, and take an interest in new pursuits.

Then, as you know, Ross MacNab died within two and a half weeks of my having informed the donor that MacNab was about to receive his first visitor; a woman who had told my secretary that she had met MacNab in the war. A fact I communicated to Ross' benefactor the day the woman first phoned. The donor rang back the next day and asked me in considerable detail about MacNab's eating habits, specifically asking what Ross took with him to the blind when spending the day outside.

In that same conversation, the donor asked me to retire six months earlier than you and I had intended, on a specifically designated date (which entailed me handing in my resignation that very day). He offered to reward us with a retirement bonus for our slight inconvenience. (Yes, and why did he wish me to leave with such speed? I asked myself then, as well as later. I would be gone, you see, when the woman arrived. I would not be there to be questioned.) It was several days after I resigned, but before Ross MacNab died, that he first told me he wished to give us a holiday trip to the Cornwall coast. I chose to see the offer as another kindness; a reward for doing his bidding.

Then, as you know, Ross MacNab died. And his woman visitor came to find me, questioning me about the donor.

The American benefactor could have caused his death. He knew Ross's habits, his medications, his thermos of coffee, his taste in pastries, and all the rest. The death would certainly be investigated. Perhaps he wanted no one at Leith House when the death occurred who had any knowledge whatever of the donor himself.

If you, my dear, are reading this letter, then I too have passed away, and it may be that the donor has helped me on my way. I am certainly the only direct link as far as I know between him and Ross MacNab.

I have purposefully kept you ignorant of this situation. My primary wish was to provide for you after my passing by leaving the funds essentially untouched. Yet, there *was* a conscious intention as well to insulate you from the donor by assuring him, at every possible opportunity, that you knew nothing of our arrangement; that the account was a hidden one, which would be found by you only at my death. I told him it would be explained to you in papers after my death as a family inheritance doled out by bankers twice a year, which I was saving for your benefit.

What, I ask myself now, does that imply about my perceptions of the donor? Did I simply lie to myself, justifying my own behavior, in believing him to be concerned about Ross? Have I suspected from the beginning that the American's intentions must have been, in part, dishonorable, or dangerous at the very worst? I don't know. I truly don't.

You must take care, my dear. You must take *very* good care indeed.

The name used by the donor is John Wagner. I am certain this is a fictitious name. I myself have tried to trace him. The telephone number he gave me to use in emergencies was an unregistered number in the area code assigned to that part of the United States known as Tennessee. The phone has been recently disconnected. It was answered by the donor, or a secretary (or such I assumed, for she only answered during business hours on the eastern coast of America). I have tried to trace Wagner through the bank, and the solicitors, and was unable to progress at all.

Use the money in the account to protect yourself. Travel for a time. Hire a private investigator to trace the donor. If the investigator uncovers useful information, take that to the police with this letter.

I cannot tell you how fervently I hope that my arrangement with the American has not placed you in jeopardy. I saw it as a means of harmlessly feathering our nest by way of a lawful accommodation. It has only been since Ross MacNab's death, which I assure you again was completely unexpected, that I saw any reason to fear for your safety or my own.

It is tomorrow we leave for Cornwall. He says he wishes to give us a special treat after all my years of service. He says he has stayed on the coast there near Port Isaac, and finds it beautiful and invigorating. He may wish us well, and be innocent of Ross' death. And, yet, on the other hand, he may not.

I have loved you always. You have given me more peace and contentment than I thought possible after my life with Sylvia. May you be safe from harm. May you still be able to love my memory after you have read of my past.

Shall we ever meet again? I hesitate even to ask, for fear that I know the answer.

Your loving Phillip, who never deserved your kindness and honest generosity.

Kate sat for several seconds with the letter in her lap, staring out the window that faced the feeder. Then she folded the letter, and put it in the envelope, before she looked at Patricia Welsh.

'I've been suspicious of Ross MacNab's death since the day he died. A friend of mine has been too. He was an American Army scout during the war, and he thinks he knew the donor then. My friend's been trying to trace this 'benefactor' for several months. It's a long story, and I can tell you only part of it, but would you let me take this letter? I'd like to send a copy of it to him, and phone him and give him the details. The man he thinks is this donor has a house in Tennessee, and other places as well.'

'You understand what Phillip means then?'

'Yes, I think I do.'

'Then you must take the letter certainly. Is that why you came today? Your concern over Phillip's death and the identity of MacNab's donor?'

'Yes. I'm sorry I couldn't be more honest before.'

'I understand. I knew nothing about it.'

'I'd like you to go away with me today. I think Phillip's right, that you need to leave your house for a while. Do you have a friend you could visit for a few weeks? Some place safe you could go?'

'I can't think where.' Patricia put the dishes in the sink, and turned off the flame under the kettle. 'Oh, there is a friend from my schooldays. A librarian living down in Sussex. I could ring her up. She's on her own. I shouldn't think it would be a terrible imposition. She *has* asked me to visit many times before this. I suppose I could phone my sister each day, to hear how Mother's getting on.'

'Could you call your friend now? And then I could drive you to the train.'

Ben took an early morning train to Chiusi, where his friend, Raimondo Ricciardi, a retired Vatican curator, picked him up and drove him north along the Val de Chiana to his family home on a softly rounded hill south-west of Sinalunga.

Raimondo turned off the narrow road into the middle of a farm field, and climbed the steep straight drive through an ancient allée of tall pointed cypress toward the entrance to La Fortezza.

The drive ran straight toward a wide stone arch, blocked to traffic by large stone urns of boxwood. And there Raimondo turned right, driving the length of an old brick wall to the parking area beyond.

They talked about the Vatican's tapestries, as they walked back toward the front entrance, Raphael's *Acts of the Apostles* in particular, commissioned for the Sistine Chapel.

Ben asked if they were ever displayed, and Raimondo said, 'Rarely. They are *extremely* delicate silk, spun with golden and silver thread. Humidity, light and temperature must be controlled, as you would expect.'

They'd crossed the right corner of the courtyard by then, heading toward the office of the inn. And while Raimondo went in to talk to the reception manager, Ben stood in the sun and stared at the ancient farming village built around a triangular square.

He gazed contentedly at the sienna-tiled roofs on two-storey brick and stone and stucco, at the arched galleries upstairs and down, at the carved stone well in the strip of grass growing in the center of the square.

Ben heard Raimondo say, 'I have arranged for your cases to be taken to your room,' and said, 'Thanks, I appreciate it,' as he turned to watch Raimondo cross the gravel toward him.

'I hope you will enjoy the accommodation. It was the original storage room of the very oldest pressing barn, and sits entirely secluded from the rest of La Fortezza. Olives were made into oil there from the thirteenth century until the fifties. The great wooden doors leading to your garden once admitted horse-drawn wagons full of ripe olives.'

'It sounds like a room I'd choose. But why did you stop making oil?'

'We continue, but much reduced, using a smaller press. The family could not maintain the farm at its grandest scale after the peasants began – how do you say . . .? – drifting to the cities, at the close of the Second World War.' Raimondo Ricciardi shielded his eyes and waved to a guest walking toward the breakfast room off to the left of the chapel. 'Would you care to stroll through the vineyards before you see your room?'

'I would, yes. It's staggering, Raimondo.' Ben had been staring at the chapel on his right across the gravel square, perfectly conceived and meticulously built, walls stuccoed, pillars and pediment carved in stone during the height of the Renaissance.

Now he turned and looked to his left, at the wide end of the triangular courtyard, and pointed to the fan-shaped stairs next to the front arch. 'What's that building over there? It's more refined than the rest, much more like the chapel.'

'The padrone's apartments. I think you would say "the home of the estate owner." We have not yet the funds to restore them, and use them only for storage.'

Raimondo turned his back to the front arch, and pointed at the long galleried brick building on his right, as he started toward the cobbled steps between it and the chapel. 'The peasants lived on the upper floor, and kept their animals below. Now we have guest rooms on both, and offices below.'

They climbed the rise at the end of the courtyard, then turned left at the back of the chapel, and walked between it and an ancient stone barn, as Raimondo told Ben that the building straight ahead was the apartment he'd made for his family.

When they approached the Ricciardis' front door and turned right around the end of the long barn, they saw the broad sweep of vineyard opening out below them, forty or fifty acres of vines – bare now and dead looking at a distance – stretching a quarter of a mile or more on either side of a white gravel track.

Ben stopped and shook his head and stood with his hands on his hips. 'It's so peaceful. So timeless. So inevitable looking. So much what it would've been a thousand years ago.'

They were walking down the dusty drive now, listening to the scrunch of their shoes on gravel, walking between the fields of vines, the rows running perpendicular to the track so they could look down their whole length.

'La Fortezza della Felicità appears much as it did. The landscape here is the same, *si*. The warmth of the sun, the sweetness of it on our faces, yes? The vines and olives growing on hills surrounding us. The old buildings being patched in the old ways, or crumbling on the ruins beneath them, as buildings have done here for centuries. The forest there ahead of us, is still in Ricciardi hands. The vineyard workers here, Carlo in the blue shirt, Paolo in the red, tying vines as their great-grand-fathers did. Pruning away more now, with the knowledge that comes.

'But the peace? Yes and no, my friend.' Raimondo shrugged in a way that told of Italy, that couldn't have been defined, the sleeves of his pale yellow sweater tied over his white-shirted shoulders, his salt and pepper hair brushed back from a well-shaped forehead, his dark eyes hidden as he squinted toward the sun, hands in the pockets of his pressed khaki pants. 'There are very disquieting developments.'

'Here? At La Fortezza?' Ben had been watching Carlo tie a length of pruned vine on a heavy horizontal wire, but then he turned and looked at Raimondo.

'There have been murders committed this year in Tuscany,

where one would never expect such things. Four women have been kidnapped and robbed. One elderly man. Tourists all of them, traveling in cars and on trains. All of them have been brutally killed. Three of them shot. One of them hung by the neck. And those who are guilty have gone undetected.'

'You wouldn't expect that here, would you?'

'No, you would not. They have been carried away from the cities. Florence. Arezzo. Siena. Which are no great distance from here.'

'No.'

'Yet, the murderers know the countryside well. They know of the abandoned buildings, the old peasant houses falling to pieces, and there they take their victims where they won't be easily found. Their bodies have lain many long days before they have been discovered. And there is an uneasiness in Tuscany now, in all the neighborhoods and the smallest village. Still – ' Raimondo Ricciardi shrugged again and smiled mildly, turning his palms toward the soft March sun – 'God is good. There is lunch waiting on the terrace of our apartment. The vines are growing well. The tourists are beginning to find us here at La Fortezza. And our daughter, Maria, is expecting a child in September.'

'Ah. Isabella must be happy about that.'

'*Si, si*, she is very pleased. The first grandchild is a gift she has long awaited. You said you need to drive to Cortona, my friend. This afternoon or tomorrow?'

'As soon as we eat lunch.'

'Yet you will return soon?'

'Tonight, or at least tomorrow.'

'Ah. It will be good to sit and talk. I want to hear about this paper process you have been working so diligently upon.'

Seventeen

It took Ben more than an hour, driving east across the Val de Chiana, to get to the bottom of the steep rock hill where Cortona clung to the top, a jagged brick and stone citadel bound by a high wall.

Ben turned left there instead of taking the Cortona road, heading toward Sodo, a cluster of houses on the fringe of the valley a mile or two north.

The one-lane roads he was on weren't on any of his maps, so he had to stop and ask directions, but he finally found the farm road that led east again between hedges and small holdings toward John Wharton's villa.

He passed olive trees, and tiny orchards just beginning to flower, as he drove slowly toward high green hills, the only car on the road, ignoring the open fields on his right below the hill that held Cortona. He was concentrating on the hedgerow on his left behind a dry stone wall, since it was the first place he'd come to on Wharton's road where there might be a house he couldn't see.

Everett's sister, Jo, had told Ben that Wharton's house was called 'The Falconer' in English, and when he drove past a pair of chained iron gates attached to tall stone pillars, he saw the words 'Il Falconiere' carved on both posts.

He drove on as though he hadn't been looking for anything in particular, then turned around a quarter of a mile further on.

He drove slowly by the gates to Il Falconiere, and stared down the curving cypress allée that kept him from seeing the house that belonged to Ted Mitchell, and John Wharton, and the man who'd called himself John Wagner when he'd blackmailed Phillip Welsh.

Ben took the first lane on his right, a quarter of a mile from the gates, trying to see the house from that side of the estate. It was an even narrower gravel farm road with two dilapidated farmhouses on his right close up to the road. But there was nothing that could've been Wharton's house between Ben and the woods in back.

He took the next tight right turn around a small simple stone church, and followed the narrow track down a short steep dappled-green incline under overhanging trees. At the bottom, the lane turned left, crossing a narrow stream, rising gently between a cemetery on the left just past a swath of woods, and a high stone retaining wall on the right, where a saint had been carved in a niche.

There were ramshackle brick cottages and small sheds just past the cemetery, with chickens and rabbits and a goat in a pen in between modest gardens.

But on the right, where the road had climbed to the top of the wall, behind olives and grape vines and berry bushes, Ben saw a large house at the back of a long field.

The gravel lane that led to it was on the left of the property, and it followed the curve of a high ridge of land that swept from left to right, from close to the road, half a mile back, to the left side of a cream-colored house half-hidden by clustered trees. Ben could see part of an old cypress allée that disappeared in a stand of woods on the right side of the house, which must have led to the locked gates he'd passed on the other road.

He pulled into the drive, then backed out and turned around, trying to see as much as he could without drawing too much attention to himself.

He drove back to the small church, pulled into the parking space across the lane, hung his camera and binoculars around his neck, put on a backpack he'd stuffed with clothes and maps, and walked back toward the working end of Il Falconiere.

He wanted to look like a typical tourist, and he took pictures as he walked, waving to a woman hanging washing on his left who chose not to wave back. He photographed the fields that belonged to Il Falconiere as he strolled past, being watched the whole time by a second testy-looking woman in a chicken yard across the street.

A quarter of a mile later, she was still watching, and there was nothing Ben could do but go on. Which he had an excuse for doing, since he'd come to a sign that pointed straight ahead to a country house hotel.

By the time he'd gotten to the black iron gate, where a brass plate on the left side said, '*Locanda al Mulino de Nibbio*' (which he took to mean Inn of the Mill), he'd decided to spend the night, and see if he could see Jenny Hunt arrive, and something of the household as well.

There were several old buildings inside the gates – an ancient villa, a brick mill, a small chapel – but Ben walked to *Recivemento* to ask for a room for the night.

It was Monday, and they were lightly booked, and the good-looking woman who was running the office took Ben up steep stone steps to a room to the left of the chapel.

He stepped through French doors on to stone floors, looked at the carved fireplace, the antique furniture, the finely arched windows – and told the woman in very slow Italian, that the room was beautiful, that he'd left his car by the church, that he'd hike for a couple of hours, then pick up his car and drive back in time to eat dinner at eight.

She smiled and left.

And Ben hung up his spare shirt, dropped his extra film in the pockets of his corduroy coat, and locked the door behind him.

He walked through the iron gate into the dusty road, then climbed up the hill on his left, following the small hand-lettered sign pointing to the hotel's vegetable garden.

He passed it shortly thereafter, and walked on along the path, hiking the ridge he wanted to be on that would wind back by Wharton's drive.

He photographed landscape in several directions the way any tourist might, concentrating on Il Falconiere once he got close enough to look down on the land.

There were three men pruning grape vines on his right, a quarter of a mile away. And when Ben climbed down through an ivy-covered thicket, and stepped out into the lane that went back to Il Falconiere, he watched them as carefully as he could to see if anyone had noticed.

He walked on toward the house, pointing his binoculars at trees and sky as though he were studying birds – scanning instead the high stuccoed walls below and in front of the villa.

There was a screening of trees around those walls, and on both sides of the house as well, so his view from up the lane was limited. But where it curved close to the north side of the house, where it was edged with tall boxwood and broad stone gates, Ben could hide in the shadows and study the pale house.

Two wings flanked a taller section with a two-sided curved staircase that led to a dark green Palladian door beneath a carved balcony. The downstairs windows were protected by wavy white-metal grills, while the upstairs windows were tightly shuttered, making the house look closed and unlived in.

The four boxwood mazes that filled the front garden were clipped but full of weeds, and the round fountain in the center was empty and covered with leaves.

Ben took pictures of both the house and garden, in case he needed them later. And had just walked to the south wing past a pair of falcon-topped pillars, when he heard a car coming toward him from the allée drive.

He slipped into the trees behind the house, and had worked his way back to the north end when a black Lancia sedan pulled up to the front door.

A humorless-looking, middle-aged woman got out from behind the wheel, as Jenny Hunt stepped from the passenger side and stretched her arms above her head.

They both pulled suitcases out of the trunk, then climbed opposite sides of the staircase, while Ben took snapshots of the driver and the car from forty feet away.

Tuesday, March 13th, 1962

Ben was thinking how much he didn't know about medieval Italy, about warring city states and armed walled cities, as he drove up the switchback road that climbed the high hill to Cortona.

He drove slowly past tiny almost vertical homesteads with three or four small olive trees, and a few short rows of naked grape vines, watching owners work the ground in several of the plots he passed.

He drove along the long side of a large elaborate walled-cemetery too, that grew out from the hill on the left on a precipitous ledge of land, just before the road turned right, and climbed even more steeply.

There were four old women there, walking down from

Cortona, scarved and dressed entirely in black, carrying flowers for the dead.

Ben downshifted into first, and wondered how many Americans could have walked down a road like that, much less made it up again.

No, we sit, eating chips and dip. Watching athletes on TV. Ironically. Getting our thrills from soap operas. Watching newscasters rewrite history.

Ah. There's the gate to Cortona.

It was part of the medieval town wall on the north-west side of the city, and Ben parked outside it, then walked through and started climbing toward the center of the city on the wide flat stones of the Via Roma.

He stopped when he got to the Piazza della Republica (an irregularly shaped square on one of the few flat pieces of ground to be found in all Cortona), and stared at his map of the city.

He was looking for the Museo dell Academia Etruscan, where the group from the University of Kentucky was meeting at nine. And he found it on the Piazza Signorelli, where an archway in the wall led through to the museum in the interior courtyard of the Palazzo Casali. There he took the stairs two at a time, and asked to be directed to the office of Professore Carlo Antoninni.

Ben had already talked to him from Siena. And before that from Florence. And he'd sent him his credentials, along with a letter of recommendation from Giovanni Balducci, with a request to be allowed to sit in on classes with the group from Kentucky. The request had already been granted. But Ben still wanted to stress again in person that he was using the name 'Benjamin West' ('West' borrowed from his best friend, who'd died the year before), in order to anonymously hunt for rare books for a well-known collector from the States.

He did not want Ben Reese used in front of the group. He did not want his real name to get to John Wharton from Jenny, or anyone else he met.

There was a lecture that first morning on Italian history, emphasizing the importance of the early Etruscans in Tuscany, stressing the conflicts between city-states later – Pisa, Florence, and Siena in particular.

There was to be a guided tour of the museum in the afternoon, and when they broke for lunch, Jenny Hunt spoke to her mother's friend, Tess Johns, who was leading the American group, to say she was going off by herself. She felt awkward with the college students, at least then, on the first day. Too young to feel comfortable, or included in any real way. She knew where to go to get lunch, and wanted to be on her own.

Ben was standing nearby, reading a notice on a bulletin board, listening to Mrs Johns' hesitation, hearing her pause and back-pedal politely. Mrs Johns said she was lunching with the director and couldn't get away. And Ben could see her thinking that Jenny was only seventeen, that she wasn't experienced with Italian men, that she was used to being chaperoned, and shouldn't go off alone.

Jenny could see what she was thinking too, and it looked like she found it galling.

Everett Adams had told Mrs Johns about Ben, and he walked up and introduced himself as Benjamin West, saying he planned to wander off on his own too, and he'd be happy to beat back the Italian men if Jenny didn't mind putting up with him.

Mrs Johns looked pleased.

Jenny Hunt looked less so.

But she still went off with Ben toward the Palazzo della Republica, walking on uneven cobblestone streets, listening to the laughter and conversation, taking in the architecture and making conversation.

They bought bread and cheese and fruit on the Via Nationale, and walked down to the public gardens, which had a spectacular view across the Val de Chiana on the south-western side of town as far as Lake Trasimeno, several miles away.

They sat on a bench and watched people walk by till they'd begun to feel cold in the wind, and decided to go get coffee in a café they'd passed earlier.

They sat in the back and sipped cups of cappuccino, gazing out a small-paned window across sienna-red roofs, watching regulars settle in to long leisurely Italian lunches – reading papers, talking intently, smoking and waving their hands.

Jenny talked about the four mares she'd bred, and how she

didn't want to miss their foaling, but had risked it anyway to study in Cortona.

Ben told Jenny about being an archivist, and studying painting restoration, and looking for an Aldine Seneca for someone he knew in the States.

'Oh, so you must be Mr Adams' friend from Ohio who worked on Jo's mural. He's been looking for that Seneca for the longest time. Not that I actually know what it is. Jo told us about you before you came to Mount Prospect, but she didn't mention your name.'

Ben had hoped she hadn't known any of that, and he answered obliquely and moved on, asking about the aunt she lived with, and what Jenny wanted to do in college, and eventually maneuvering himself around to asking about her stepfather.

He already knew by then that Jenny was direct. She had opinions. She had enthusiasms (horses, painting, Appalachian folk music). She saw no reason to mince words, even when she talked about her aunt.

'Aunt Alma tries hard, and she's a kind person, but she's never been anywhere but Lexington. Her family lost everything in the Depression, and she never married, and she's never had a job, and she's easy to overwhelm. Fussy. Vague. Pushed around by my stepfather because she feels dependent.'

'It might be hard not to be. Jane Austen was an impoverished aunt, you know, who got shuffled between relatives. Maybe that's why she wrote about dependents as often and as well as she did.'

'Did you have to study Austen, as an archivist?'

'No. My wife did her doctorate on her.'

'I haven't read much about her. But I do think Aunt Alma caters to John when she doesn't need to. I tell her to do something fun. Get a job she likes, or travel. John doesn't own the house, and she has money from Mother for raising me, but she still lets him push her around. I know she loves me, and she does the best she can, and I try not to be impatient.'

Ben nodded, and said, 'Going through the Depression probably left some scars.'

Meaning that. Having lived through it himself.

But that's youth too. It's all simple. It's all obvious.

*Decisions that affect other people for years, no reason to hesi-
tate there. Not until you've lived long enough to make painful
mistakes yourself.*

'He's nice to her. Usually.'

'Your stepfather?'

'Yessir. Patient, but long suffering. Patronizing might be a
better word. He's patronizing toward me too, but I try not to
say anything. I b'lieve it's better to get along with him than
start a huge fight.'

'He's not unkind to you, is he?'

'No, he's good to me in his own way. He's let me come
over here once a year since I was thirteen. And he buys me
things when he travels sometimes. He's not the cruel stepfather you read about in books.'

'So it could be a lot worse.'

'Yessir, it certainly could.' Jenny Hunt took a rubber band
out of the pocket of her slacks and fastened her long blonde
hair in a ponytail, then flipped it back behind her shoulders, while her blue eyes squinted against the sun stabbing
in at the window. 'John's distant. He's very busy with his
business. Businesses, I should say. He bought a terracotta
pottery that makes pots and urns over near Pienza. That's
so he can use the trips and the house here as a tax right-
off at home.'

'Really?'

'Something like that. Taxes, or profit-and-loss offsets, or
something. He has a business in England too, or he's trying
to start one. Or he's exporting a lot to England, I'm not sure
which. Anyway, he lives his own life. And he's hard to know.
But he leaves me alone most of the time, and that's about all
you could hope for.'

'My family's not very close either. I'm the weird one in
the bunch. The one who left and does peculiar things.'

'John thinks I was stupid to keep my mother's horses. But
it's my house in Versailles, from my mom and dad, so he
leaves that part of my life alone.'

'Does he visit you often? Do you spend Thanksgiving and
Christmas together, or does he stay pretty separate?'

'Depends on the year. He came up for Thanksgiving, and
I went down to his place outside of Knoxville for Christmas
Day. Aunt Alma and I both.'

'Did you do something together for New Year's Eve?' Ben looked nonchalant, sipping his cappuccino, wiping the corner of his mouth.

'Not this year. He was in England for New Year's. He brought me back a pair of riding boots we'd ordered from a company there, so I wouldn't have to wait for the mail. He didn't come home till the middle of January. I think he was in Europe too, but I'm not sure. My birthday's the seventeenth, so he brought the boots up to me from Tennessee that afternoon, and he took me to dinner at the Lafayette Hotel, and then drove on to Louisville to call on a customer there the next morning.'

'That was nice of him, wasn't it?' Ben told himself to keep his face straight and not look overly gratified that Ted Mitchell was known to be in England when Ross MacNab died.

'Could I ask you one other thing, Dr West?' She looked at him intently, before she dropped her eyes.

'Sure. You can also call me Ben.'

'Thank you. When you go to look at that Seneca book would you take me with you? I know I shouldn't ask, but it sounds like—'

'Let's do it tomorrow. I'll try to make an appointment for the break between morning class and your tour of the city.'

'Thank you. That's very kind. Were you in an accident?' Jenny was staring at the scar on Ben's palm, and the index finger that didn't bend. She looked sad for him, but not at all self-conscious, or as though she thought it was too personal to ask.

Ben laughed and said, 'It was more intentional than accidental,' as he picked up the check.

'Oh? Were you in the Second World War? My daddy was too old to go, but John was.'

'1942 through 1945.'

'Europe, or the Pacific?'

'Europe.'

'So was John.'

'There were quite a few of us over there.'

Jenny laughed as she stood up and pulled on her coat.

'Is your stepfather coming to see you while you're here?'

'No. He doesn't call either. Not very often. He's somewhere

in Asia right now. He's invented some new kind of special method for making machine tools. Not that I know anything about it. I've never been too interested.'

'I don't know much either, but when I've gone to manufacturing plants and actually seen how things get made, I've always found it really interesting. Even the lowly pencil. You'd be amazed at how complicated they are to make.'

'Would I? Maybe I ought to go see John's plant. I did when I was small, but I don't remember a thing.'

Five minutes after one of the hotel's British racing-green Rolls-Royces had swept John Wharton around the Italianate fountain and deposited him under the large gold letters spelling out THE PENINSULA above gold and glass doors, Wharton had already crossed the marble lobby, climbed the balustraded stairs, walked into his elegant English-looking room, thrown his suit coat on a chair, pulled off his green paisley tie and unbuttoned his French-cuffed shirt.

He rubbed his temples as though they ached, and stroked both sides of his short black beard with the fingers and thumb of one hand. He brushed his hair back with both hands too, turning his head from side to side, examining his temples in an antique mirror.

He decided the grey wasn't any worse. That it must've been the lighting in the restaurant. That except for the roll above his belt, he looked damned good for forty-six.

When I'm eating at home, and playing tennis all the time, it'll come right off the way it used to.

Wharton turned toward the broad bank of windows that faced the hustle of the harbor. But he didn't move any closer, and he didn't watch the boats, or the city lights glittering on the bay. He pulled his shirt out of his trousers, and shifted his cufflinks from one hand to the other.

He was asking himself why Adams would take somebody from a university to see the house. And why he hadn't heard about it till that morning. Alma knew she was to keep him informed. And Wharton didn't like the sound of it. He didn't want strangers in a house where he had personal things. *Now that Jenny's older, with friends who wander in and out, I should've taken what's left of my belongings down to Knoxville before this.*

It's eleven here in Hong Kong, so it must be five in Cortona. And I better call now, if I'm going to, before the girl gets up here.

He poured himself two fingers of twenty-year-old Scotch, then looked at the harbor lights floating on the water, while recalculating his rate of return after he'd paid his middleman.

We figured all along that the US ban on selling Mao machine tools would raise the cost of doing business, but from what Chang got out of them today, we may be able to set our margins higher than we expected. If we play our cards right. If we stick to our guns.

The Reds were tough negotiators. There was no doubt about that. But they needed what he had, and he was betting he could pull it off. No other broach maker in the world could compete with his technology.

But they'll catch up in the next two years, and now's the time to make a killing.

It was one of the risks he liked. Deal making with an edge of intrigue.

For the status quo holds no appeal. I don't want to watch my step. I have no interest in playing it safe. But my wife couldn't accept that. Ruth was nothing if not an admirer of middle-class respectability.

When Chang said, 'If we don't do it, someone else will,' he was only stating the obvious. And what the Reds make with my machines is none of our damn business.

They obviously weren't coming after the US. Not with nukes any time soon. And not business-wise either for a long time to come. Mao's trade ministers weren't fools. They wanted to make the *next* deal, not just the deal today. But they wouldn't play by the rules either. Intellectual property restrictions didn't mean squat to them.

So Chang's the right guy to handle it. He'll avoid the normal types of double-cross, having perfected them himself. Anything more far-reaching I'll deal with on my own.

I need to call Jenny now, before I get interrupted.

John Wharton placed the call, then hung up and lit a cigarette. He sat down at the desk and read a three-page cost analysis from his manufacturing manager in Knoxville, underlining and writing comments, until the phone rang twice.

'Yes, operator, thank you . . . Hi. How was your flight? . . . Good. So how's Janetta taking care of the house? . . . Then you stay right on her case . . . What about this college course you're taking? . . . You're not walking around by yourself, are you? . . .

'Oh? What's he do for a living? . . . Where? . . . Ohio's all you got out of him? You usually squeeze more than that out of an ordinary stone . . . Jo's mural? . . . Then he must be the guy Alma said Ev took to the house. . . . What? Did you say Ben West?'

John Wharton was standing between the bed and the desk staring at the mirror across the room. 'Benjamin West? Not Reese? . . . You're sure? . . . No, it's just that I . . . Find out if he was in the war . . . Oh, yeah? Then ask him what he did. Rank. Division. That kind of thing. I mean it. Ask him tomorrow, and I'll call tomorrow night . . . No, I'm just curious . . . I've got to make another call. Have a good time, Jen. Don't forget to ask West. Wait! Ask what college he's at too . . . Find out, OK? Be sure to ask him tomorrow.'

There was a knock on the door a second after Wharton had placed his call to New York City, and he opened it and looked hard at the girl in the blood-red dress, before he pointed her toward the chair in the corner by the king-sized bed. 'You speak English?'

'Yes, yes. Very good English.' She put her hands on her hips just above the side slits and smoothed the tight silk brocade higher, before she sat and crossed her legs.

She watched John Wharton as she showed them off – smooth, honey-colored thighs, fine calves, narrow ankles, tiny feet in stiletto-heeled black silk sandals. She tucked her chin demurely as she smiled up at him, her lips red and glistening, her teeth white and fine, her black-lined almond eyes large and serious-looking, as she adjusted one of the white jade sticks that held her hair on top of her head.

'You want a drink? Wait a second.' The phone had rung once, and Wharton picked it up. 'Give me Grady . . . No, not Miller, Grady.' John Wharton gazed down at the girl while lighting another cigarette, keeping the receiver cradled against his shoulder. 'Get a drink if you want it.'

She was shaking her head and smiling at him as Wharton spoke into the phone.

'I've got a job for you, and I want it done fast. Put as many people on it as you have to. I don't care what it costs, I want you to trace a guy . . . wait a minute.' John Wharton put his hand across the mouthpiece and looked at the woman in the chair. 'Wait in the bathroom. Turn on the shower, and close the door. Turn on the fan, too. I'll get you when I'm off the phone.'

She got up and went. And John Wharton waited to speak till he'd heard the shower. 'I want you to trace a guy named Ben Reese. R-E-E-S-E . . . Right. He was a scout in Europe during World War Two . . . I understand, just find out where he lives and what he does. I want anything you can come up with. Find his parents. Find out who he's married to. Who her family are. Anything personal you can dig up . . . By phone, in person, I don't care, whatever it takes to get it done fast . . .

'He may work in Ohio, but I don't know where. He may be an archivist in a university . . . archivist . . . A-R-C-H-I-V-I-S-T. That's at least an angle you could try. I'll know more tomorrow, and I'll get back to you then . . . I'm in Hong Kong at the Peninsula Hotel if you come up with anything. On second thought, I want to hear back tomorrow, whatever you've got then.'

Wharton gave the phone and room numbers, then hung up and lit another cigarette while staring out at the night. He stood there long enough to smoke another, and finish the last of his Scotch.

Then he opened the bathroom door and said, 'You can go. I've changed my mind.'

'You don't like me?' She'd undone the frogs that fastened the top of her dress and she was smiling, sliding the shimmering silk off her smooth round shoulders.

'Out. Now. It's none of your damn business what I like or don't like.'

'You pay me anyway! You pay me!'

Wharton grabbed her by the upper arms and pulled her up against him. He bent over her, staring down into her dark eyes, hissing softly in her ear. 'This is a very fancy hotel you're in, sweetheart. You make plenty big money if you're *careful* and the wrong people don't hear what you're up to. So if *I* were you, I'd shut my little red lips and wiggle right out the door.' His face was red and hot-looking and his mouth was a tight thin line.

He let her go. And the girl slid past him sideways, out through the door to the hall.

Eighteen

The smell of the shop was what Ben noticed first as he turned to close the door, the spicy musky almost smoky smell of paper and leather that had made him smile since he was six, when he first crossed the creaking wooden floor of a rural Michigan library (which he'd then visited twice a week till he left to go to college).

The stationery shop looked just the way he'd thought it would too, in Italy. Dark wooden shelves lined with finely crafted hand-bound books in pale pastels and rich leathers, leather-bound address books lined with marbled end-papers, crisp thick stationery in elegant boxes – being straightened now, on counters in the back, by a plump, pleasant-looking fortyish woman with tortoiseshell glasses and dark auburn hair who was talking on a phone while she worked.

As soon as she hung up, Jenny bought a teal blank book from her for taking notes on her field trips, which the woman asked her about, easily and intelligently in excellent melodic English, as she wrapped the book in marbled paper.

Ben listened absently, wondering idly what Kate would've bought – realizing as soon as he started how little he really knew about her, about the small daily likes and dislikes that are a lot of what we are to live with.

'May I help you, signore, in any way?'

'I'm here to examine a volume of Seneca that Francesco Mostardini is holding for me. I phoned and made an appointment yesterday afternoon.'

'Of course, professore. *Uno momento.*' She smiled with what looked like well-intentioned amusement, and turned toward the glass door behind the high desk at the back of the room. She unlocked the heavy brass lock, turned on lights beyond the door, and ushered Ben into a larger room that was brick floored and ceilinged and lined with heavy carved bookcases.

'I, *professore*, am *Francesca* Mostardini. There has been a typing error perhaps?'

'I probably misread the letter from the bookseller in Florence.'

'*Si, si*, it is easy to do. Though some, of course, simply expect to find a male proprietor, and read the name accordingly.'

'Even though it was two women from New York who revolutionized rare book buying after the Second World War.'

'*Si*. They did. Truly. Buying, with deep knowledge, great numbers of antiquarian books in Britain and Europe. My father, may God rest his soul, worked with them many times. So . . .' She removed a small package from one of many drawers in a huge carved apothecary cabinet, then folded back the green velvet cloth protecting a small quarto volume.

Francesca Mostardini's short well-tended index finger, half-covered by a gold-crested signet ring, glided appreciatively across the smooth cover before she handed the book to Ben.

'Here is a Seneca of the sort you require. It is an Aldine first printing of the philosophies from 1513. You will see the Aldine colophon of the anchor and the dolphin on the title page, which first appeared on the 1502 Dante. The book was bound to order by Angelo Citterio for the English Lord Cairnorvan. It was bound, as you will no doubt perceive, in the very finest of soft and supple veal.'

'It's exquisite.' Ben was running his hands across the shining pecan-colored leather, smiling to himself as he looked at the tooling – the repeated relief of a complicated Greek key that edged both the outside and the inside of the covers, the inside clearly stamped in gold, though the outside had lost its color. 'Would the outside have been stamped in gold leaf originally?'

'We believe so. It would have been usual for a leather worker of such distinction, working to order for a wealthy aristocrat, to have used gold leaf, yes, outside as well as inside. Silver leaf, perhaps, to suit a specific taste. Now, I shall leave you alone to examine the offering.' Francesca smiled with dignity, pulled her cashmere cardigan higher on the shoulders of her matching grey silk blouse, and stepped into the front room.

Ben read the description and presentation of provenance in the document lying on the table, examined the cover with considerable care, looked at the watermark on every page as well as the Latin printed across it, with the magnifying glass on his key ring.

He called Jenny into the back room, showed her the binding and the colophon, the way in which the selvages were sewn and several details of the printing itself.

He then took the Seneca into the front of the shop, where Francesca Mostardini had just said goodbye to a customer, and asked her the selling price. She mentioned a figure that made Jenny's head snap around, as Ben nodded his without batting an eye.

'I am unlike many of my countrymen, professore. I do not enjoy . . . how do you call it . . . ? The practice of haggling. I prefer to offer a work at such a price that a modest profit is provided for my establishment, while offering an honest assessment of a work's true value.'

'It's a very fair offer, and I accept. I can give you a deposit of one hundred American dollars, if that is acceptable, and arrange for a wire transfer of funds to your bank from my American buyer's account.'

'*Si*. That would be most satisfactory.'

'Where do you teach in Ohio?'

Jenny and Ben were walking toward the museum where the group was meeting to tour Etruscan sites, two of them very close to Sodo, before the tour of Cortona.

'In a small private university. We have a surprising number of those in Ohio. That's something I'd like to study, the history of college foundings in early pioneer Ohio.'

'I know this may sound funny, but is your name West, or Reese?' Jenny's hair was blowing around her face, and she held it back with one hand while turning to look at Ben.

'That's an odd thing to ask.'

'I know. My stepfather called me last night from Hong Kong. And when we talked about my course work, and I told him about you, and that your name was West, and you'd been in the war in Europe, I think he misunderstood me, and he asked if your name wasn't Reese.'

'I see.' Ben stared straight ahead as he walked, his grey eyes hidden and his jaw set, his mouth deliberately neutral. 'What'd you tell him?'

'West is what I understood it to be, but he wanted me to make a point of asking.'

'You told him the right thing.'

'Good. So are you coming to the burial sites with us?'

'No, I've got to organize the money transfer and finish some other work for an archivist friend.'

'There was something else John wanted me to ask, but I can't remember what it was.'

'You're going to miss your bus if we don't get a move on now.'

Thursday, March 15th, 1962

'You must be Maggie.'

'Yes.' Maggie Parsons had opened Ben's front door and was considering a tall thin woman in her thirties she'd never seen before.

'I'm Ben's cousin, Martha. Martha Reese Ryan? I'm his dad's brother Billy's daughter.'

Maggie raised her eyebrows, but didn't say a word.

'I live in DeKalb, Illinois, and I haven't seen Ben for years, but I'm on my way to visit my husband's mother in Cincinnati. She's had surgery, and I'm going there to help out, and I thought I'd stop by and surprise him. Sorry to bother you. I'll try to find him at his office.'

'He's away for spring vacation. He won't be back till next Tuesday.'

'Oh. I didn't think about that. It was a last-minute kinda trip. I haven't seen him since before Jessie died, and I wanted to surprise him, like I said.' She shivered slightly in her thin-looking raincoat, in the west wind tearing across the porch, as she shrugged her shoulders half-apologetically.

'You want to come in for a cup of tea? You've got quite a drive to Cincinnati.'

'Sure, if you've got time.'

'I was making myself a cup. I'm leaving for Findlay this

afternoon, so you almost missed me too. How'd you know my name?'

'Aunt Mernie. Ben's mother. I write to her every month or two, and we talk once in a blue moon, and she told me about you.'

'Never met her myself, but I've chatted with her on the phone.'

'That's just what she said.'

They were sitting in the living room ten minutes later, sipping their tea and looking ill at ease.

'Sure was sad about Jessie. Did you know her?'

'No. Know people who did.' Maggie took a lemon slice out of her tea and added a spoonful of sugar.

'Musta been a real nice lady.'

'Yeah.'

'Sounds like Ben gets to travel a lot with the kind of work he does.'

'Yep. Goes all kinds of places. Enjoys that a lot.'

Martha nodded and blew on her tea. 'Where's he gone to this time?'

Maggie looked at Martha for a minute, before she said, 'Italy.'

'Boy, I'd like to go there. 'Member that movie with Audrey Hepburn and William Holden? Maybe it was Gregory Peck. When she was this princess in Rome? Be fun to see Venice. The gondolas and all that. Where'd he go in Italy? Ben, I mean.'

'Tuscany. Staying near some real small place called Sina-something. Sinalunga. Been other places too, while he was over. Staying with a friend now who's started some hotel. Used to work for the Vatican.'

'Is that where the ceiling's painted all over, the place that's real famous?'

Maggie, who'd been born and raised a Roman Catholic, said yes, she thought it was, while trying to keep every last hint of horror out of her voice.

Neither of them said anything else for a minute. So Maggie swirled the teapot and passed a plate of brownies.

'The family was real worried when Ben got hurt in the war. Looked like he wasn't gunna make it for a real long time.'

Maggie said, 'I guess they did a bunch of surgeries on his nerves, and what not, and from what I've heard, they figured for awhile he wouldn't be able to do much of anything. Course, he worked harder at his physical therapy than most anybody would. Least that's what a friend of his told me.'

'I'll bet he did. His mom was real worried about whether he oughta get married then, and all that. Course now she wishes he'd marry again.' Martha Reese Ryan ate the slice of lemon in her cup and wiped her hands on her napkin. 'I don't s'ppose he's dating anyone?' She raised an eyebrow inquisitively and laughed out loud. 'Mothers are the last ones who get told, you know, and the first ones to be hopin' their children'll get busy and have kids. Some anyway. Some mothers can't let go.'

'I wouldn't say he's dating anyone per se. He's got a friend who lives in Scotland. An American lady he knew in the war. She writes books, and they see each other some, and talk sometimes on the phone. She was married to a friend of his who died years ago.'

'That wouldn't be someone named Carrie, would it?'

'No. Kate.'

'Ummm. Wilson? There was a Kate he went to—'

'Lindsay.'

'That's not the one I was thinking of. Course she didn't live in Scotland either. My husband was stationed in England during the war, and he got sent up to Scotland after he was hurt. Before he got shipped back to France, he walked all over on them walking trails. You don't happen to know where she lives? I thought maybe my husband mighta—'

'On some lake somewhere. Kind of north, but in the center.'

Martha nodded and set down her cup. 'Well. Thanks for the tea. Will you be talking to Ben before he comes home?'

'Doubt it. Not unless there's a change of plans.'

'Tell him I stopped, and I hope he's doing well.'

'Sure. Too bad he had to miss you.'

'Thanks again.'

She was half way down the front walk when she turned and waved to Maggie, who was watching her from the open door with an uneasy smile on her face.

*   *   *

A heavyset man in a homburg hat and grey tweed overcoat was standing in a phone booth on the main street of Hillsdale, Ohio, stamping his feet, and rubbing his gloved hands, waiting for his call to go through.

'Yeah, I'm still here . . . Mr Wharton? . . . Al Grady. We've tracked a guy named Ben Reese who was an army scout in Europe in World War Two to Alderton University in Hillsdale, Ohio . . . Right. He's in Italy now staying with a friend named Raimondo Ricciardi outside a place named Sinalunga, in a hotel called La Fortezza della Felicità. I've spelled that out in a Telex. He's comin' home next Tuesday. He's lived here since 1951, but . . . no, his wife's been dead for . . .

'No *real* close friends. Not since somebody named Richard West died . . . There *is* a woman writer friend. An American living in Scotland on Loch . . . Right. How'd you know? That wasn't easy for us to track down. Her name's . . . Nope, you got that right too . . . I've Telexed you Reese's family information, army record, employment record and educational background too, to your hotel there in Hong Kong.'

Friday, March 16th, 1962

Kate was sitting at her desk staring over her IBM electric at the clouds high above Loch Rannock, thinking about how to describe Georgina's house on Scotland's east coast, and fictionalize the grounds so they'd be as interesting as the real ones, but not be recognizable – when there was a knock on her studio door.

That was something of a surprise since her father-in-law was away in Aberdeen for a week, and only a handful of people would have known where to find her studio if she weren't in the house.

Kate opened the door by the fireplace, and looked out on a man she'd never seen before – a short, very redheaded postman in a neatly pressed uniform, holding a telegram in his hand.

'Good morning, madam. Would you be Mrs Lindsay?'
'Yes.'
'The sender has requested a reply.'
'Thank you. Where's Tommy?'
'He has a very bad case of influenza.'

'Tell him I hope he feels better soon.' Kate opened the telegram with a cold hard knot in her own chest, worrying about her father and whether he'd had another heart attack, feeling a rush of relief when she saw it came from Ben.

> Emergency. Please come. Tickets for 8:07 a.m. flight March 18th from Prestwick to Heathrow at British Airways desk at Prestwick. Tickets for flight to Rome plus Money Order at Alitalia desk Heathrow. Friend Bob Boyd will meet plane in Rome outside customs. Tell no one your destination. Ben Reese

Kate took the return telegram form and wrote, 'See you March 18th. Kate.'

'Yer telephone's still out, is it?'

'All of Loch Rannoch's out, and down toward Aberfeldy too. Our nearest neighbor stopped by this morning to tell me we're all cut off, but he didn't know what had caused it.'

'A lorry slid on an icy patch, in the wee hours of the morning, and rammed a piece of equipment. They say they may have to send to Manchester for the part, and it could be quite a considerable time before they set it to rights.'

'I guess that's what we have to expect, if we live in the middle of nowhere. Thank you for walking to the woods to find me, by the way.'

'Oh, yer very welcome I'm sure.' He touched his cap and closed the door.

And Kate stood, staring at the fire, wondering what the emergency could be, and hoping Ben wasn't hurt.

Sunday, March 18th, 1962

Kate was exhausted by the time she got to Rome. She'd had to get up at three to drive down to Prestwick to catch the flight to London.

She'd then sat in Heathrow, with what seemed like thousands of other tired frustrated people, while her plane to Rome was postponed twice. She hadn't been able to sleep in the airport, or on the plane, either one, and when she landed in Italy she felt hot and irritable and groggy.

She had no idea who Bob Boyd was, much less what he

looked like, and she was standing outside customs scanning the swarm of faces hoping that finding him wouldn't take long – when she saw a tall dark-haired man, with a neatly shaped beard wave as he walked towards her.

'Mrs Lindsay?'

'Yes.'

'I'm Bob Boyd. Ben gave me a good description.'

Kate smiled and said, 'I'm afraid to ask what it was.'

Boyd looked mildly taken aback.

And Kate said, 'I'm just kidding. Ben's a little like me. Actually, I'm worse. He's direct, and I'm blunt.'

'Then you may assume, Mrs Lindsay, that he likes the way you look. Let me take your suitcase.' He pulled his sunglasses off the top of his head and settled them on his nose while he talked, before he reached for her bag.

Kate thanked him, and handed it to him, and then asked if Ben was hurt.

'No, he's fine. The only information he was willing to part with was that he's found someone he's been looking for, and he had to stay where he was. Let's get out of here as fast as we can so we miss the worst of the traffic.'

Fiumicino Airport was south-west of the city, and they were driving north with Rome behind them, in a black Fiat 1100, before Kate asked Bob Boyd how he knew Ben, and where they were heading.

'I'm an archivist from the States. I met Ben at the Brooklyn Museum of Art when he was doing post-doc work there. My specialty is frescos, and I'm working for a year in Florence. Ben's staying at an old farm estate that's being turned into a hotel near Sinalunga, and he found frescos there in the private chapel that he knew I'd want to see. I came down on Thursday, and then whatever this is that he's involved in came up, and he asked me to pick you up. He didn't tell me anything about it.'

'How soon will we be there?' She was wondering why he was wearing dark glasses. It was overcast now, and sprinkling, and there were darker clouds straight ahead.

'Two and a half hours, maybe three. It may seem odd that I'm wearing sunglasses, but I've been fighting a bad eye infection, and my eyes are sensitive to light.'

'Oh.' Kate yawned, and tried to find a comfortable way to lean her head on the seat.

'Why don't you take a nap? There's a picnic blanket on the back seat. You could use that as a pillow.'

'Thanks, I think I will.' She folded it up and stuffed it by the window and settled her head against it. She was drifting away even then. Seeing Bob Boyd's face as he'd walked toward her in the crowd and wondering why he'd looked familiar when she'd never seen him before.

She began to wake up when the car slowed down, then straightened her head when it stopped – when she heard the emergency brake get pulled on, close to her left thigh.

She saw a small trattoria on her right in the twilight – a small stuccoed restaurant, surrounded by trees and shrubs – just as Bob Boyd got out of the car and slammed the door behind him.

He walked around and opened hers, and said, 'I wanted to get some bottled water and stop and use the bathroom. Do you want to come in too?'

'Yeah, I do. Thanks. Where are we now?' There were no other buildings nearby along that narrow road, but she could see the lights of a village down the hill behind them in the darkening grey dusk.

'We're just north of Chiusi. A lot of restaurants don't have American-style bathrooms, but this one here does. I'll meet you by the car.'

When Kate came out, she couldn't see Bob Boyd anywhere, and she stood by the Fiat rubbing her neck, trying to remember if he'd been wearing his sunglasses when they'd gone into the restaurant.

Then she thought how good it had felt to splash water on her face and spray perfume along her throat. And she was wondering why alcohol on skin feels relaxing when you're hot or tired, and what that meant about human physiology – when she was grabbed from behind and a cold wet cloth was pressed across her nose and mouth.

She had enough time to decide it was ether, before she watched herself – a tiny miniature picture of herself – in a sickly-sweet dreamy haze swirl down in a cold black pit.

It had been a tense three and a half days for Ben, once he knew that Wharton had told Jenny to ask about his name.

Surprise was what he'd counted on. And any chance of that was gone.

Once Ted Mitchell knew that somebody who at least *might* have been Ben Reese was talking to Jenny, Ted would make sure one way or the other. And then he'd make the threat go away, if Ben couldn't stop him first.

Mitchell, being Wharton, had money enough to track Ben with investigators if he had to. So a whole lot of ugly things could start happening any second.

Ben had called Maggie that same night, Wednesday the 14th, but she hadn't been home. He couldn't get her on the 15th either. But he had on the 16th, at midnight in Italy, and heard about the woman pretending to be his cousin (a cousin who existed, but looked nothing like the woman Maggie'd seen). Ben grilled her in great detail, and told her not to talk to *any* stranger, no matter what was said.

Then he started trying to get Kate.

He'd watched the Wharton- Mitchell house too on Thursday, to see if Mitchell would appear. For he couldn't find out from Jenny what Mitchell might be doing, since she'd left with her group that morning for Florence, and wouldn't be back till Monday.

By Thursday night Ben had hired Raimondo's nephew, Marco, to take a room at the hotel down the road from Il Falconiere, and watch the house from up on the ridge.

Marco saw nothing of Mitchell Thursday night. Or Friday, when Ben was trying to get the money transfer worked out for the Aldine Seneca. It wasn't till that Friday afternoon that the money was in Francesca Mostardini's hands, and the Aldine Seneca was in Ben's.

Marco didn't see Mitchell that night.

And Kate didn't answer her phone.

No one answered on the 17th either.

And neither did Marco see Mitchell.

It hadn't been until that afternoon, Sunday the 18th, at five, that Ben had gotten David Lindsay at the house in Scotland, and learned that David had been in Aberdeen for a week, that the phones had gone out on Loch Rannock on Thursday and had only come on that afternoon. That Kate was gone, but had left a note, written that morning at 3 a.m., saying she'd gotten an urgent telegram and would be away for a few days. She was fine, and she'd phone David when she could. All she could tell him was she'd be with a friend he knew whose first name began with 'B'.

Ben hung up and said, 'Damn!' Before he walked out of the office into La Fortezza's courtyard.

The bell in the campanile struck the half hour as he stood there staring at the chapel without seeing or hearing anything. A maid climbed the stairs to the verandah above him, a waiter came out of the restaurant, smiling and saying *'Buona sera'* to him, a middle-aged French couple walked down the fan-shaped stairs from the padrone's house talking quietly with their arms around each other's waists – before Ben turned and crunched across the gravel toward the small stuccoed church.

It was cool and musty smelling. And Ben walked around it before he sat – looking at the carved plaster, and the beeswax candles, at the raised wooden altar, and the sculpted stone font, at the six minor medieval masterpieces (three saints he knew nothing about, and three Madonnas and Child).

He sat then in the back with his eyes closed thinking about Kate, telling himself that it *could* be nothing, that she could be with someone David knew in Scotland whose name began with 'B'.

Yeah? Then why couldn't she say where she'd gone? Mitchell knows who she is, and where she lives too. He'd know from Phillip Welsh. Once Mitchell found out she knows me, he'd try to get to her first, and use her to reel me in.

While I wait like a snagged trout for Mitchell to twitch the line.

He knows where I am from Maggie. And I'll bet he's already got Kate.

And all I can do is sit here. There's not another blasted move I can make, except sit right here and pray. Keep her safe. Please. Keep him from hurting anyone else. And help me turn back from wanting to kill him with one quick blow to the throat.

It's one thing to stop him. To protect her, or somebody else. It's another to actually want to feel him die right in my hands.

If I can make that happen, of course. If *I'm given a chance to get to Mitchell in time.*

The door opened and an Italian couple came in talking in hushed tones before they dipped their fingers into a tiny shell-shaped stone of holy water set in the wall near the door. They genuflected in the aisle before they approached the altar and stared at the fresco behind it of the Madonna and Child.

Ben walked out into blue-green dusk wanting to run for miles, needing to burn off the restlessness he had to control soon.

He knew it would all take concentration. Rational thought. Discipline. Careful preparation. And he stood there thinking, by the ancient well in the grassy center of the courtyard, fingers tapping the carved curved edge.

Then he turned and went into the office, and told the woman at the desk he was expecting an urgent message. Possibly that night. Possibly the next day. It was a matter of life and death that they bring him the message immediately. And everyone working in reception needed to have that explained. He also asked if he could eat early, in the first seating at seven. And was it convenient to see Raimondo?

Mr Ricciardi was away in Siena until seven thirty or eight, but they could have him meet Mr Reese in the dining room as soon as he returned.

'*Multo Grazie.* I'll be in my bedroom till dinner.'

Ben walked across his large white room, past the stone fireplace and ancient armoire, to the two heavy arched wooden doors, and closed them in front of the glass. He lit the fire, and put on his rubber-soled desert boots, then pulled a black wool sweater over his thin black turtleneck.

He checked the two wires he kept in the unstitched fold of his belt (the one coated with diamond dust, the plain one made of heavier metal), then dropped his large Swiss Army knife into the right-hand pocket of his black cords.

He set the alarm for 6:45, lay down on the white crewel bedspread with his shoes hanging off the end, locked his hands together on his chest, concentrated on breathing slowly, and willed himself to sleep.

*   *   *

He had to eat sometime. There was nothing else useful he could do, and being hungry wouldn't help.

He told himself worrying wouldn't either. So he read a translation of Da Vinci's notebooks while he ate pheasant, asparagus, salad and fruit, and drank two cups of coffee.

Ben had just signed the check, when a waiter brought him an envelope, and he already had it torn open by the time he'd shot into the sitting area between the restaurant and the hotel office.

> If you want to see Kate alive, drive toward Pienza. After you pass the quarry on the right, take the third farm track on the left. Come alone and unarmed. Tell *no one*, or her death will be on your head.

Ben was at the desk two seconds later asking how it was delivered.

'A chambermaid brought it. I questioned her as you asked, Signore Reese. She parked behind the restaurant, and walked toward the lane that approaches the front entrance. A car drove from the shadows of the trees at the back, and a man handed her the envelope and five one-thousand lire notes. He did not exit the car. He instructed her to bring the letter to reception. She did not see him clearly, Signore, except to see that he had a . . . how do you call it? . . . A beard, is that right?'

'Thank her for me, and share this with her too.' Ben gave the receptionist several one-thousand lire notes, and asked if Raimondo had gotten back.

'One minute before the note came. He went to his apartment to wash. He should be here to join you in only another moment.'

Ben ran the length of the courtyard, and up the incline next to the chapel, then turned left at the top, between the back of the chapel and the big stone barn on the right.

Raimondo's house was straight ahead of him. And he was pulling the bell rope beside the arched door almost before he'd stopped running.

Raimondo came out a second later, saying, 'Ben—'

'Can you come to my room right now?'

'Of course, my friend. Now, certainly.' He took one step

into the house, said something quickly to his wife, then ran down the cobblestones after Ben Reese.

Ben had laid his flashlight on the bed, and was pulling the heavier wire out of his belt, wrapping it around his waist, twisting the ends together in front, while Raimondo Ricciardi read the note, and said, 'Is it the killer who has kidnapped tourists in Tuscany?'

'No, it's the person I've been tracking.'

'We must call the police immediately!'

'No, Raimondo, I can't take a chance with Kate. Do you know the place he's talking about?'

'*Si, si.* It is strange that, for this is a property recently purchased by a close friend to restore as a home for his family. I have gone with him to examine the buildings and advise him as to the work. It is remote. It is difficult to find the farm lane.'

'How can I tell if I've—?'

'You must look for a tree stump on the right-hand side, a hundred meters or so along the lane. That will show you that you have found the correct drive. The lane is long. Three quarters of a kilometre I would say from the Pienza road to the first of the farm buildings. It will be deserted. The restoration work has not yet begun.'

'What can you tell me about the buildings?'

'There are three structures. Brick and stone. Stucco on some surfaces. All the buildings crumbling. First there will come a barn. The floor above is gone. The one big wagon door rotted entirely away.

'The second building is the largest. It was a peasant home for two families on the upper floor, and there, above, there are many rooms, as well as two stairways. One outside. One inside. There are many different byres under those rooms, on the ground floor, where many types of animals were kept.

'The third building is another barn with high doors on both ends. Both rotted away, I think. Yes, and there is a fourth building I forgot, perhaps ten meters beyond that, a brick barn where tobacco was smoked with fires in pits in the floor.'

'Anything else I need to know?'

'The peasant apartments are in very bad repair. Upstairs, in the second building, large holes are in the floor. Walls are missing.

Many tiles have fallen from the roof. It will be a dangerous place in the dark. Even so, there should be a moon tonight, after the clouds pass, and I will be coming with you, so—'

'No, Raimondo. I've got to do this alone. But first I need a piece of the blue plastic sheeting we put on paintings to study brushwork.'

'That I have in my office. Yet still, I must—'

'I need your cudgel too – your long walking stick with the heavy knob on the end.'

'It is there as well, next door to your room here.'

'Could I also borrow the windbreaker you've got on? I need something black and lightweight that's got a lot of pockets.'

'Of course, my friend. I shall be removing it now.'

'I need a length of strong light rope. Maybe cotton, half to three quarters of an inch in diameter, and something like eight-feet long.'

'That we will find in the barn between my office and my home.'

'A coil of strong rope too, fifty or sixty feet of it.'

'That too will be there, yes. Come, we will make a start. It-tis good we are still a farm, no? So we have what you require.'

It took them ten minutes to collect what Ben wanted, and for Ben to fasten the blue plastic sheet across the lens of his flashlight. He zipped it into a pocket, while he told Raimondo he needed horseshoes.

Raimondo stared and shook his head, as he handed Ben the keys to his sedan.

'Didn't I see some in the long shed behind the restaurant? Between the restaurant and the parking area? The place where you keep the old ox cart?'

'I do not remember the horseshoes, but we shall go and see.'

There were three horseshoes on the wall. And Ben took two, tying one to each end of his eight-foot cotton rope.

'I shall pray for you my friend. I shall—'

Ben was gone before Raimondo had finished the sentence, running through a soft drizzle to the parking area entrance at the end of the long shed.

He spun Raimondo's Alfa Romeo around in the gravel, shot down the long drive, down the steep hill between the two rows of cypress. He braked hard, turned right, climbed halfway up the same hill on a side road that angled away to the left along the long side of the property, curving left and then back again, climbing toward the road that led south-west to Pienza.

Nineteen

It was a dark wet one-lane country road, twisting tightly, climbing steeply, making Ben look at his watch and ask how it could take fifteen minutes to drive five miles to the stone quarry.

He'd just said, 'Nuts! I can't have missed a turn, can I?' when his headlights caught a black-lettered sign with 'Cava Pietra' in the name.

The road curved to the left after that, and started to level off just before he came to an unmarked Y-intersection, where he bore to the left (hoping he was right), and that that way led to Pienza.

The rain had stopped and the moon was out, but there was mist swirling in the hollows, which made it harder to tell what was an ordinary farm lane and what was a driveway to a country villa hidden away from the road.

Ben made one wrong turn and turned back again. Right before the engine started coughing and choking and strangling suspiciously on what sounded too much like air – leading Ben to look at the gas gauge, at a needle dead on empty.

He moaned, and slapped the wheel once, as he worked at maneuvering the car before it coasted to a stop, willing it almost, past the left berm, away from the steep sheer drop down the right side of the road.

He took the key out and moved fast – checking the wires on the outside of his belt, feeling for the flashlight in his coat pocket, pulling on his dark knitted cap, climbing out of the car. He tied the horseshoe rope around his waist on the outside of his coat, rubbed mud across his face, set the sixty-foot coil of heavy rope over his right shoulder, and then picked up the wooden cudgel.

It was half a mile later that he came to what looked like a likely farm track, and when he found himself next to a

burned-out tree stump a hundred yards down the lane, he
smiled to himself, and thanked God, while he ran, that he'd
stumbled on to the right lane.

It led straight ahead into an overgrown woods, and the next
quarter mile was a dark walk through rustling trees, dank and
mushroomy smelling after the rain – the whole wood thick
with sound (the creaking and clattering of tangled bare
branches scattered by gusting wind, the squeaking of bats, the
beating of wings, the scratching and shuffling of foraging
animals that stopped when he got close).

The footing wasn't good anywhere – jagged stones in rutted
packed dirt, slippery mud slicks in low spots between rocks,
potholes deep enough to break ankles. And Ben had just
thought, it's a good thing I've got decent night vision – which
was one of the ways the army picked scouts – when he came
around a right-angle turn and startled a wild boar in the underbrush entirely too close for comfort.

The belligerent bellowed screech ripped the night like a
rifle shot, and Ben jumped before he could stop himself,
swinging the cudgel up in front of him, while the pig thrashed
through brush and vines, sticks cracking under sharp hooves,
as he charged off on Ben's left, instead of straight at him.

Ben lowered the stick, but listened for twenty seconds,
before he started down the path again – which took him
suddenly to the end of the woods fifty yards further on.

There he could see a straight line of silvery road, a half a
mile or more in length, stretching away in front of him, cutting
an overgrown vineyard in two.

The moon was bright enough at that moment for him to
be seen against the stony track, so he edged into the shadows
of a shallow ditch on the right of the road that followed a
thick hedgerow along the ends of the vines. There were
strips of mist lying in low spots, but he could see over
them, and move fast, and concentrate on the buildings on
the gentle rise in front of him at what looked like the end
of the road.

When he'd gotten close to the first barn, he crouched and
ran from the end of the hedge to the north-east corner, on the
right of a big empty doorway.

Ben stood with his back against cold crumbling brick and
held his breath and listened – to nothing but cool wet wind

blowing out of the south-east, rushing around the buildings, swishing underbrush and rattling trees close behind the barn.

Ben waited. Watching the shadows on the outside of the building, before he twisted his head to the right around the open door.

It was black inside. The moonlight hardly reached past the threshold – except where one small high window let a thin thread of pale light spill out on the dirt floor.

Ben watched and listened and worked out the shapes in the darkness. Old tires. A tank lying on its side. Stacks of boards or beams. Jagged piles of fallen brick.

Nothing breathing. Nothing coming after him.

No Kate there to worry about.

He exhaled slowly and listened again, then ran across the open doorway and froze with his back against the strip of south-east wall.

He stood, straining to hear beyond the wind. Staring, a few seconds later, over his right shoulder at the two-story building thirty feet away.

It was the one that made the most sense, from what Raimondo had said about it. Apartments above, animal stalls below. Nooks and crannies and hiding niches. Where anyone approaching could be seen from entirely too many places.

There were three stone arches two-thirds of the way down its long north wall, with what looked like some kind of porch area behind them, under the upstairs room. There was a small-paned window centered above each of the two pillars that supported the arches, and he watched those windows carefully, but couldn't see anything useful – not at that distance, at that angle.

He back-tracked and circled the barn on the north side, working his way through weeds and tangled shrubs, till he could see the arches of the second building straight ahead of him, when he bent his head around the barn's north-west corner.

It did look like a porch of some kind, beyond the arches on the first floor – twenty-five-feet wide or so, and maybe eight-feet deep – the back wall solid, except for a narrow half-open door near the right end.

Ben couldn't see the end walls of the porch. Or the floor behind a row of tall thick weeds. He couldn't see the ceiling, or anything inside the upper windows, but at least he knew there was a first-floor doorway. Where Mitchell could hide on either side.

Ben edged back the way he'd come to the east end of the barn. Then crouched before he sprinted across the sloped and stony ground to the north-east corner of the porch building – where he stood and listened again.

There were no sounds except the wind, rushing and fluttering through empty doors and broken windows, rattling a shutter above him once in a sudden strong gust. That, and the call of an owl somewhere in the sweep of woods to the south.

Ben studied that end of the porch building, the small barred ground-floor windows (five feet above his head because of the hill's incline), the two tall second-floor windows directly above those – small-paned casements that opened in, some of the glass still intact.

The one on the left had a wrought-iron grill attached to the wall outside it, forming a kind of balcony across the bottom of the window. There'd been a grill on the right window too that now lay on the ground, and Ben pulled on its rusting bars to see how strongly it was made. Then he went off to finish the reconnaissance that still had to be done.

He scouted inside and around the south barn, and the tobacco-curing barn too. And there he found a locked black Fiat parked behind the west end.

He sprinted back to the west end of the porch building (which didn't have windows, or any other way in), crept down the north wall till he'd reached the west end of the porch. There he looked over his right shoulder, his back against brick and stone, and saw at the other end, facing him, the bottom steps of inside stairs curving toward the upper floor.

He looked at the porch ceiling next – at a long black hole where the upper floor should've been, where a fifteen-by-eight-foot section of ceiling had fallen in, exposing an eight-foot length of wooden beam that crossed the center of the porch to meet the outside wall.

The floor of the porch between him and the stairs was completely littered with rubble. And he told himself not to even think about those stairs, as he crept around the west end and turned down the long south wall. The steps were too open above. There was too much rubble to cross quietly, protected on the north from the wind.

There were four broken doors on the south wall, into the tangle of animal byres. And he saw what he could through all of them – the deep borderless blackness, except for the outline of the porch door on the north, with moonlight grey behind it.

He ran to the outside staircase near the center of the south side – a steep, U-shaped, stone and brick stairway, bordered by waist-high walls that followed the angle of the stairs. The treads were littered with broken glass and shards of brick and stone, but they led to a six-foot wide double doorway, the right-hand door standing open, pushed in on the second floor.

Ben studied what he could see of the steps and the upper doors, from where he stood in the shadows, then examined the weeds and shrubs growing close to the bottom stairs.

He rounded the south-east corner of the building (studying the grill on the window again, as he sidled along that east end). Then turned the north-east corner.

There were patches of soft gravelly mud there between the corner and the arched porch, caused by the slope and the last working downspout. And there Ben took off his windbreaker, then zipped it up fast, and sat on his heels with it draped over his head touching the ground all around, aiming his flashlight at the mud.

He crept carefully toward the arches, keeping close to the wall, following two fresh sets of footprints – one male, one female, the woman's showing she had been pushed and dragged toward the first-floor porch.

Ben switched off the light, then stood and put his coat on. The wind wasn't as strong here as on the south or east sides, and he couldn't afford to make a sound.

He slid his back silently along the wall to the east end of the porch, where he could just see the west end – the solid brick wall without windows or doors.

He couldn't see much of the floor from where he was, because of the weeds at that end, but he kept his back on the wall and looked up at the hole, hoping to see the ceiling from that angle and study the beam as well.

He could smell Kate. He could smell her perfume.

And then he heard her cough up above him. Somewhere not too far beyond the oblong hole.

He moved east away from the arches and the porch, slipping fast around the corner of the building, till he came to the window with the balcony grill, saying *thank-you*, twice, silently, because Kate was still alive.

So what makes the most sense? That Mitchell expects you to use the stairs, inside or out. Which presents a classic military problem with one textbook solution. Get yourself up there anyway you can, without using the stairs.

Not that I've got many options. Without sophisticated gear.

Ben had dropped to the ground and taken off his desert boots, and was putting on the two pairs of dark socks he'd stuffed into a coat pocket. He pulled on black leather gloves, then stood and studied the wind while he uncoiled the rope.

When the next loud gust came at him out of the south, he threw one end of the rope against the lash of the wind – gritting his teeth at the clang of rope on metal – lapping several feet of it over the grill on the upper window.

Something screamed and flapped up above him, a startled screech owl from what he could see – broad wings, yellow eyes, big blunt-headed body – flying out the window across the night sky.

Ben waited, listening, clutching the rope in his hands, back plastered against the wall, holding his breath and praying.

Nothing else happened in the next two minutes.

No sound. No movement up above. Just the night ticking past, tearing into his insides, with Kate still caught in Mitchell's hands.

He had to jump to grab the short end of the rope. Twice. Which infuriated him. Listening time after time to the clang of rope hitting metal in his head – hoping the wind had muffled the sound, knowing it hadn't altogether.

He pulled the rope down as quietly as he could, held one end in either hand and hung there for several seconds, bouncing before he climbed four or five feet to test the strength of the railing.

It was old and brittle. He could feel the metal stressing, then start to pull away from the wall.

Kate Lindsay stood in the center of the upstairs with a noose around her neck and a washcloth stuffed in her mouth, three or four feet from the hole in the floor above the north porch.

Her wrists were tied by two ropes attached two feet behind

her, ten feet away on either side, to two new heavy metal rings drilled into thick wooden wall posts. The ropes weren't forcing her arms above her head (and she'd told herself to be thankful for that), but out to her sides just lower than her shoulders a foot behind her back.

She could have eased the strain on her arms and her neck, on her shoulders and her chest too, by stepping backward toward the hole, but she didn't trust herself to do that. Not when she couldn't see it, or be sure how stable the edge was.

She'd been telling herself not to forget that hole behind her, or the deadliness of the noose around her neck. Because even though it was loose now, a dead weight on her collarbones, a death threat if she stood still – one push from Mitchell, or one moment of lost concentration, and her neck would snap before, *or* after, her arms were pulled from their sockets.

Let it snap fast, please. If that's what has to happen. Don't let me hang a long time before I finally die.

She wasn't herself, and it scared her. She wasn't as groggy as she'd been, but the sharpness wasn't there. The clarity, the speed, the brain she took for granted ticking over on its own.

She didn't think she'd been given as much ether as she would've had with surgery, but how long she'd been gone Kate couldn't have said. Her hands had been bound behind her on the car floor and kept her from seeing her watch.

The ether had made her vomit in Mitchell's car, before he put the gag on her, and that was a consolation. Mitchell had been disgusted, which had made Kate laugh out loud.

She was watching him watch her now. Tall, tense, the hand holding the Luger raised in front of him as he listened for a second sound that would tell him Ben had arrived for sure, as well as exactly where.

The wind had picked up in the last hour, and it'd been talking to the house, making eerie unexpected noises through broken windows and slapping shutters, through the animal pens downstairs, in the scratching of branches against outside walls.

But there had been a second, a few minutes before, when it sounded as though there was some other noise at the east end of the building. A soft clang from something metal, then the owl screeched and flew out the bedroom neither she nor Mitchell could see.

Mitchell had been sitting on a wooden bench, inside the right side of a huge fireplace in the bigger of the two kitchens – waiting behind what was left of an east-west wall.

He'd been able to see both doors from there – the one to the porch stairs behind Kate, and the south door to the outside stairs that Kate faced from the north.

When Mitchell had heard the owl, he'd stepped outside the fireplace, and was still standing eight or ten feet away from Kate, partially hidden from the porch stairs, where he could cover both doors, and Kate even easier. And the tenseness in Mitchell's body did not make Kate feel at all secure.

Grey watery moonlight came and went from the windows behind her, and Kate's eyes had long since adjusted to the dark, and she could see Mitchell's sharp white face above the border of beard.

He seemed to be willing himself to see and hear more than any human does, and the edginess of his eyes and hands looked lethal to her then, as though one loud breath, or one raised eyebrow, would make him shoot her dead.

The cough had almost brought it down on her. When she'd thought, for one split second, that she'd heard someone down below her, and she'd coughed one quick cough to communicate everything she could. Mitchell had whipped the barrel at her eyes, and more than half a minute passed before he'd turned away.

He'd wanted to kill her then.

She'd seen it. And he'd known she had.

But she'd also told herself again that Mitchell needed her alive, and was only trying to intimidate her.

Because if Ben saw me dead, he'd kill Mitchell right then. He'd be free to at least, if he didn't have me to worry about.

Mitchell must know that. And that he doesn't have the training to fight Ben hand to hand. Though getting at Mitchell without knowing where I am would make it hard for Ben.

Please forgive me for my selfishness, Lord. For never forgiving the people I haven't. For all the times I didn't do what I knew I should've done. Please don't let me die like this, if it's your will. And don't let Ben get hurt. Not because of me.

Kate was staring at Mitchell. Her arms aching almost more than she could stand. Her arm sockets screaming. Her collarbones ready to snap. Her neck and chest making her want to cry.

She told herself not to for the hundredth time. *Don't you even* think *about giving this jerk the satisfaction.*

Mitchell was staring at her. Raising the Luger slowly. Pointing it at her face.

The chimneys had crumbled. The windows were rotten. The roof had half its tiles.

So the rope's pretty much useless. And Kate's too close to the hole by the north steps, where I'd be too easy to see.

That leaves the outside stairs. Littered like a bombsight. But the wind's strong there, and that'll help. Just don't let the walking stick bang against the steps.

Ben buttoned the top button of his coat, pushed the cudgel down inside the back of the neck so it lay between his shoulder blades with the knob caught on his collar.

He untied the horseshoe rope wrapped around his waist so the ends were looped but not knotted, then blackened his face with more mud. He pulled the knitted cap further down on his ears and face, picked up the rope he'd just finished coiling, and edged his way toward the north side to stage a small diversion.

He crept to the porch, tight up against the wall, where, with one fast purposeful dash, he slung the end of the long rope over the exposed ceiling beam in the broken patch of ceiling.

Then he sprinted back the way he'd come till he'd made it along the east end wall, and turned the south-east corner. The entrance to the outside stairway was straight in front of him, but before he started toward it, he threw a chunk of broken brick over the roof to the north side as near the arched porch as he could get it.

He crouched and ran to the outside stairs, working around brambles and bits of ruined wall, then started climbing the lower stairs, painstakingly on his hands and knees, below the waist-high walls.

He climbed seven steps to the landing. Feeling with his hands. Moving the largest shards of glass with thinly gloved fingers. Shifting pieces of brick and stone so he could move silently. Sitting long enough on that landing, with his back against the inside wall, to lob a chip of stucco over the broken roof.

Ben was thinking about his options, picturing the ten or twelve feet of second-floor wall between the double door on the right end and the wood-shuttered window on the left, figuring that Mitchell would've planted himself where he could see both stairs.

The left side might make sense. But you gotta find Kate before you make a move. And here you've gotta be quiet.

Ben slipped the cudgel up out of the neck of his windbreaker and laid it carefully on the left side of the stairs, hooking the knob on the edge of the tread below the landing by the door.

He crawled up the last set of stairs – feeling for glass, rearranging shards and pieces of brick – till he was kneeling on the third stair, where he could lean forward and brace himself on his hands, and his head would reach the landing.

He'd be able to look to his left and see beyond the door from there, just at floor level, without being easy to see. He took off his gloves and shoved them in a pocket, then gathered the rope with the horseshoes on the ends into his right hand. He picked up a gravel-size piece of stucco with his left, and lobbed it over the roof so it landed on the ground on the north-eastern corner. As it hit, he leaned forward on the outer right edge of the stairs, twisting his head to the left till he could see that section of the second-story floor.

He could see Kate outlined in the moonlight from the two windows in the far wall above the first floor arches – both arms pulled to the sides, and what looked like a rope looping down around her neck from somewhere up above.

He could see the whole of the right side of the room – and Mitchell wasn't there. There were dark places in the right-hand wall that must've been doorways to other rooms where Mitchell could've been hiding. Though the eastern doorway to the porch stairs would've been hidden for him from either, and it made less sense that he'd hide there, than the west side of the room.

Adrenaline was screaming through Ben, turning him into a raw nerve, making him notice every whisper of wind and change of sound and light – and he saw Kate's body straighten slightly, almost imperceptibly, and her head rise a fraction of an inch, and he knew Kate had seen his face just above the landing.

She turned hers to his left, then back to center and left again, and even though Ben couldn't see her eyes, he knew she was telling him that Mitchell was there, somewhere on Ben's left.

Ben raised his left fist with the thumb up.

And she glanced to his right then, twice, as though she were trying to make Mitchell think that all she was doing was easing her neck, and the looks to the left hadn't meant anything.

Ben picked up the cudgel in his left hand, stood up on the third stair where he couldn't be seen from the second floor, crept up two more, threw chunks of stone – the first on the roof in front of him, the second on the north side, the third on the east end – while he rushed on to the landing.

What happened next took one split second. He lunged toward the closed left-hand door, battered the wall hard with the cudgel ten feet or so to the left of it, while swinging the horseshoe rope above his head.

A bullet slammed into the left end of the wall, but Ben still kicked the left-hand door open and threw the horseshoe bolo straight at Mitchell, fifteen feet away.

There were two shots more from the Luger. One before, and one just after the bolo pinned Mitchell's arms against his body – one horseshoe slamming his chest, the other hitting the back of his neck – knocking him down on a pile of broken brick.

Neither shot did damage. The Luger clattered out of Mitchell's hand, and Ben kicked it hard across the room. Then he grabbed Mitchell and shoved him on his chest, tying the ends of the bolo around his wrists behind his broad-shouldered back.

Ben picked him up and shouted, 'Butcher!' twice, close to Mitchell's face. Then he knocked the back of his head against the wall and threw him down on the floor.

Mitchell was out cold when Ben stared down at him, fury on his own face, his whole body seething with outraged adrenaline, as he pulled the wire from his belt loops and tied Mitchell's ankles together.

Ben yanked the noose over Kate's head and threw it down on the floor, then untied her wrists as gently as he could and lowered her arms slowly.

He picked her up as she began to fall and carried her away from the hole in the floor toward the wall opposite the fireplace, slowly easing her down on to plaster-covered tile. He pulled the washcloth from her cracked and bleeding mouth and rubbed her wrists and arms.

'You OK? Can you talk? Can you feel anything in your arms?'

Kate nodded painfully and licked her lips before she whispered, 'Shoulders,' a second or two later.

Ben sat on his heels behind her and massaged them till he felt her shudder and silently start to cry. He knelt beside her and wrapped his arms around her. And she turned and sobbed against his chest, in ripping, tearing animal sounds that shook her whole body.

Ben rubbed her back and said, 'It's OK, Kit. Everything'll be OK,' while he watched Ted Mitchell over the top of her head.

Mitchell was conscious. Ben had seen him move. And he took out his flashlight and trained it on Mitchell, who stared at Ben with cold disdain before he looked away.

Ben put the arm holding the flashlight around Kate again, and he could feel her making herself stop, taking control, swallowing, sniffing, clearing her throat, inhaling slower, less-jagged breaths.

Ben never took his eyes off Mitchell while he drilled the flashlight in his face.

'What happens to you, Mitchell, in the next ten minutes depends on how well you answer my questions. You understand what I'm saying?'

Mitchell gazed at him with a cool self-satisfied smile.

And Ben eased Kate closer to the wall, getting himself ready to move. 'Answer me!'

Mitchell nodded slowly, after he'd looked away from Ben.

'How many GIs did you kill?'

'Why should I tell you?'

'Because I'm looking for an excuse. Because I've wanted to get my hands on you since 1945. Because I'll beat you to death in a painful and methodical manner if you don't cooperate soon.'

Mitchell didn't say anything, and Ben let go of Kate. He handed her a handkerchief and helped her sit against the wall.

Then he turned to face Mitchell. 'You're about to get what you deserve, and I can't say I won't enjoy it.'

'Four.'

'Two on the recon with me?'

'You knew that.'

'The others before or after?'

'Before.'

'You murdered MacNab.'

Mitchell looked at him neutrally for a minute and then nodded.

'Did that make you feel strong and powerful, murdering someone like him?'

'I took care of him. I paid him back for saving my life. If it hadn't been for me, he would've—'

'Been alive today. You pushed Phillip Welsh off the cliff in Cornwall too.'

Mitchell didn't say anything and Ben stepped closer.

'Yeah.'

'And what about your wife? Did you murder her for the money?'

'I didn't get her money.'

'I'm not in the mood, Mitchell.'

'I didn't kill Ruth.'

'Good. That's something. So what German technology did you steal?' He didn't say anything, and Ben took a step closer. 'You listening to me, Mitchell?'

'Breakthrough techniques for the manufacture of jet engines and other high temperature alloys, like Inconel 718 and Rene 44. Rene was such a bitch to machine, they named it for a Madame in Schenectady, who was well known to the guys at GE where the early work was done.'

'And Ted Mitchell thinks that's amusing, like he did when he was a kid. What other German science did you steal?'

'Magnetic recording technology.'

'And that you sold to start your metalworking business?'

'We all stole German technology. The Americans, the British, the Soviets. How was what I did any different from them?'

'You murdered for it. That's a minor detail.'

'And they didn't? Bombing the crap out of Europe?'

'The US and Britain took whatever science we could get

to help us end the war. Hitler kept saying he had secret weapons, and the Allies had to find out what. We also had to find out if he had the bomb, for very obvious reasons.'

'Wait a minute, at the end—'

'It did degenerate after the war, I'll give you that.'

'So that was an attempt at objectivity?'

'We justified it as war reparations. We were rebuilding Europe single-handedly, you'll recall, and trying to deal with Stalin. He was force-marching every German scientist he could find off to the Russian Motherland, and imprisoning all of Eastern Europe, while *we* at least gave the scientists a choice, and only took—'

'So I did what we all did.'

'No, you took it for *you*, and murdered your *own* men to keep them from talking!'

'That made a big difference, did it, in the carnage around us then? They could've died anywhere, any second of any day.'

'I took out two untrained men under you, and I would've gotten them back if *you* hadn't shot 'em in the back.'

'So *that's* what's eating you, I ruined your precious record!'

'No, you're a murderer, and a traitor, and under military law alone you'd be court-martialed and shot.'

'Everything I took helped the US! Our economy has been fueled by the advances in machining and metalworking, and I'm responsible for a lot of it. And the tape-recording industry too, that's changed a few things. That's given jobs to one or two people. If I hadn't brought that back—'

'And sold it to make a nest egg for yourself!'

'Somebody else would've.'

'Where have I heard that before? Berlin? Nuremburg? Moscow? Did you always want to be rich and important? Is that what this was all about? Or was it the excitement too? The thrill of seeing if you could pull it off?'

'You're a self-righteous prick.'

'Convenient for you, the murders happening now in Tuscany. Giving you kidnappings to copy when you killed us.'

'I land on my feet, and make good decisions fast.'

'It'll be interesting to see how you handle humiliation. Public scorn and humiliation. The Italian police. The British police. The American military police too, they're going to be *very* interested in you. It's quite a little tangle, isn't it? Deciding who'll get you first. The papers'll have a field day. Every paper in the US will be full of Ted Mitchell, alias John Wharton, alias John Wagner. The papers in Scotland, and Italy too, and maybe even—'

'Shut up!'

'Did you ever think about what you did to your parents? Do you have any idea how much she grieved for you? When you'd taken up your new identity and neglected to mention it to her?'

'My heart bleeds! You don't know what a pain in the ass my mother was when I was in college. If I could've shut her up then I would've.'

Ben started toward him, pushing the flashlight in his pocket, ready to shove his thumbs into Mitchell's throat.

'Ben, I need a bucket! I think I'm gonna be sick.'

There was a battered enamel pan in the stone sink on the south wall, and Ben brought it to Kate and held it for her while she vomited.

There was a noise then, on the outside stairs, the sound of footsteps on broken glass, and Ben ran to the wall beside the double door and listened hard with the cudgel in his hand.

It was then that Mitchell squirmed sideways, turning himself and rolling toward Kate along the hole in the floor. His ankles were still wired, but he smashed his legs into hers, trying to kick her toward the jagged edge of the broken collapsed floor.

She started scrambling to get herself up, using the east wall, pushing herself toward Ben – but Ted Mitchell kicked at her again, harder than he had before, even though he couldn't reach her.

And that was when the floor broke under him, the shattering rip like a clap of close thunder, as the edge of tile and rotting wood cracked and crumbled underneath him, spewing him on to a pile of broken stone fifteen feet below.

Ben had seen what Mitchell was doing before Raimondo stepped through the door, and was almost to Kate when Mitchell fell.

Ben leaned against the east wall where the floor was still stable, and aimed his flashlight down through the haze of brick and stone and stucco dust that was swirling up from the rubble. He kept it trained on Mitchell's skull – crushed side down, seeping on the stones – watching Mitchell twitch twice, and then lie still.

'Ben!' Kate sat frozen, staring at Mitchell, her back against the wall, shaking again and looking sick – ten feet from Raimondo Ricciardi, who'd stopped dead in his tracks. Ben touched Kate's cheek, and stroked her hair for a second, looking across at Raimondo. Then he started down the north stairs toward the body in the rubble-piled porch.

Twenty

B en thanked the young waiter who was holding a wicker basket out to him, and Maria too, at the front desk, for arranging the picnic lunch. Then he stepped out the open door and went to meet Kate.

He'd left her sitting on the fan-shaped steps of the padrone's house with her elbows on her knees and her chin in her hands smiling at La Fortezza, stretched out in front of her like a ginger cat in the sun.

He'd watched Kate eavesdrop nonchalantly as two black-haired girls in grey and white uniforms trotted along the second-floor veranda above the main restaurant, laughing and teasing in smooth watery voices, carrying clean linen to the rooms.

But Kate wasn't on the steps when Ben came out with the basket, and he went to find her, back where she'd said she might be. He walked through the front arch and turned right on the cobblestones, opening the crested wrought-iron gate that led back around to the old padrone's garden, to the spring grass and bare wisteria and irises slicing their way toward the sun along a low stone wall.

Ben crossed to the opening in the middle of that wall, at the top of a stone stair, and saw Kate down below him in a patch of sunny ground. She was walking around the herb garden, bending stiffly to read the wooden labels, humming something that sounded like an Appalachian folk song, or an old southern-style hymn.

Ben watched her for a minute in silence. Seeing her again in that broken building – limp and bloodied with a noose around her neck, arms dragged back behind her, Luger set to shoot away her face, eyes asking Ben to make her safe.

'Hey.' He smiled as he looked down at her. And she straightened as though she ached in a lot of places, and told him she'd be right up.

They walked around the end of the big barn toward Raimondo's vineyard, watching dew-covered vines glisten in the morning sun.

They spoke to two men tying old growth on wires, then stared to their left across the Pienza Road at the wheat field shining in the narrow valley, trying to think of a word for green that had anything to do with foot-high wheat with sunlight shining through it.

They gave up by the time they'd come to the woods that grew thick at the end of the vineyard, where they turned right into a farm track edged with wild flowers and ivy.

They talked again about Mitchell, in the cool green in the shaded woods, trying to appreciate how fortunate they'd been that Raimondo had arrived when he did – in time to see the floor break away and be able to say that neither Ben nor Kate had shoved Mitchell off.

'Because you know the police would've wondered about us if Raimondo hadn't been there.' Ben picked one white wild flower, one of thousands in Raimondo's woods, and handed it to Kate.

She inhaled the scent, and thanked him, and slipped it through the top buttonhole of her cream-colored blouse. 'It still makes me sick when I think about it.'

'What does?'

'Mitchell.' Kate shivered and swatted a gnat. 'Twitching there on the porch. The spike from the broken beam sticking into his head.'

'Then tell me what it's like to live in Scotland. The thought of that makes me feel better.'

She did then, for several minutes, before she asked Ben about finding the Seneca. And the family that had owned the jewelry.

That led to all kinds of other things, to the history of La Fortezza, and the generations who'd lived there before Raimondo, all of which had found artifacts buried across the land.

'I guess most of Italy's like that.' Ben listened to a bird

call, somewhere close above them, before he spoke again. 'They've had hundreds of years of living on top of each other, so wherever you dig, even planting a garden, you pull up pieces of other people's lives.'

'Raimondo told me they'd found several Etruscan artifacts, but he didn't say what kind.'

'Pitchers, and vases, and sculptured heads. His grandfather gave most of them to a museum somewhere. Siena maybe, or Chiusi.'

'America's so young. When you think of England even, with the Celts and the . . .'

They started there and talked on at least half an hour, as they walked through the woods, sprinkled with evergreens and hung with ivy – until Ben led Kate out to a spit of open land he'd found the week before.

They climbed over dead logs and around tangled brush, inching into the warm sun that felt like summer on their skin, following a curving ridge to a small mound-shaped hill covered in soft spring grass under widely spaced dark green cedars, swaying high on thick bare trunks.

They found a flattish spot on the northern edge and laid Raimondo's quilt on the ground, then sat staring off on their right at the broad Val di Chiana. They gazed at the small tiled town of Sinalunga clinging to a hill much closer on their right, at the gentle green-edged strip of narrow valley lying just below their feet, the center just plowed a warm rich brown, being picked upon now by a flock of white birds.

It must've been almost eighty, and the sun was lapping at their skin, as they lay back with their hands under their heads and watched the clouds above the trees.

It was Kate who spoke first. Rolling on to her left side to look at Ben, propping her head on her hand. 'How did you think Jenny took it? Was she traumatized by Mitchell's death?'

'I don't think she was crushed, but it had to be a shock. Hearing your stepfather's fallen to his death, and "Oh, by the way, he was also an imposter who murdered several people," has to be fairly unsettling. Personally, though, for her, I don't think it was that much of a blow. I think she's spent her life living around him, trying not to get too close. She's an inter-esting kid. And I bet she does something worth doing.'

'It'll be embarrassing when she gets home, though. Being

the center of some very messy gossip. Teenagers take that sort of thing harder than you or I would.'

'How are *you* doing, by the way? Does everything seem to be healing?'

'I'm OK. I'm still sore, but the aspirin, and the ice, and the hot baths help. I wonder who'll inherit Mitchell's houses. And his businesses too, of course. Jenny, or someone else?'

'He had real relatives. The ones he let think he was dead. It'll be interesting to know what his will says, and what the legal implications are. You can't profit from a crime, for one thing. And he started with stolen technology.'

'I forgot about his own family.'

'What's his mother going to think when she hears he's been alive all this time, but didn't bother to tell her? That's worse than thinking he's dead. The obviousness of the disregard. I probably ought to call her before it hits the US papers.'

'Did you get along with her when you met her?'

'Sort of.' Ben paused and smiled ironically. 'Not really. It'd probably work better if I called his sister. Help me remember when we get back from lunch.' Ben sat up and took out the picnic – the cheese and mushroom and tomato focaccia, the green salad, the tiny oranges, the thermos of cappuccino.

They ate and laughed and leaned back in the sun. They talked about dogs, and David Lindsay. About Kate's father and whether he should retire. About what she needed to learn still to write the book about Georgina's murder. Then she asked about Harrison Hall. And Ben told her the board was evaluating the business sense of medical offices versus high-style apartments.

They were quiet then for a few minutes. Watching the world grow greener. Listening to the breeze in the tops of the cedars. Watching bugs crawl on grey-green moss.

Kate picked up an ant and slid it off on to Ben's wrist, while she said, 'You're awfully quiet.'

He looked at her dark arched eyebrows and her interested blue eyes and the teasing lips sidling into a small smile, before he glanced away.

'I got a call from my secretary at Alderton this morning. She woke herself up in the middle of the night to get me on the phone before I left, and what she said doesn't bode well.' Ben didn't say anything more.

And Kate waited longer than she wanted to before she said, 'Well?'

'Roger Simms, the Alderton library director, has been asking her for information about me, and so has President Harper. Everett Adams phoned her too yesterday, and told her to tell me he wants me to call as soon as I get home.'

'That's not necessarily bad, is it?'

'Not Everett, no. But with me getting home a day late because I had to talk to the police, Simms and Harper will see it as another excuse to hassle me.'

'It's not as though you could help it. And didn't you plan to leave today anyway?'

'I was supposed to fly out of Rome this morning and be at work tomorrow. Now I have to take a late train to Rome, and fly out tomorrow morning, which means I won't get home till tomorrow night.'

'What's Simms been asking?'

'He told Janie to turn over whatever personal calendars of mine she can find. He wants to know how many days I've taken off for personal time in the last five years. The fact that I worked most of my sabbatical last year doesn't seem to matter to him.'

'Why do you keep the calendars?'

'I have stuff in them I like to hold on to. Names of people and phone numbers and notes to myself about things I want to study. I keep them in a cabinet in my office, and if she's told to find them she'll have to. He'll compare them to records in Personnel, and see if he can catch any discrepancies. He can't, on any reasonable level, but I don't document everything I do for the university. Speaking to history groups for the library. Doing research for donors. I don't explain all that to the personnel people. We've always just worked on the honor system, which, obviously, in a principled society, is the way it ought to be. Though whether we've *got* a principled society is open to serious debate.'

'I bet you could fight that.'

'I wasn't there, though, was I, to keep him from taking them?'

'Was that all he wanted?' Kate was looking at Ben with serious eyes and a worried forehead, as her shiny mahogany hair blew across her mouth.

'He also asked for a list of apprentices I've had in the last five years too. And all lists of artifacts. And any gifts I've been given personally by donors over the years.'

'Something's up, Ben.'

'Yep. They know they can't fire me, so as near as I can figure, they may try to make me take a non-faculty position in library administration. Which would mean no summer vacation, no sabbaticals, very little time to do my own work, while I still act as Alderton's archivist.'

'Doesn't sound good, does it?'

'Nope. But it could be worse. I could have a noose around my neck, and be standing on the edge of a precipice. You've done really well, by the way, coping with what Mitchell did to you.'

'I'm in Italy. At La Fortezza. Expenses paid by Mr Mitchell. The sun's out. The food's excellent. I'm *not* hanging by the neck above a hole in the floor, because of Ben Reese and the goodness of God. So I'm telling myself not to think about it till I'm back in the cold in Scotland trying to finish a first draft.'

'Still, you've handled it amazingly well.' Ben was peeling his orange, looking hard at his hands.

'Thanks. That means something coming from you. You want any more water?' Ben shook his head and Kate put the lid on the bottle. 'So how are *you* doing? You've had Mitchell sitting there in the back of your mind ever since the war. How is it now to be done with it, and know he won't hurt someone else?'

'Very good. On that level.' Ben didn't say anything else.

And Kate couldn't let it rest. 'Yes?'

'I *wanted* to hurt him. I wanted to crush his windpipe. I wanted to drive the bridge of his nose up into his brain.' Ben stopped and looked at her.

And Kate couldn't think of a thing to say.

'I might have too. I think I might have killed him, if you hadn't asked me to find you a bucket.'

'Then it's a good thing I was sick. Right?'

'Yeah, but I don't like it.' Ben rolled over on his stomach and picked a long blade of grass. 'I did things in the war I don't ever want to do again. That's nothing surprising. Anybody who was there would say that. But what I did was impersonal. Necessary. What had to be done by someone, even if it wasn't me. This got to be personal with Mitchell. And when I saw you – ' Ben didn't look at Kate's face, but he turned in her direction and leaned his head on his hand – 'with a noose around your neck, and your arms forced back behind you, and the smile on his face while he justified killing Ross MacNab, I wanted to make him hurt.'

'That's natural, wouldn't you say? Wouldn't almost anybody?'

'Yeah, but I didn't want it to be me anymore. You and I believe things that make more demands than that.'

'Yes, but—'

'I know he had to be stopped, and executing him legally, by court-martial or civil authority, would've been fine with me. It would've been OK to kill him myself, if I'd had to, to protect you, or me, either one. It was *wanting* to. It was wanting to make him hurt.'

'We aren't perfect here, Ben. None of us.'

'I know.'

'We can't control our feelings every second. All we have is will. All we control is our actions.'

'True. I've said that to people myself. But—'

'I don't think you would've killed Mitchell. I think you would've made yourself stop.'

'Maybe, but once you start, with a history like mine, it's not so easy to stop.'

'What does that mean?'

'Combat. You're trained to kill, not wound. Once you start, you finish it. It's adrenaline too. Bringing it all back. Anyway, it's a good thing I didn't have to find out what I would've done.'

'Yeah, but—'

'I'm just glad I'm not staring at life from inside an Italian jail.'

'Oh, I know, me too.' Kate lay down and put her arm under her head and looked at the side of Ben's face. 'Anyway, you didn't kill him. And as *you* always say—'

'Speculating won't help.'

'Do you think Ross sent me the eye?'

'I think so. Not that we've got any proof.'

'I do wish I could've talked to him.'

Ben said he would've too, if he'd been her, and turned over on his back.

'So what would you do if they make you an administrative employee instead of a member of the faculty?'

'I could move to another university. I could become an appraiser. I could go to work for a museum. But I *do* like working with students. And with all the different kinds of unexpected stuff donors give to schools. It keeps me from having to specialize in one particular field. I like being my own boss too. The way I used to be. And having a real sabbatical that lets me concentrate completely.'

'You could become an investigator.'

'Maybe. What kind did you have in mind?'

'I don't know. An atypical private investigator?'

'Divorce work wouldn't be *my* idea of a good time.'

'No, but what about art crimes? Museum crimes? That sort of thing.'

'Maybe. I don't know. It's not what I would've chosen.'

'It looks to me like you like solving puzzles in every conceivable form.'

'Right. That's part of what I like about being an archivist. Solving the puzzles of the pieces themselves. What *are* they? Where'd they come from when? Who made them?' Ben raked his hair back out of his eyes and rolled over on his side facing Kate. 'I guess maybe I could set up some kind of business. With all the people I know who are specialists in all kinds of areas. Coins. Paintings. Books. Something like a clearing house business maybe, doing what I do now for other people for hire.'

'For museums and auctions houses?'

'Yeah, and collectors too. But I don't have capital to get it going. And I don't have much real business experience.' Ben looked at his watch and squinted into the sun, then sat up and looked at Kate. 'Anyway, we better get going. I've still got some packing to finish before Raimondo drives me to the station.'

'It's too soon.'

'I know.'

'It feels so good lying in the grass.'

'We better go, though, and then we can take our time walking back.'

'I think you want to go home.'

'I do want to see Max. I've felt bad being away from him when we were just getting used to each other. But it sounds like he's adjusting really well. I talked to Walter yesterday, and Max is flying around his paddock exactly the way he used to.'

'I'm glad he's doing well again.'

'I'm glad *you're* staying a couple more days. Raimondo and Isabella will take you interesting places, and introduce you to their friends, and it ought to be a lot of fun.'

'I'll be fine on my own. And if I get bored I can always work.'

'You're as bad as I am.'

'Yeah, I think I am.'

When they were standing by Ben's door, Kate had said, 'Goodbye, Ben. Thank you again for everything,' and was starting to walk away.

Ben said, 'Look. Down to the right by the doormat. There's a lizard lying in the sun.'

Kate saw it then, and smiled. But as soon as she moved toward it, it shot up the vine on the right side of the door and disappeared in a chink between stones. She laughed and turned around, and found she was standing against Ben.

He smoothed both sides of her hair back behind her ears, and ran one finger down the line of her jaw, then traced the curves in her upper lip, before he wrapped his arms around her, and pulled her tight against him. He kissed her long and hard, like he'd been thinking about doing that for a very long time. And he kissed her forehead for half a second, and her mouth again, softer this time, and longer, and then he kissed the hollow of skin pulsing between her collarbones.

He pulled himself back and stared down at her. And then he slid his arms around her and rocked her from side to side with his chin buried in her hair.

Kate sighed and listened to his heartbeat, and the sound of his voice with her ear against his bones, when he finally spoke again.

'Did I just do a stupid thing?'

'I don't think so. Do you?'

'I don't know, Kate. I don't want to do something that

makes it hard for us to talk the way we do now. I want to talk like this for a very long time, and I don't want to jeopardize what we have now by changing it before we—'

'We aren't going to stop talking. Anyway, you know what they say.'

'Do I? Who?'

'Some Indian tribe, I think. Other people say it too. That when you save someone's life, you're responsible for them for ever. That's not quite right – it's more poetic than that. So we have to stay in touch in *some* way. Christmas cards. Change of address notices. Announcements of births and deaths.'

'What if you got the person in trouble to begin with?'

'Ah. Well. There is that.' Kate leaned back and looked up at him. 'How'd you get me in trouble?'

'You knowing *me* is what led Mitchell to you.'

'Ben, that's not how it started. Mitchell knew who I was from Welsh, and decided I was a threat. He didn't want Ross to talk to me about the war.'

'It was both. That, and you knowing me that finally brought him down on you. Anyway, do you want someone to be responsible for you?'

'Not really, not the way the saying makes it sound.'

'No. I wouldn't either.'

'Though . . .' Kate kissed the cleft in Ben's chin, and the left side of his neck. And then she kissed his lips. 'I guess it depends on what you mean. You've called me Kit twice, you know. The way Graham did. Once in Tryon and once here. There was once in New York too.'

'Have I?'

'I wonder what that means.'

'I have no idea. But I s'ppose it might not be a bad thing, to spend more time, and get to know each other.' His voice let her know he was mocking himself.

And Kate said, 'No, that wouldn't be a bad thing.' Then she laughed, half a minute later, after holding him close against her.

Ben looked down at her and smiled. 'Have I missed something important here?'

'Well, you just *know* that when we both start thinking about this, you in Ohio, and me in Scotland, we'll begin to worry about what we both meant, and how the other might've misunderstood, and how we don't want to make a mistake and get too involved too soon. And we'll never talk to each other again.'

'Oh, we'll talk. One way or the other.' Ben laughed and kissed Kate's earlobe. 'Though about what I couldn't say.'

Kate said, 'Very funny!' before she closed her eyes and smiled.

Acknowledgements

First, I'd like to thank Ed Weilant at Bowling Green State University's Science and Technology Library for his help in researching the American and British Technical Teams in Europe during, and after, WWII, as well as the history of tape recording, mid-century electronics and airplane design and manufacturing. Ed's very good at what he does, and makes technical research fun.

Much of the information about broaching machines, heat treating, and the development of jet engine metallurgy came from Andrew Nelson, a man with many years experience in machining and grinding, who loaned me his books, explained what was in them, and told me interesting stories (Rene in Schenectady) among them.

A very good friend of ours, Antonio Ricciardi, who grew up in Florence, answered innumerable questions about Italy, made excellent suggestions, and did the Italian translations.

Fortunately for me, Dr Harold Rossmore, a distinguished professor and industrial microbiologist (as well as a long-time family friend), now sadly deceased, who talked me into attending 'Art, Biology and Conservation 2002, A Symposium' at the Metropolitan Museum of Art, where I learned about bio-based forms of decomposition that affect all manner of artifacts, including stone, paper and oil painted murals.

At the Met, Tomlyn Barnes guided me through a spectacular tapestry exhibit (about which I knew nothing) that included the Raphael 'Acts Of The Apostles' referred to in *Watches*. A curator in the Met's Education Department, Tomlyn was extremely knowledgeable and helpful, and also guided my research there into early Italian jewelry making, Ghiberti in particular.

The house I describe as Mount Prospect, as well as the log cabin on that same ridge, do exist near Versailles, Kentucky (and the bloodstain story's true). Jim and Sharon Rouse let me stay in both, and invited interesting people over to give me a flavor of the area. I met them through my friend Betsy Pratt, who now lives in the log cabin, but used to own the house that Ev takes Ben to see. She helped me in countless ways, and the three of them, together with the land, the horses, the houses and the history, make me want to move to Versailles. The anecdote about the builder of the dry stone walls in Versailles is true. It came from Jonelle Fisher's book, *A Soul Remembering*, and refers to the real Legrand Lee.

I was able to travel in Florence, Pisa, Siena and Lucca, and learn as much as I did as quickly as I did, by joining a Rockford Institute Study Tour. Their itinerary and lectures were extremely helpful.

The settings in Scotland were found over a period of years with the help of Dr David Munro, Director of the Royal Scottish Geographical Society, who's helped with most of the Ben Reese books. Like Traquair, Leith House does exist, has a sad and interesting history, and is open to the public.

Locanda La Fortezza is based on an inn near Sinalunga called Locanda dell'Amorosa. (Pictures of it appear on my website: www.sallywright.net.). It's beautiful, and historically interesting, and it's close to many isolated wine growing villages well worth visiting. The food is excellent; our room in the pressing barn was lovely; the owner and the staff were very helpful; the woods and vineyards are as I described them (and we did startle a wild boar). The ruined buildings (half a mile behind the inn) led me to write the book I wrote.

The inn where Ben stays near Cortona is based on La Falconiere (the name I used for Wharton's house). The rooms and food are exceptional, and the owner's falcon and boxer dog made the stay even more enjoyable.

Pam Strickler, my long time agent, was especially helpful during the years between the publishing of *Out of the Ruins* and *Watches of the Night*, when publishers were bought and sold, and editors departed. She gave good advice and made practical decisions throughout.

I'm very grateful to Sheena Craig, my editor at Severn House Publishers, for her commitment to *Watches of the Night*, and the sixth Ben Reese (to be published in 2008), as well as her very perceptive editing.

I've been indebted to John Reed for years – the archivist and ex-World War II scout on whom I've based Ben – who still answers my questions, gives me good suggestions, and makes me appreciate, without ever intending to, what his generation did for mine, as well as those that come after. In *Watches* he helped with the mural work, the paper preservation techniques, the choice of the Aldine Seneca, and the inner workings of academe.

John found the bodies at Malmedy, was wounded the way Ben was in the Saarbrücken Forest, was flown-out under the Piper Cub, and recovered the way Ben did – helped by his wife, an exceptionally fine English professor, much respected by her students.